The Unmarked Road

The Unmarked Road

By

George Cadwalader

Fireship Press

THE UNMARKED ROAD : BY George Cadwalader

ISBN-13:978-1-61179-247-8: Paperback
ISBN 978-1-61179-248-5: ebook

BISAC Subject Headings:
FIC014000FICTION / Historical
FIC032000FICTION / War & Military
FIC0012000FICTION / Action

Cover Design: Kevin King

Address all correspondence to:
Fireship Press, LLC
P.O. Box 68412
Tucson, AZ 85737

Or visit our website at:
www.fireshippress.com

DEDICATION

To my wife, Yara, and our two sons, George and Thomas, both of whom became Marines.

AUTHOR'S NOTE

A risk in superimposing a work of fiction on real events is the possibility of doing an injustice to the actual Marines who served in the billets I've assigned to my fictional characters, and who fought in the battles I've had my characters fight. So I need to emphasize that what follows is entirely a work of fiction and my only reason for using actual units, places and engagements is to make the story more realistic.

My own tour in Viet Nam as a Marine Corps Captain serving in 1965 as an advisor to the South Vietnamese Marines was cut short by a mine explosion, and the rest of my war was fought in the Philadelphia Naval Hospital (PNH) where I remained for the better part of the next two years. My actual time "in country" was spent almost entirely in Four Corps south of Saigon. I never got to Da Nang or to Chu Lai or up into the Quang Tin Mountains, and I hope my descriptions of these places are close enough to make them recognizable to those who were actually there.

My descriptions of PNH are probably closer to the mark, although I never did set foot on the ninth floor, home of the Psychiatric Unit, where I have set part of my story and which, whenever we passed it on the elevator, gave rise to a lot of bad jokes, all intended to mask our feelings of uneasiness. Attitudes have changed for the better since those days, and we can be thankful that the men returning from Iraq and Afghanistan bearing the psychic scars of war are no longer dismissed as "wingnuts" as they were then. This is the story of one such man who came back from Viet Nam wounded in both body and spirit.

A list of all those who helped in the writing of that story would be longer than the book itself, and I wish I could thank them all here. Three who deserves special mention are my friend, Kevin King, who, among a great many other things, designed the book's cover; Chris Page, my editor who brought order to the manuscript; and most of all, my wife, Yara, who made the whole thing possible.

CHAPTER ONE

Philadelphia Naval Hospital, Fall of 1969

John Caleb was struggling to focus his eyes. Two hazy figures wearing white swam in and out of his field of view. One was tall, the other short—that much he could make out.

"What have we got here?" asked Tall.

"*Caleb, John, no middle initial. Gunnery Sergeant, USMC,*" said Short, reading from a clipboard. "*Date of birth, 14 February, 1940.* Isn't that Valentine's Day? You want the rest?"

Tall held an x-ray up to the light. "I can see the rest. It's a wonder they didn't take that arm off when they got him to Clark. Wee Willie thinks he can save it?"

"He's going to try. We had him down to the OR for some debriding today. All kinds of shit still in there. Dirt, shrapnel, dead bone, it's a mess."

"How about the hand?"

"Not much left of it."

He heard a curtain being pulled closed and they were gone. Time passed. He lay unmoving, a once-powerful, hawk-nosed man whose Marines had first called him the Indian because of his ancestry and later K-Bar because of his reputation with a knife. Gradually his vision cleared. The hazy orb above his head took shape as an IV bottle and he groggily traced its plastic tube down to where it disappeared under the tape on his left arm. From beyond his cubicle he could hear the sounds of other men in pain.

Then Short was back, bending over him. Even through the haze Caleb noticed instinctively that the man had his Lieutenant's bars pinned on cockeyed. "John!" Short was calling, "Talk to me! Do you know where you are, John? Can you tell me where you are?"

It came back to him. He remembered waking up in an Army field hospital and then later finding himself back in Da Nang. He'd been vaguely aware then that something was wrong with his right side but it wasn't until he'd been flown back to Clark in the Philippines that he'd seen for the first time the mess of mangled meat that had been his right arm and hand. They'd cut open the cast, and the sight of his mutilated arm encased in blood-soaked plaster had conjured up images of an Egyptian mummy.

"That's your ticket home, Marine," the Air Force doctor who'd examined him had said. He'd realized then that it was bad. You didn't have to be long in country to know that if they could patch you up fast enough to get you back in the game, they'd med-evac you only as far as the Philippines or Japan. It was only when you were down for the count that they sent you home.

He'd left Clark on an Air Force Starlifter full of moaning men, and he recalled at some point in that interminable journey seeing an arm flop heavily out of the stretcher above his own. That arm's dead owner was carried off at Iwakuni. Then it had been on to Travis Air Force Base in California, and from there to McGuire AFB in New Jersey, where they'd loaded him on an ambulance for the final leg of his journey to the Philadelphia Naval Hospital.

In his mind's eye he saw again the ambulance doors flung open, men in green hovering over him, and a wide-eyed intern who'd asked him what he did for a living.

"I'm a Marine, Sir," he'd said.

"I mean, what did you do before you were a Marine?"

"Lobsterman."

"So you must be from Maine?"

"No, Sir. Massachusetts. Woods Hole, Massachusetts."

They'd wheeled him away to the operating room. The last thing he remembered before going under was a female voice saying, "You'll get used to it, doctor!" and another voice—he thought it was that same intern's—answering, "Sure, but what about him? How's a lobsterman going to get used to having only one hand?"

After that, nothing.

*****

His dream began happily. He was seventeen again. He and the neighbor girl were lying on an improvised bed of burlap bags in the loft above the shed where his father kept their fishing gear. He was on top of her and their clothes were scattered all around them. The smell of her hair was mingled with the smell of fish. He heard the door opening below them and his father's footsteps.

"You up there, Johnny?"

Jesus! His heart was pounding. He lay stock still, but not the girl. She started to squirm. "For chrissake, be quiet!" he whispered.

"You're squashing me, Johnny!"

But then instead of the girl it was a little NVA soldier who lay pinned beneath him, smelling strongly of fish. He could hear other NVA on the trail not two feet from where the two of them lay hidden. He held his knife against his prisoner's throat, forcing his face down into the mud and hoping he'd have sense enough to stay quiet. But he didn't. So he shoved the knife home and the man beneath him went soft like a punctured air mattress. He felt warm blood spurting on his arm and jerked his knife hand back.

He came to with a corpsman lying across his chest trying to pin down his injured arm. Short came bursting through the curtain, took one look and groaned, "Oh shit! He's bleeding again." Would you like me to shoot them?"

"He's one strong motherfucker," said the corpsman. "I couldn't hold him."

"When's he due for more morphine?"

"Not for another hour."

"Give it to him now."

Caleb felt the sting and then the familiar metallic taste in his mouth. The pain began flowing away, starting at his shoulder and running down his arm until all that was left was a dull ache. He was vaguely aware that they were working on him again. He could feel the jab of the needle and the tug of sutures being pulled tight, and then the light was out and he was alone again.

He fought off sleep, wishing back the pain that would save him from slipping into more hellish dreams. But the morphine did its work. His eyes closed, all the things he wanted to forget came flooding back, and he came to once more with the same corpsman struggling to hold him down. A nurse came in with another shot. He told her no. He'd rather have the pain.

"No can do," she said. "Wee Willie's night orders say ten milligrams of morphine every four hours, and in these parts Wee Willie's word is law."

So passed his night in a seesaw back and forth between pain and nightmares.

*****

"You awake, Gunnery Sergeant?"

If I wasn't already, thought Caleb, *I am now*. He'd been having a brief respite from his hell, an interlude when the morphine-damped pain had crept back to where he no longer had to fight off sleep but had not yet crested to the point where the sweat would pour off him and his jaw would ache from the effort of not crying out. He looked up angrily and checked himself when he saw the enormous, craggy faced Navy captain who was standing by his bed. Caleb read *Williamson/Orthopedics* woven with blue thread on a white jacket and figured that this must be Wee Willie. Half hidden behind this giant, he thought he could make out another figure, but the light was in his eyes and he wasn't sure of it.

"Yes, Sir," he said, his own voice sounding very far away. "I'm awake."

"Bad night?"

"Not so good, Sir."

"Let's have a look at the damage." Wee Willie pulled up a stool, sat heavily down, and stuck his hand out behind him, waving it impatiently.

"Scissors!" he barked, making Caleb jump. "Pay attention, Miss Reardon! I'm not waving at you!"

A striking Lieutenant Junior Grade materialized out of the glare. Her eyes met his. She nodded towards the captain and made a face. But Caleb wasn't going to let her into his pain-centered world. Instead he rolled his head sideways and watched numbly as Wee Willie snipped away at the blood-stuck gauze that bound his cast together. The JG stood at the giant doctor's elbow holding a tray of instruments. "Trick is to anticipate," Wee Willie muttered. "You want to know what I'm going to need before I even know I need it."

A rivulet of blood began snaking its way down the white plaster. Unasked, she passed him a gauze pad to wipe it up.

"Attagirl."

Doctor and nurse were now working in silence, the only noise coming from the snip of the scissors and the clink of instruments rattling on the tray. Then the top was off the cast and Wee Willie was shaking his head. "Lord, Gunny," he rasped, "what a mess you've made." He turned to the nurse. "Who sewed him back up last night?"

Miss Reardon leafed through the pages on her clipboard. "I think it was Doctor Blankenship, Sir." She flipped a few more pages. "Yes, Sir, it was Bob. Here are his notes."

Wee Willie swiveled furiously around to face her. "You will *not* use first names in my department," he growled. "You two can do whatever the hell you want on your own time, but when you're on duty he's 'Dr. Blankenship' to you and you're 'Miss Reardon' to him. Understand?"

"Yes, Sir." She was biting her lip.

He turned back to his work. "Might as well clean this thing up while we're in here, Gunny," he said. "Might hurt a bit. OK?"

Caleb nodded.

"Forceps, Miss Reardon."

It did hurt. But not unbearably, and the stab Caleb felt shoot through his arm when scab or dead tissue resisted the pull of the tweezers seemed somehow to flatten the deeper pain which never went away. Still, it was no picnic. Miss Reardon stood by his head, gently mopping the sweat from his face. He could hear the catch in her breath each time the tweezers hung up on some stubborn piece of meat.

"Well, that's about it," said Wee Willie, shoving himself away from the bed so suddenly that his nurse had to pirouette out of the way. She grabbed the instrument tray from where she'd set it on the night table and held it out uncertainly to him.

"Put that thing down and come over here closer." Wee Willie leaned down, stuffing his nose almost into Caleb's bloody dressings and drew a deep breath loudly through his nose. "Now you do it. See what it smells like."

She bent slightly, and sniffed.

"Closer! Get your nose right down in there!"

Miss Reardon bent further, giving Caleb an unobstructed view down her blouse. Her face was now so close to his that he could see the down on her cheeks and the anger in her eyes.

"Smell OK to you?"

"Sir?"

"The wound, goddammit, girl! How's it smell?"

"I… I don't know, Sir."

"*You don't know!* What the Christ do they teach you people today? First thing I learned…" Something caught his eye and he stopped in mid-sentence. "How in hell did I miss that?" Caleb felt the jab of the forceps again. He looked down but could see only meat.

"Piece of your uniform," Wee Willie grunted, pulling free a length of bloody green thread. "Yours or somebody else's. Want it back?"

Caleb grinned feebly.

"How about you, Miss? Souvenir from the war?"

Miss Reardon looked beguilingly disgusted. Wee Willie swung around again to face her. "Know what's the trouble with young doctors today, Miss?" he demanded.

"No, Sir. I don't." There was an edge to her voice.

"Well, I'll tell you. Young doctors today, they're too christly high and mighty to use their noses. But if you're willing to use that pretty one of yours, you're going to find most times that you can smell trouble long before you can see it." He nodded towards Caleb's arm. "That one still smells pretty good, but before we're done today I'll let you take a whiff of a couple that don't." He looked up at her over his glasses. "Learn to tell the difference and you'll know something even that wise-ass boyfriend of yours doesn't. OK?"

Caleb watched the color rise in her face. "That's uncalled for, Sir," she snapped, her eyes flashing. "And something else, Sir. Something else they didn't teach us in nursing school. They didn't teach us that doctors would try to embarrass us in front of our patients or patronize us by. . . by calling us girl, Sir!

Wee Willie's face showed the ghost of a smile. "Seems they didn't teach you not to talk back to your superiors either, did they? Now hurry up and bandage this guy back up. We're running late already."

She worked swiftly and well. Wee Willie looked over her shoulder scowling. "Don't use all the damn gauze in the house, Girl!" he growled, "You ever find yourself in a field hospital full of wounded men, you're going to be pulling that stuff out of the shit can to use it over again."

She glanced at Caleb with the same 'Isn't he a jerk?' face she'd made earlier. This time he did grin back at her and then wondered right away if he should have. He'd also had to toughen up a lot of wet-behind-the-ears kids, and the only way he'd known how to do that was to be a hard-assed sonofabitch himself.

Alone again, Caleb occupied himself by trying to summon up a mental image of Miss Reardon. He could get bits and pieces. He remembered she had green eyes. High cheekbones. Wide mouth. He was less certain about her hair. *Black,* he thought. *Good figure.* Of that he was sure. But the whole picture eluded him.

That effort occupied him until the agony in his arm reached a point where all he could do was to grit his teeth and roll his head from side to side as he counted down the minutes until the shot which he both craved and feared.

*****

Later that same day or perhaps the day after—Caleb had no way to know—Wee Willie and Nurse Reardon were back at his bedside.

"It ever get cold over there, Gunny?" Wee Willie was asking.

"During the monsoons it did, Sir. Heat was worse."

"Coldest I ever been was in Korea. We had about a half hour to get our KIAs into body bags. Otherwise forget it. After that all we could do was stack 'em up like cordwood." Wee Willie poked at the puckered flesh below Caleb's elbow. "Feel that?"

Caleb winced.

"Only good thing is they didn't stink," Wee Willie muttered as he worked. "Not like Iwo. Christ, there you could damn near see 'em rot." He poked again, lower down. "Here?"

Caleb felt a searing jolt shoot up his arm. "Jesus Christ!" he muttered through clenched teeth.

The giant doctor laughed outright. "Time to call on Jesus would be if you *hadn't* felt that. But you're lucky. You've got a lot less nerve damage than I'd have predicted from the pictures. That's the good news. Bad is that you've lost your thumb. Anybody told you that yet?"

Caleb digested this information in silence. He thought back to a time when he'd been in high school. His science teacher—he'd forgotten the man's name—had drawn the outline of a hand on the blackboard and was standing with his back to the class drawing big, screeching chalk circles around the thumb. And then he'd pirouetted theatrically around to face his students. "Ladies and gentlemen," he'd announced, "I give you the opposable thumb, the humble digit that launched us on the long march towards civilization!"

The image faded, leaving Caleb to wonder at what point in Viet Nam he'd got himself turned around and started back towards the place where that long march towards civilization had begun. If there was a God—and he was undecided on that question—it occurred to him that taking away his thumb might be a precisely tailored bit of divine retribution.

Wee Willie interrupted this reverie. "Looks like your first finger's got to go too," he was saying. "All the other holes you've got in your legs and side are going to leave you with some pretty impressive scars, but there's nothing there that time won't heal."

"Yes, Sir," said Caleb weakly. He tried to visualize where this latest bombshell would leave him. No thumb and three fingers. That would take some getting used to. Wee Willie read his mind. "As to that hand, no worries. What I can do is take your middle finger and move it around so it opposes the other two. Looks like hell but it works."

But for Caleb, fighting back the image of his own arm terminating obscenely in a lobster claw, this news provided little consolation. "How long, Sir?" he asked. "How long until I can get out of here?"

"Depends on you, Gunny," said Wee Willie. "Here, let me show you why." He nodded towards Miss Reardon, who stepped forward carrying an x-ray and smelling of soap. She bent awkwardly across the bed, trying to keep her weight off Caleb's arm while holding the film where he could see it. Wee Willie leaned massively over her shoulder, tapping the back of the film with his pencil. "That's the bone in your upper arm," he said. "What's left of it."

Caleb looked at the bone's image, black against gray, with a large gap between the two jagged ends. "Seems there's a piece missing, Sir," he said.

"There is. About two inches of it. Which is why I've got to build a bridge across that gap, and I can't do that until you stop your thrashing around."

"It's the morphine, Sir," he said, trying to sound less desperate than he felt. "If you'd quit giving me the morphine, I'd quit having the nightmares."

Wee Willie just shook his head. "Morphine's not your problem, Gunny. We've all seen some bad shit in this business. Comes with the territory. You just gotta put it behind you. Put it behind you and let me get on with saving that arm. OK?"

*****

They rolled him back down to the operating room where Wee Willie cut off his trigger finger. He woke up with his hand on fire and Wee Willie, knowing that it would be, upped his dose of dope. They'd shifted him over to Demerol, the theory being that by rotating between painkillers he'd be less likely to become addicted to any of them. Regardless of which they used, the nightmares always returned.

They tried stronger restraints but he fought so hard against them he did himself more damage than before. He lost all track of time. There was no day or night, only an endless round of shots and torments. All around him he could hear the moans of other men and, to his shame, he sometimes added his own voice to this doleful chorus. Then, unmercifully, would come sleep and more hellish dreams. The antiseptic smells of the hospital would give way to the rank stink of decaying jungle vegetation and he would be back in Viet Nam again. Even in sleep he could not escape the place.

*****

He was lying behind a fallen log, his rifle resting across it. Sweat running into his eyes had so blurred his vision that he'd blown an easy shot. The man he'd hit was still floundering feebly in the little pool below. He watched the water turning red with blood. Another figure appeared out of the jungle and tried desperately to pull the wounded man up the muddy bank. They'd get so far and then they'd both slide back into the water.

Heat radiating off his face was again fogging the lens of his scope. He'd wipe it clean with his sleeve only to have it fog up again before he could center this second VC in the cross hairs. "Goddammit!" he was muttering when he heard the voice of his best friend—something that even in his dream he knew was impossible. "Don't do this," his friend was pleading. "If you've got any heart left in you, don't do it."

"I've got to," he argued. "Can't you see? If it's wrong now, then all the others were wrong too."

They were fighting now, struggling for the rifle. He pushed his friend savagely out of the way, grabbed back the rifle and aimed again. The image in his scope cleared. He could feel his finger tightening on the trigger. The Springfield bucked painfully against his shoulder, waking him up.

"Shit!" said the corpsman. "He's got his cast wedged between the mattress and the bed frame."

"I thought we'd tied him down," said a second voice out of the darkness.

"We did. He broke the straps. Go get the nurse, will you? I don't want to try to get this thing loose on my own."

*****

The two doctors met in the hospital cafeteria. "I never got your first name," said Wee Willie to the misshapen little man sitting across the table from him. "Or if I did, I've forgotten it."

"Ernest," said the other man. "So named because my parents hoped I would grow up to be a dutiful, studious son. I was a very great disappointment to them."

"My son, the doctor," laughed Wee Willie, crudely mimicking a Yiddish accent. "I thought all Jewish mothers wanted their sons to be doctors."

"Did I mention that I was Jewish?" asked Ernest Throttlemeyer evenly. "I don't recall that I did. But to answer your question, the last my parents knew of me before they joined Hitler's six million, I was doing cartwheels with a troupe of Bulgarian acrobats." He grinned. "Becoming a clown had always been my childhood ambition. Seemed a clever way to turn a liability into an asset."

Wee Willie found himself uncharacteristically off balance. "Sorry," he mumbled and then headed for safer ground. "Myself, I began life banging nails. Probably still be at it if it hadn't been for the war and the GI Bill." He slugged down a great gulp of coffee before adding an afterthought. "Get right down to it, there isn't a helluva lot of difference between working with wood and working with bone. Except for the politics, that is. Damn sight less politics when I was a wood butcher."

"Life does take unexpected turns, doesn't it," said Commander Throttlemeyer. "As proof of that, I'd offer the fact that the two of us are sitting here today."

Wee Willie sat contemplating his cup. "I guess you know I was against your appointment to the staff here?" he asked finally.

The Commander nodded. "Surprising, really, that the CO went ahead with it in the face of what I understand was your characteristically outspoken opposition. He seems scared to death of you."

"He is," said Wee Willie bitterly. "But that candy-ass son of a bitch'll have the last laugh. He writes the fitness reports."

A group of high-spirited nurses swept into the cafeteria, took one look at Wee Willie, and stopped their skylarking. Commander Throttlemeyer raised his eyebrows. "Seems everyone else is scared to death of you too."

"But you're not?"

"No," said Commander Throttlemeyer, "I'm not. Deformity builds a thick skin. But I am interested in why you were so opposed to my coming here."

"Not fair to the lifers," grunted Wee Willie. "Man devotes his career to the Navy. Then here comes this hotshot civilian and right off the bat they give him the same rank the rest of us worked a lot of years to earn."

"Yes, I can see how that might be a problem. I suppose, though, that you could argue that the Medical Corps didn't have much choice in the matter. You'd find it a bit hard to lure a full professor away from academia if all you had for bait was the same Lieutenant's commission you'd offer his students." The little man grinned mischievously. "Maybe I should have held out for more rank."

Wee Willie snorted so indignantly into his cup that the contents went up his nose, unleashing a thunderous sneeze. "Any of that hit you?" he asked, wiping his eyes. "No? Good! Fact is, Commander, we don't need you here. Far as I'm concerned, if a Sailor or Marine qualifies for your kind of medicine he's by definition of no further use to the military. So I say discharge him to the VA and let them look after him there."

The PA speaker on the wall behind them began a staticky crackle and the cafeteria fell suddenly silent. Then a metallic voice: "Captain Williamson, Captain Williamson, please call Extension 438, Extension 438, Sir."

All around them conversations picked up again. "Initiative!" grunted Wee Willie. "What the fuck ever happened to initiative? Kids I got working for me won't even take a crap without checking with me first." He heaved himself to his feet. "Get you more coffee while I'm up?"

"Thanks, but one cup's my limit."

"Shows you're no Navy man."

It struck Commander Throttlemeyer as he watched his enormous colleague make his way like a great ship through the sea of white uniforms that his new acquaintance was very much an anomaly in a medical staff which, as he'd been quick to notice, affected a studied disregard for all things military. "Squared away"—he'd heard that term used by the Marines, and it seemed to fit Wee Willie, at least in so far as it applied to his bearing and appearance.

The Commander cast a guilty eye over his own disheveled khakis and contemplated making an effort to become a bit more squared away himself. The realist in him knew that no amount of spit and polish would make him look any less the clown. But then again, he'd always tried against long odds to remain an optimist. And now, as a newcomer to the Navy, he was petitioning for membership in a different fraternity, so perhaps here the rules for acceptance were different.

Wee Willie returned, grinning broadly. "Know what we used to call you guys when I was with the grunts?" he laughed.

"Grunts? What are grunts?"

"Marines are grunts. But don't call 'em that yourself. It's kinda like nigger. If you're black, you can call yourself nigger. If you're not, it's a fighting word. Same way with grunt."

"I see. At least I think I do. But you still haven't told me what the grunts call psychiatrists."

"Wizards!" guffawed Wee Willie, slapping his knee. "Wizards and wingnuts!"

"Wingnuts?" asked the commander. "I take it those would be the wizard's patients?"

"Yup, they are. Most times, once a grunt goes to see the wizard, he'll never live it down. Nobody wants him in the same foxhole."

"So where does that leave us with this fellow Caleb you wanted to talk to me about? If he's a wingnut, why not just discharge him to the VA?"

Wee Willie looked genuinely surprised. “Gunny Caleb? No wingnut there. The guy’s a legend.” He paused, realizing that he was caught in a contradiction, and then bulled ahead. “He’s been through a lot. Just having a few nightmares, that’s all. I thought you might have some magic for that.”

“I might,” said the Commander. But just so you know, it won’t be quick. We wizards seldom effect overnight cures.”

“Well, you’re going to have to this time. If I don’t get that arm of his into traction very soon, he’s going to lose the goddamn thing.”

Wee Willie got up to leave. “One other thing,” he said, “some people in high places think it might be a good idea if Caleb were kept under wraps for a while. That’s another reason for moving him up to your ward.”

*****

Caleb had become as sensitive to sounds as a blind man. With nothing to look at but the IV bottle, he spent his conscious hours tuned in on the noises that came from outside the curtains. He knew from the jingle of jars and bottles to anticipate the agony of dressing changes, and he could tell from the rush of feet when one of his unseen neighbors was in trouble.

To pass the time, he tried to predict from the sound of approaching footsteps who would next come through his curtain. Easiest to spot was Wee Willie, whose lumbering tread was a dead giveaway. Another he never missed was the elderly nurse Lieutenant Commander he called Squeak because her orthopedic shoes creaked. Then there was Short, whose footsteps sounded as laid back as the man; and Nurse Reardon herself, who tripped along sounding as if each step came just in time to catch herself from falling on her face.

His one recreation became to add new faces to his catalog of footsteps. So, when at some point in his timeless existence, he heard the sound of an unfamiliar shuffle headed his way, his ears pricked up. He opened his eyes to see a large ugly face smiling down at him from over the top of his still closed curtain. Then the face disappeared, there was a crash, the sound of running feet, and a good-humored voice waving away offers of help.

His curtain parted and the owner of this extraordinary face appeared beside his bed. Caleb's first thought was that the morphine was playing tricks on him. The man who moments before had been tall enough to look over the curtain was now nearly a dwarf whose head was so out of proportion to the rest of him that Caleb found himself averting his eyes as he would to avoid staring at a freak. Ashamed at this reaction, he made himself look back at this oddly proportioned, white-coated little man. The image of his own distorted self reflected in a fun house mirror came back to him and he smiled at the memory.

Caleb had a cruel grin, made so by a scar that cut like a shifted fault line across his mouth so that what started as a smile on the right side of his face ended as a leer on the left. He saw pain flash momentarily in the other man's eyes and recognized that his grin had been misread. His first reaction was guilt; that quickly gave way to anger that now, on top of his other troubles, he had to feel badly for someone else, particularly for someone else who, as he now noticed, was wearing a Commander's oak leaves.

The improbable Navy Commander smiled apologetically. "I've upset you." His smiled widened. "Odd, isn't it, how we react with indignation to the things that make us uncomfortable?"

Not knowing how to answer this, Caleb said nothing.

"Well, it is odd," the Commander continued good-naturedly. "I mean, take our own situation here. If I read it correctly, you are upset with me because my own ludicrous appearance has made you feel embarrassed for staring at me. Yes? Have I got that right?"

Caleb felt himself being goaded out of his pain-centered existence and he wasn't sure he liked it. But he did have to admit the little man had called it right. "Yes, Sir," he said. "That's pretty close."

"So you see then why I find it odd? On reflection, doesn't it seem to you that the wrong one of us feels himself the aggrieved party?"

"Yes, Sir," said Caleb again. Fourteen years in uniform had taught him how to say 'Yes, Sir' in a way that could mean anything or nothing at all.

"Yes, Sir, *what*?" prodded the Commander. "What are you agreeing to with your Yes, Sir?"

"I was out of line, Sir."

"Out of line? How?"

"I was thinking of something else, Sir."

"Still, you saw that you'd hurt my feelings, didn't you? I'd not have expected that. But you're quite right. Even the most hardened freak never really gets used to being laughed at. Or at least this one hasn't." He grinned, held out his hand, and withdrew it when he saw the impossibility of shaking hands. "Well," he said, "now that we know each other so well, I suppose I should introduce myself. I'm Commander Throttlemeyer, Captain Williamson's counterpart in Psychiatry. He's asked me to see if I can help you shake your nightmares."

Loud alarms went off in Caleb's mind. His face took on an obstinate expression.

"Nobody's saying you've gone off the deep end," said the Commander, "But Captain Williamson isn't going to be able to do much for your arm if you keep yanking out his stitches."

Caleb said again what he'd said so many times before. "Take me off the morphine, Sir, and I'll quit having nightmares."

"Maybe you'd stop having the nightmares, but the demons which cause them will still be there. I might be able to help you exorcise those demons."

"I don't need that kind of help, thank you, Sir."

"I think you do. But that's really neither here nor there, isn't it? You're a Marine, my friend. You go where you're sent."

CHAPTER TWO

They moved him up to Ward Nine with the wingnuts. The only advantage was that there he had his own room. They wheeled him into it, parked him next to a window, set up his IV, and left him alone to study his surroundings. He saw the bars on his window and the hastily patched fingernail scratches on his walls, and he smiled ruefully at the images these things conjured up. But he was glad for the window and the chance to look out onto a world with more colors in it than white. Glad too to have his own shower until he remembered he couldn't get up to use it.

A thickly muscled black corpsman arrived with a tray. Judging from the fading light outside, Caleb judged it would have to be supper. The Corpsman's name tag said *Randall, J: Hospitalman Apprentice*.

"Chow time, Gunny," grinned Randall. "You OK with this or you want I should feed you?"

"No to both, Doc. I'm not hungry."

"You gotta eat, man. You got Jell-O here an' all kindsa good shit." He held out a spoon full of soup. "Here, open up!"

Caleb was not going to let himself be fed. So he went at it himself, trying to eat left-handed without fetching up on the IV tube in his arm.

Randall stood watching him wrestle with the Jell-O. "You doin' good, man! Practice some more an' you might even get some in your mouth." He consulted the clipboard hung at the foot of the bed. "Says here you ain't shit. Fuck man! I gotta tell you everything? Any fool know you gotta shit same as you gotta eat."

"Doc, where I come from it's the E-7s who tell the E-2s when to shit!"

“Maybe so, but you don’t shit real soon, this E-2’s gonna be stuffin’ an enema up your E-7 ass!”

Caleb smiled despite himself. Randall fussed around, dumping Caleb’s piss pot and cleaning up the mess he’d made with his food.

“You like this work, Doc?”

“No Suh, I do not. But we all gotta do some time in a hospital before they send us on for more school.”

“How’d you end up working on the psych ward?”

Randall chuckled. “Time to time a patient up here’ll get rowdy an’ we got to settle him down. Could be that’s why they got me up here on Nine. But I don’t mind workin’ with you wingnuts.”

That last Randall said with a grin, and Caleb decided to let it slide.

Randall started toward the door and turned back. “You seen the Vulture yet, Gunny?”

“The Vulture?” Caleb asked, startled. “What’s the Vulture?”

“Vulture ain’t a what, he’s a who. He’s the Commander! He’s the *man*, Gunny!”

“So why do you call him the Vulture?”

“’Cuz he look like one.”

“Like hell! You ever seen a vulture? Vulture’s got a tiny little head.”

“They be bald, don’t they?”

“Yeah.”

“Got a big-ass beak?”

“That too.”

“So that’s why we call him the Vulture.”

A nurse came in with his shot and the last image that flashed across Caleb’s mind before he was engulfed again in the morphine fog was of a carrion-covered vulture waiting just out of his reach until he would become too feeble to chase it away.

*****

He was a boy again, eight years old and going out the farmhouse door to fetch eggs from his aunt’s chicken coop. “Keep an eye out for any hen with yoke on her beak," she called after him. "She'll be the one's been breaking the eggs."

"What'll I do if see her?" he called back.

"Catch her if you can."

"Then what?"

"Lord help me, Johnny," she laughed. "Do I have to spell it out for you? Put her in that crate by the door and I'll kill her after I've done the milking."

He spotted the culprit right away, cornered her after a brief chase and picked her up. She pecked painfully at his arm, but his aunt had taught him what to do. He flipped her over on her back and she settled into a trance, staring up at him unblinking with yellow reptile eyes.

He knew what to do now too. He'd seen his aunt do it many times. All it took was to tuck the hypnotized hen under one arm, grab her by the neck, pull down hard, snap her head back and twist. Do it right, his aunt always said, and they never feel a thing.

He hesitated, wondering if she'd be angry. *No*, he thought. *She'd be proud.* Killing's no fun, she'd told him, but somebody's got to do it.

So he did it. But it didn't work. He was big for his age but the hen was big too. She got a wing loose and beat hard at his face as he bent forward, pulling and twisting desperately at her neck. And then, just as she was about to slip from under his arm, he felt a snap and the bird went limp. He looked down at the head that now hung loose from his hand and recoiled in horror to see that the body he was holding was no longer that of a chicken.

He woke up lying in a pool of his own blood.

*****

Wee Willie came by in the morning and was not pleased.

"It's the dope, Sir," said a shamefaced Caleb. He had to believe that. Otherwise he really was a wingnut.

Wee Willie looked at him thoughtfully. "OK, Gunny," he shrugged, "I'll show you what you're asking for.

"Nurse!" he called over his shoulder. "Get me a dressing kit, will you?"

Squeak was accompanying Wee Willie on his rounds that day. She unwrapped the kit. Wee Willie again selected forceps and probed into the raw open wound on Caleb's forearm as he'd done before. But this time he probed harder. Caleb flinched.

"Feel that?"

"Not too bad, Sir," he said through clenched teeth.

"No?" Wee Willie dug deeper. Caleb felt the tweezers rasp against something hard. Every muscle in his body jerked tight at the spasm of pain that shot through him.

"Still OK?"

Beads of sweat were running down his face. He nodded.

"Well, hang on then. Because this will hurt."

Caleb forced himself to watch. Beneath pooling blood he could make out a piece of dull white bone.

Wee Willie was twisting the tweezers this way and that trying to get hold of it. His bushy eyebrows knit closer and closer together until finally they met in a straight line across his nose. "Son of a bitch!" he muttered. He paused, considering the problem, then poked again tentatively at the bone.

Watching him, Caleb flashed back to a long ago day when he and his father had hit granite while setting a fence post. He remembered his father standing back to consider the problem of that rock and looking much the way Wee Willie did now. He saw his dad again as he'd tapped at it with the post spade, listening for the dull thunk that meant a seam along which the stone would split. He heard the repeated ring of iron against hard granite, then the thunk, and then it was himself gasping "*God damn!*" as Wee Willie drove the tweezers deep into the meat of his arm, twisted, wrenched hard, and came away triumphant with a big bloody fragment of dead bone.

"Sponge," said Wee Willie matter-of-factly. The ashen-faced Squeak slapped one into his hand and he set about mopping up the blood that now poured from the cavity vacated by the bone.

"Ordinary pain serves a purpose," Wee Willie went on, "but real agony—agony so godawful it becomes debilitating—that's always seemed to me to be one of nature's mistakes." He paused to mop up more blood, then looked up at Caleb over his glasses. "Sorry to do that, Gunny, but you asked for it! What you felt just now is pretty much how you'd be feeling all the time without the pain killers."

"We could try, Sir," Caleb pleaded. "If it got too bad, I could always go back on them."

"Wouldn't work. You felt how your muscles seized up when I dug for that fragment? That's the body's instinctive reaction to stabbing pain. We cut out the dope and you'll just pull yourself apart even worse than you're doing now."

*****

"You going to be able to do anything for my boy?" asked Wee Willie when next he met the Commander in the cafeteria.

"Too early to say," replied the Vulture. "If I had to make a preliminary diagnosis based on what I've learned of his record, I'd label him the classic psychopath. Cold-blooded killer, incapable of any feelings, including fear—that kind of thing. But somehow all that doesn't square with the nightmares, does it?"

Wee Willie shrugged. "You're asking the wrong man."

"It is a bit of a puzzle. I can't recall ever reading anything in the literature on the subject, but, empirically, you'd have to think the true psychopath would be less prone to nightmares than the rest of us. So I expect Caleb may be a deeper well after all."

"Gonna be a deep well with only one arm if you don't do something quick," muttered Wee Willie.

"Rather a mixed metaphor, that one," laughed the little doctor. "But let me remind you, my dear fellow, that we wizards deal with afflictions which are every bit as real as a broken bone and take every bit as long to heal."

"Maybe I should just cut off his arm and be done with it. That what you're telling me?"

"It may come to that. But compose your soul to patience. All modesty aside, I'm really quite good at what I do."

"Yeah? So what exactly do you do?"

"Do I detect a note of sarcasm? If so, I'll overlook it. To answer your question as it applies specifically to Sergeant Caleb, I see my task as helping him to become more comfortable in his own skin than he is now. So you mend his body and I'll mend his soul." The Vulture looked levelly at his counterpart. "I'll let you decide which one of us has the harder job. Yes?"

Even Wee Willie, for whom language was a blunt instrument, could feel the steel that lay behind that 'Yes'. *Cocky little bastard,* he thought. But he liked that. He liked a fighter. So he was finding it hard not to warm to this unusual man. Still, he wasn't yet ready to lower his guard. He'd spent too many years as an enlisted man and then graduated from too unpretentious a medical school to ever feel at ease with his more urbane colleagues; his abrasive manner was his defense against what he knew to be the talk that went on behind his back. So without excusing himself, he blew his nose loudly into his napkin, inspected the results, got up from the table and left.

*****

"I understand Wee Willie's made you a convert to pain killers." The Vulture was studying Caleb's clipboard. He saw his reluctant patient's expression and changed the subject. "Another nightmare?"

"Yes, Sir."

"Remember anything about it?"

"No, Sir." Which he realized was a very unconvincing lie.

"Nothing at all?"

Caleb had been trained to resist interrogation. *"Name, rank and branch of service,"* the instructor had told his class before they'd been subjected to two very realistic weeks of hell. *"If they break you to where you got to give them more than that, buy yourself time. Feed 'em bits and pieces they can't use."* With that advice in mind, Caleb considered his reply. "It was something about killing a chicken," he said finally. "One of my Aunt's chickens."

The Vulture hoisted himself into a chair where he teetered with his short legs barely reaching the floor. "Something about killing a chicken?" he said. "Is it that you don't remember what it was about killing a chicken, or that you don't want to tell me what it was about killing a chicken?"

"Yes, Sir."

"I'm not sure that answers the question. But spare me another of your 'Yes Sirs,' will you, Gunny? You won't hurt my feelings one bit if you dispense with the Sir."

Career NCO that he was, Caleb believed in the sanctity of protocol. "That wouldn't be right, Sir," he said primly.

"Say I were to ask you fifty questions in a row. Would you answer each one with Sir?"

"Yes, Sir."

"Forty-nine to go!" laughed the Vulture. "I had to stand on a stool," he went on. "Fell off the damn thing."

"Sir?"

"I had to stand on a stool to see you over the curtain."

"Hardly seems worth the trouble, Sir."

"For me just getting up on a stool is trouble. But I wanted to see you before you saw me."

Caleb looked puzzled.

"Yes, I grant you it does seem odd. But people do tend to react unpredictably in the presence of the deformed and that, for me, becomes something of a professional liability. So I always try to sneak a look at my patients before they get a look at me."

Why is he telling me this, Caleb wondered? *Is it to encourage the same candor on my part? If so,* he thought, *good luck to you, Sir*. But then it occurred to him that perhaps the little man's own candor about coming to terms with his twisted body was intended to prepare him for having to do the same thing with his own. He shook his head, trying to banish the thought that now he too was deformed.

"You were asleep when I first saw you, Gunny."

"I heard you coming, Sir." It was a point of honor. Caleb was still alive because his senses were sharper than most men's.

"You looked to be asleep to me. You know what they say, don't you? 'The face of a sleeping man is the window to his soul.'"

Caleb grinned. "The face of a sleeping man generally has its mouth open and is drooling on the pillow."

"Which proves the point doesn't it?"

They both laughed. But Caleb was quick to get his guard up again. He'd had only one really close friend in all his years of active duty. It had been an improbable friendship—he, the taciturn Yankee loner, and Jacob Hume, the irreverent drop-out physicist from Brooklyn—but it had been Hume who had taught him the fun of conversation simply as an end in itself. It was a very unYankee-like recreation, and now this improbable Navy Commander seemed to be trolling for him with the same lure.

"*Look out for the nice guys*," his escape and evasion instructor had warned, and he'd been right. The bad guys had tied his hands behind him in a hammerlock and hung him up with his toes barely touching the ground. And then after they'd repeatedly kicked his feet out from underneath him each time he'd refused to answer their questions, they'd left him hanging. The nice guy had taken over when the tendons in his shoulders had felt about to snap. "*This isn't even real, Corporal*," he'd said. "*It's just a training exercise. So why put yourself through this kind of shit? Just answer a couple of questions for me so the CO won't get on my ass, OK?*" He'd been close to agreeing before he saw the trap. "*Caleb*," he groaned. "*John, no middle initial. Corporal, USMC, 1693904*," upon which the nice guy also had kicked his feet out from underneath him.

So he hid again behind his 'Yes, Sir.'

"You get a lot into those two words," smiled the Vulture. "I read suspicion and maybe even a bit of contempt. So I better make my pitch before the next 'Yes Sir' comes along to tune me out entirely.

"You see, my training tells me that whenever you find yourself unable to confront some awful experience—whenever you try to bury it —you start to build up what for lack of a better expression you might call a head of psychic steam. That steam's got to vent somehow, Gunny, and in your case I surmise that it vents through your nightmares."

Caleb said nothing.

"Any of that make sense?"

"No Sir. Not to me."

"Why not?"

"OK Sir, let's say it does make sense. Then the nightmares are the cure, not the problem. Let me ride out a few more bad nights and I should have the steam pretty well vented off. Right?"

"Quite a clever rebuttal. But of course if that were the case, how many bad nights would depend on how much pressure's in the boiler. If I'm not mistaken, your argument does concede that there is pressure in the boiler. Yes?"

Point for the other team, thought Caleb. "Sure there's pressure, Sir. Everybody carries around a head of steam. But they keep the lid on it, same as I would if I wasn't all fucked up with dope."

"Not my bailiwick, Gunny! You'll have to take that one up with Captain Williamson. I'm here about the steam." The Commander paused, rummaging through his briefcase. "I brought along your *Service Record Book.* Mind if I look through it?"

"What if I did mind, Sir?"

"Then I'd have to remind you that for the duration of your stay here Captain Williamson and I share the role as your surrogate commanding officers." The Vulture adjusted his glasses and began leafing through the manila folder. "No next of kin?"

"None, Sir."

"Father? Mother? Both deceased?

"Yes, Sir."

"You mentioned an aunt? The one with the chickens?"

"She's dead too," said Caleb curtly. "Can we leave it there, Sir?"

"Yes." The Vulture muttered. "I suppose we'll have to." He leafed through more pages. "You've been to a great many schools. Parachute School, Underwater Swimming School, Ranger School, Mountain Warfare School, and that's not the half of them. Isn't that somewhat unusual?"

"I was in a Reconnaissance Company, Sir. That's about all we did was to go to schools. Pretty good fun, most of them."

"For you, perhaps. For me, fun is not the word that comes to mind when I contemplate leaping from an airplane." The Vulture continued thumbing silently through the record. His hands seemed to be invested with all the grace nature had denied to the rest of him and, as Caleb watched him turning the pages, he was reminded of a time years before when a well dressed stranger had come calling on his father. It had been a one time visit. Nothing, or at least nothing discernible to a small boy, had followed from it. But he'd never forgotten the difference between the two men's hands. They'd sat at the kitchen table with documents spread out between them and he, who'd thought all grown up hands were rough and work-hardened like his father's, had been mesmerized by the other man's long white tapered fingers and the way they seemed to float from one paper to the next, before settling on one of them, caressing it smooth, and pushing it along with a gold fountain pen across the table for his father to sign. His own father by contrast had seemed all awkwardness, that gold pen almost lost in his huge hands as he formed the letters of his signature.

Over the years Caleb had come to see those two sets of hands as symbolic of the difference between ideas and action. It was the difference between the thinkers and the doers, and he, who counted himself among the doers, had convinced himself that the only way to understand a place was to go there yourself. So now, as he waited for this wizard to finish pawing through his past, he was thinking that someone who knew nothing of war was no more competent to cure him of his nightmares than would an architect who couldn't swing a hammer be competent to build a house.

"This from Page Eleven," recited the Vulture, interrupting Caleb's reverie. "Honor graduate from Parris Island in May of '57. Then we have a meritorious promotion to corporal." He ran his finger down the entries. "Couple of Letters of Commendation. And here's another meritorious promotion. This one to sergeant." His brow furrowed and Caleb knew what was coming. "'*10 May, 1965, Reduced to the rank of corporal.*' That had to be only a month or so after you first got to Viet Nam." He turned back to the *Record of Duty Assignments*. "Yes, it was. You landed at Da Nang on the eleventh of March." He looked up inquiringly.

"It's all in there, Sir. Page Thirteen. That's the *Record of Convictions by Court Martial* in case you can't find it."

"Page Thirteen isn't actually on page thirteen," noted the Vulture. He read silently for a moment. "You beat up a Vietnamese officer?"

"That's what it says, Sir."

"What it says specifically is that 'Sergeant John Caleb, U. S. Marine Corps, on active duty, did, on or near the city of Da Nang, the Republic of South Viet Nam, on or about 14 April, 1965, assault First Lieutenant Than Hu Duc, Army of South Viet Nam, a friendly foreign power, by repeatedly striking the said First Lieutenant Duc with his fists.'" The Vulture closed the folder with a snap. "What was all that about?"

Feed 'em bits and pieces they can't use, Caleb's instructor had advised. So what the hell? Talking helped him forget the pain.

CHAPTER THREE

He'd been a squad leader in the Second Platoon, Delta Company, First Battalion, Third Marines, and on March 11th, 1965 they'd slogged in full combat gear across the Da Nang beach to be met by politely applauding schoolgirls. His battalion was one of the two making up the 9th Marine Expeditionary Brigade which was the first unit of American ground troops to be committed to Viet Nam.

Caleb had been a Marine for eight years and had been shot at a couple of times in the Dominican Republic, but that hardly counted as combat. So he was happy that day to be relieved of the worry that the little brushfire in Viet Nam would be put out before he got there.

In the beginning it wasn't much of a war. They'd been told that their only mission was to provide security for the Da Nang airfield in order to free up more ARVN troops who would do the actual fighting. Second Platoon laid wire, filled sand bags, built bunkers, sweated and bitched about the desk-bound warriors in Washington who wouldn't let them off the leash. Their Platoon Sergeant had fought in Korea and knew better. "Won't be too long," he predicted, "before all you hard chargers will be wishing you were still back here inside the wire!"

"Shee-ut, Gunny!" laughed the platoon clown. "I ain't seen one of these Slopeheads yet stands much over five feet."

"Give any one of them a rifle and he's just as big as you are."

"I'm turrible afeard! Just lookin' at them rat-assed little rice farmers sets me to quakin' in my boots!"

Their Gunny shrugged. "OK, wise ass. But don't say I didn't warn you. There's some hard-eyed motherfuckers waiting for you out there."

"One o' them hard-eyed motherfuckers is up at the battalion CP right now," someone else chimed in. "ARVN just brought in a guy they're sayin' is a real live Viet Cong."

Caleb went up to the CP for a look. The shirtless prisoner stood silently with his arms tied behind him while the battalion's Vietnamese liaison officer, Lieutenant Duc, strutted back and forth in front of him, yelling questions. 1/3's own intelligence officer watched while Duc drew a bloody line down the suspect's bare chest with the point of his knife.

The prisoner winced but didn't open his mouth. Duc flipped the K-Bar around in his hand and knocked the man's front teeth out with the handle.

"Jesus Christ, Sir," Caleb muttered to the S-2. "Are you going to let him kill that guy?"

"Cool it, Sergeant. It's his war."

The prisoner went down to his knees. The ARVN officer kicked him forward onto his face and walked around behind him, flashing them a big gold toothed "watch this" kind of grin. He stuck his knife up the prisoner's ass and twisted it. Then he jerked him back up onto his knees and kept on yelling questions while the man who might have been a Viet Cong sat rocking in agony in a fast widening pool of blood.

Caleb had seen all he could take. He slammed Duc onto the ground. The ARVN officer rolled back up onto his feet like a cat, his knife in his hand and murder in his eyes. Caleb caught him by the knife hand and would have broken his wrist if the S-2 and a couple of others hadn't pulled the two men apart.

They locked him up in the battalion's makeshift brig where he spent a sleepless night contemplating a career in ruins. The battalion Sergeant Major came by the next morning and found him sitting dejectedly on his bunk. The older man shook his head in wonder. "You should be proud of yourself, kid," he said. "It's not every Buck Sergeant can cause a flap that gets all the way up to MACV."

"I'm fucked, aren't I, Sergeant Major?"

"If regiment had its way, you'd be flappin' in the breeze. I don't know how the Old Man did it, but he's convinced the higher ups to settle for a summary court. Regiment's the convening authority and the Old Man himself is gonna be the court martial officer."

Caleb knew that a summary court was the least severe of the three military courts, but it was a court martial nonetheless. "What's the worst that can happen?" he asked.

"You get busted down a pay grade and forfeit two thirds pay for a month."

"No confinement?"

"Like I said, Sergeant, you're one lucky son of a bitch. Summary court can't confine an E-5." The Sergeant Major held up a paper. "I got the charge sheet here. Violation of Article 138, Assault on a Superior Officer. Technically the Old Man's got to serve this on you himself, but he's asked me to do it. He wants to get this damn thing under the rug quick as he can."

Caleb accepted the charge sheet without reading it. "So what's next?"

"You got to decide how you're gonna plead. Old Man says to tell you that's up to you. If you want to plead not guilty, he'll play it by the numbers. Call witnesses. Take depositions. The whole bit."

Caleb laughed mirthlessly. "Trouble is, I am guilty."

"So that's how you're going to plead?"

He nodded.

"Then the court'll be at 1300 this afternoon. I'll come get you."

Caleb spent the morning squaring away his uniform. The Sergeant Major came back at 1245 and he followed him silently back up to the CP with two brig chasers in tow. "One thing the Old Man hates worse than a fuckup," said the Sergeant Major over his shoulder. "That's an ass-licker."

1/3's CO was Lieutenant Colonel Otis E. Kant. He'd won a Navy Cross in Korea and there were two stories about why he was called the Ice Man. One had it that he was cool as ice under fire and the other that he was the coldest, most ambitious, calculating son of a bitch in the entire Marine Corps. Caleb didn't know which story to believe. He hoped it was the first one.

They stopped in front of the Colonel's tent. "Wait here," said the Sergeant Major, "and may God have mercy on your soul!" He ducked under the canvas. Caleb heard murmured voices from inside and the Sergeant Major reappeared to beckon him in.

The Colonel was reading at his field desk. Caleb reported as ordered. The Colonel continued to read. Caleb stood at attention, his heart pounding.

"At ease," said the Ice Man finally.

Caleb snapped to parade rest. The Ice Man looked up at him. He was a dry stick of a man with skin drawn so tightly over his face that the veins in his forehead stood out like a road map. Sunlight filtered through green canvas gave him a greenish tinge. In all, thought Caleb, the man about to decide his future looked more like an accountant than a war hero.

"See this bundle of crap, Caleb?" said the Ice Man, holding up the thick stack of papers he'd been reading. "This is the *Summary Court Martial Guide* which I'm supposed to follow to the letter to insure you get a fair shake. It tells you that you have the right to refuse trial by summary court in which case regiment will decide how to dispose of your case. It also goes into some detail to make sure you understand the implications of your guilty plea."

He put the papers back on his desk. "There are just three of us in this tent," he went on. "You, me and the Sergeant Major. So what I'm proposing is that we shortcut this proceeding. You understand that what I'm saying now is off the record and that if you agree to it you'll get a written record of trial that will include a good many pages of questions by me and answers by you that you won't recognize because I didn't ask them and you didn't answer them."

"Yes, Sir," said Caleb, wondering if he was being set up.

"You understand also that you could probably overturn the sentence I'm about to give you and in the process hang me higher than a kite by claiming, and claiming quite correctly, that I've denied you due process?"

Now Caleb really was lost. "No, Sir," he said finally. "I'm not sure I do understand that."

"I'll spell it out for you. First thing is that you've opened up what could turn into a huge can of worms. ARVN's pissed at you. MACV's pissed at you. About the only good thing is that somehow the press hasn't yet got wind of this affront you've caused to our comrades in arms. With me so far?"

"Yes, Sir."

"So I guess you can see why I want this thing to just go away. I don't want to have to call Lieutenant Duc as a witness and I don't want a bunch of reporters sitting in on an open trial. To avoid all that, I'm willing to risk you blowing this whole thing wide open." He paused. "Look at me, Sergeant!"

Caleb had his eyes fixed on a point above the colonel's head. He looked down into cold gray eyes.

"I've read your record and don't think you will play games. If I did, we wouldn't be having this conversation."

"I won't, Sir."

"I'm still going to hit you with the maximum sentence this court allows. You understand that too, don't you?" The Ice Man paused and then added "Corporal."

"Yes, Sir. I guess I've got that coming."

"We're also going to have to get you out of sight. Lieutenant Duc's expecting to see you up before a firing squad and I haven't disabused him of that impression." He turned to his Sergeant Major. "You got that taken care of, Top?"

"Yes, Sir. Got his orders right here." The Sergeant Major passed them across the desk. The Ice Man glanced at them briefly. "You're going to Chu Lai, Corporal. Second Battalion, Fourth Marines. That's my old friend Pete Riccio's outfit. He tells me he was your company commander back at LeJeune. Spoke highly of you."

"The Wop, Sir?" In Caleb's delight at the prospect of again seeing his favorite officer, the words were out before he caught himself.

"Colonel Riccio," the Ice Man corrected dryly.

"Yes, Sir, That's... that's who I meant, Sir."

"Very well then," said the Ice Man, "I suppose we can consider this court martial adjourned."

Caleb could hear the Sergeant Major gathering up his papers. He came uncertainly to attention, not sure if he'd been dismissed.

"Hold it, both of you!" barked the Ice Man. "We're not quite done here yet. I want to hear what exactly you were thinking of yesterday, Corporal."

Caleb drew a blank. He froze, staring off into space.

"You better say something," the Ice Man prompted. "You've caused me a great deal of trouble and I want to know why."

"The Lieutenant was torturing that man, Sir!" Caleb blurted.

"So he was. And what if he'd learned something that might have saved your own squad from walking into a minefield? Would that change your high-minded position?"

Another blank. Another long silence. Behind him, the Sergeant Major was clearing his throat again. Caleb remembered his warning about ass-lickers. "No, Sir," he said finally, "It wouldn't. We had classes on the Geneva Convention at NCO School. Aren't we…?"

The Ice Man shrugged. "Nobody plays by those rules. Not us. Not them. The only conventions that stick in wartime are the ones neither side dares ignore. We don't use nerve gas so they won't use nerve gas. Laws or morality haven't got a damn thing to do with it."

Caleb knew he was on shaky ground. Was he supposed to agree with that heresy or was it a test to see if he wouldn't? He decided to say what he thought. "We are trying to fight a moral war, Sir. That's why we don't fire at their temples…"

"Look where it's getting us. The VC are holing up in those temples we don't destroy and the NVA are building SAM sites on the dikes we don't bomb."

So what's he saying? Caleb wondered. That we should be blowing up their temples? We're American for chrissake! "What about the people we've come here to help," he demanded indignantly, forgetting the 'Sir.' "Those are their temples and their rice paddies, aren't they?"

"Come off it, Corporal! All you'll see from that foolish altruism of yours is a longer war. You'll get more planes shot down, more destruction done, and a lot more people killed on both sides. All that in the name of fighting your moral war!"

Caleb was about to say if that was the price for decency, then so be it. But he saw the contradiction there and felt suddenly less sure of himself.

The Ice Man sensed his ambivalence. "There's only one moral principle in this game," he said quietly. "That's to get the goddamn thing over with. Torture, atrocities, killing women and children, whatever it takes to end it, that's what we do."

Caleb just shook his head, not believing what he was hearing.

The Ice Man smiled thinly. "I'm not telling you to shitcan your sense of decency. I'm just saying you can't let those high-minded principles of yours stop you from doing your job. Is that clear?"

"It's not, Sir."

"You'll figure it out soon enough. Now get out of here. Your fool stunt's cost me enough time already."

Caleb did a stunned about face and marched out.

Outside, the Sergeant Major handed him a set of Corporal's bars. "Old Man was hoping he could just get you quietly out of town," he explained, "but he had to bust you down to corporal to throw regiment a bone."

"When do I leave, Sergeant Major?"

"This afternoon, but first we got a little show to put on for Lieutenant Duc." So the two brig chasers marched Caleb over to his tent and stood outside while he packed his gear. Then he took his place between them with his sea bag over his shoulder. "Prisoner, march!" commanded the senior man. They paraded him back through the Battalion CP, past a scowling Lieutenant Duc, and on to the airfield where he was released by his guards and flown to Chu Lai where the Second Battalion, Fourth Marines had just arrived from Hawaii.

*****

Caleb looked out his window and saw the rush hour traffic backed up on Broad Street nine stories below. Beside him the Vulture sat silently writing in his notebook. The pain, held at bay while he'd relived that long ago day, was making up for lost time and he had to clamp his jaw hard shut not to show it.

"Your Ice Man advances a very Machiavellian argument," said the Vulture without looking up. "Much the same one, really, that the Nazis used to justify putting my parents in the gas chamber."

The comparison was jolting enough that Caleb's pain gave way to anger. "That's a cheap shot, Sir!"

"It's not, Gunny. What both positions have in common is the belief that evil can be justified in the service of a greater good. Your colonel condones atrocities if committing them will expedite the end of the killing. The Nazis condoned far worse ones in hopes of purifying the race. If you agree that both saw themselves as pursuing worthy ends, then the link's not that far-fetched, is it?"

"I don't buy it, Sir. The Nazis were. . ."

"Thugs and sadists? Some were, to be sure. But there were also highly educated men among their ranks. Idealists even. Within the SS there were men who would have infinitely preferred assignment even to the Eastern Front, but who stayed at their posts by the ovens, convinced that they, as the best and the brightest, had the moral duty to carry out what they believed to be the repugnant but necessary task of improving mankind." He smiled sadly. "In their eyes, they were killing my parents to make the world a better place! You see the irony in that, don't you?"

But Caleb was no longer listening. He'd developed a theory that his pain came metered out—a fixed amount every four hours—so that any put on hold while his mind was otherwise occupied got added on top of the rest once he again became aware of it. Which was what was happening now. The pain had taken over and his resolve was gone. He heard steps approaching and looked hopefully towards the door. But it was only Randall coming in to remind his boss of a Department Heads meeting which was about to begin.

"Good Lord!" said the Vulture. "I forgot all about it. My apologies, Gunny..." He didn't finish but instead quickly left the room, returning seconds later with a syringe. "I'm a little rusty at this kind of thing," he said apologetically, "but if you're willing to risk my botching it up, I'll... I'll give it a shot."

Caleb's jaw was too tightly clenched shut to attempt an answer.

"Give it a shot! Get it? I thought that was quite a good joke," the little man grinned. "Rather takes the edge off when you have to explain it."

"Just... just give me the goddamn thing!"

The Vulture unhooked Caleb's chart from where it hung at the end of the bed. "A bit early yet. You've still got a half hour before you're due. Maybe I ought to wait?"

"Oh, for chrissake!"

The Vulture expertly injected the morphine into Caleb's left arm. "There," he said. "Now let's hear no more about how you don't want the painkillers. Yes?"

But Caleb was already asleep. The Vulture nodded towards the door and Randall came in to take his place by the bed. "Don't you worry none, Suh," he whispered. "He even move, an' I'll be on him like flies on shit!"

That night he had no dreams he could remember, surfacing from sleep to find Randall sitting beside his bed.

"What time is it, Doc?"

"2350. 'Nuther ten minutes you be gettin' another shot."

Being reminded brought back the pain. He spent that long ten minutes waiting for the dope and when it came he fell back into unconsciousness. Randall's relief came on at midnight.

"How's he doing?" the new man asked.

"Doin' good! But I ain't. I'm ready for my beddy."

"Don't forget your log entry."

"Shit!" said Randall. "I ain't never gonna get outa here!" He picked up the clipboard and wrote: *Slept real good. Mumbled something. Sounded like homer. Said it twice but I couldn't make it out.*

*****

"Does the word 'homer' bring anything to mind Gunny?" The Vulture was perched in his usual place beside Caleb's bed

"I dunno, Sir. Baseball maybe. Why do you ask?"

"Something you said in your sleep. But maybe it wasn't homer. Anything close to that ring a bell?"

Caleb felt himself naked. *Name/rank & branch of service* might hold them off while he was awake, but God knows what they were finding out about him while he was asleep. He shook his head.

"No matter. Let's go on."

"No Sir. Let's not."

"I see. Well then, that's it for today, isn't it?" The Vulture packed up his papers and said good-bye.

That night Caleb had another nightmare.

*****

He was with a girl he'd known in high school. They'd been swimming and now they were walking through the New England woods. She was ahead and he behind her carrying a picnic basket and watching how her dress clung to her still wet bathing suit. But then, in the way of dreams, the woods gave way to rice paddies and instead of on a wooded path they were walking along a dike between flooded fields. He saw the trip wire before she did. He could hear himself yelling. She stopped in mid stride, lost her balance, and fell forward. He struggled to catch her but found his arm pinned down. There was a blinding flash and she disintegrated into a red haze.

Then the light above his bed was on shining painfully in his eyes and his room was filled again with white-clad figures.

*****

Short had gone Mexican. He'd grown a huge Pancho Villa mustache and affected the mannerisms that went with it. "*Ola, Amigo*!" he grinned as he and Miss Reardon swept into Caleb's room the morning after that last nightmare. "How they hangin'?"

"I'll let you know next time I stand up, Sir," said Caleb curtly. He'd decided he didn't like Doctor Blankenship, in part because of the man's un-officer like ways but also, he had to admit, because that irreverent doctor had evidently snagged Miss Reardon. It was not that he was jealous. Only that he thought she deserved better. Or so he tried to convince himself.

"*Chistozo*, Juan!" laughed Short. "A joke, no?"

Caleb didn't answer. Even as a civilian he'd not liked strangers calling him by his first name. But having an officer do so was infinitely more insulting.

"Soooo..." said Short, "Our man's his usual talkative self. Open the casket, will you Nancy? I had to sew him up again last night. Hung over and half asleep I was at the time, so let's see how I did in the cold light of day."

Miss Reardon set about unwrapping the gauze, met Caleb's eyes and smiled.

"Seems it's my bad luck to be on call every time you throw a nutty on us, Juan," said Short. "Getting so's I'm putting stitches on top of stitches."

Miss Reardon lifted the top of the cast. "It's getting pretty soggy, Bob," she said, setting the blood soaked plaster down on the rollaway table. "Maybe you should get him down to the cast room?"

"Yeah, remind me, will you?" Short bent over the open wound. "Wee Willie seen this yet?"

"I don't think so. He's been in the O.R. all morning."

"He'll give me the usual ration of shit when he does. But *que sera sera*. You might as well close him up. Nothing more we can do here."

She picked up the cast. "This thing's disgusting," she said, wrinkling her nose.

"We'll send him down for a new one." Short paused reflectively. "No. On second thought, let's let Wee Willie do it. If he's gonna piss on me anyway, why bother?"

"Maybe because it's your job to bother, Bob."

He shrugged, then turned back to Caleb. "Hey, *Amigo*, you heard about the veterans' march? Thousand of 'em going down to DC to throw away their medals. Bunch of the guys on the ward want me and Nancy here to go down and represent them."

Miss Reardon had finished with Caleb's cast. "Can we sign you up?" she asked, dazzling him with her smile. "With your record, the press would mob you."

Caleb didn't answer. The thought of active duty Marines participating even by proxy in peace marches seemed to him disloyal, and he wanted no part of it.

"You'd be among friends," Short urged. "We've been passing a bucket around the ward and it's already half full of ribbons. Letters too, Nancy's been collecting them."

Randall had come in with Caleb's lunch. "You be haulin' all the Gunny's medals to DC," he said as he left. "You'd best get yourselves a bigger bucket."

"But that's the point," said Short. "We need you, Buddy. Think about it, OK?"

Caleb was trying to sit up. They'd only seen him flat on his back and now, somehow, he seemed a much larger presence.

"I'm not sure you're supposed to be doing that," warned Miss Reardon. She started towards him and then stopped short, realizing with a start that the man in the bed had suddenly become the man she'd been hearing the rumors about.

"Let me ask you something, Bobby," Caleb was smiling his half smile/half leer. "It's OK if I call you Bobby, isn't it, Good Buddy?"

"Yes.... Sure. I mean, why not?" Short's good humor was showing signs of strain.

"So what I'm asking, Bobby, is what with you being a superior officer and all—you know, superior as in smarter because I'm betting that's how you think of yourself—is it really your job to convince a bunch of shot up eighteen year old kids that the war they fought is wrong or immoral or whatever else you guys are calling it? I mean, that's got to make them feel real good about themselves, won't it?"

"Very clever speech, *Amigo*. We can debate the war some other time. But I'll tell you now where you got it wrong. First, I don't buy any of your military bullshit, OK? I'm not an officer. I'm a doctor, and the only reason I'm even wearing this clown suit is that it got me a free ride through medical school."

"You took the oath. You wear the suit. That's the deal you made, Good Buddy."

"That's not the deal I made."

"No? Then you're not just an asshole, Bobby. You're a dishonest asshole."

"Hold it right there, Sergeant! You're way out of line!"

"Why's that, Bobby? You just said yourself you're not an officer."

*****

"Guess I'll have to chew Caleb a new asshole," grinned Wee Willie when he and the Vulture met again. "But I wish to hell I'd been there to see him tuck it to that wise-ass!"

"We may have a problem. Doctor Blankenship's been down to see the legal people."

"No shit! How'd you find that out?"

"Randall. He's dating a yeoman in the legal office. Your man wants to run Caleb up for disrespect. I guess you know the Gunny's already been court martialed once for assaulting an officer?"

"Jesus!" The two doctors sat silently drinking their coffee. "More?" asked Wee Willie. "Or are you still on one cup a day?"

"What do you mean, one? Salty old sea dog like me, I'm up to two!"

The Vulture reached for his mug but his hand suddenly began to shake, causing the cup to rattle loudly against the table. He surveyed his trembling fingers dispassionately. "Odd. Been happening quite often lately." He grinned. "Maybe I should stick to one cup!"

"Lucky thing you're not a surgeon. You want cream?"

"Cream and sugar."

"Waste of good coffee, putting that crap in it. Be right back."

Wee Willie returned to find his unlikely colleague smiling. "I have a solution. I'll tell the legal officer Caleb's nutty as a fruitcake. You can't very well charge a wingnut with disrespect, can you?"

Wee Willie raised his mug in salute. "Seems you wizards are some use after all." He gulped down his coffee in one shot and pushed away from the table. "See you later, my friend. I gotta go round up my sex goddess and make the rounds."

"Sex goddess?"

"Reardon."

"Lucky man! You get to consort with sex goddesses while I am left to exorcise demons."

"Well, get on with it!"

*****

A stone faced Wee Willie came lumbering into Caleb's room with Miss Reardon in tow. "I'm told you wised off to Lieutenant Blankenship," he roared even before he was entirely in the door. "I'll not tolerate that kind of disrespect in this department, Gunnery Sergeant! He's an officer and you'll treat him as such. Do I make myself clear?"

Caleb stiffened. "Yes, *Sir*! Maybe if the Lieutenant acted like an officer, it'd be easier to remember he is one, *Sir*."

"Dig yourself in any deeper, Gunny, and you'll be facing Office Hours."

"Yes, *Sir*!"

Miss Reardon bent over Caleb's arm unwrapping his cast. Wee Willie looked over her shoulder. "Who did rounds this morning?"

"Doctor Blankenship, Sir. He was up all last night on call and then did rounds this morning."

"Good Heavens, that does stretch the limits of human endurance, doesn't it? Do you think he was just too exhausted to notice this filthy cast?"

"The cast room was... was booked up, Sir."

"Did he get the Gunny's name on the waiting list? Seems to me there weren't any patients in the cast room when I got out of surgery."

"I... I don't know, Sir."

"Well go get your young man and we'll find out."

Minutes went by. Caleb lay looking at the ceiling. "Permission to speak, Sir," he said finally.

"Shoot, Gunny."

"Sir, the scuttlebutt is that a bunch of Marines on your ward are contributing their ribbons to that veterans march in DC. Somebody's getting to those kids, Sir. They wouldn't be doing that on their own."

"I know. Some of my own goddamn staff are behind it. But my hands are tied. Legal Officer tells me it's too hot a potato to touch. First Amendment rights. All that kind of shit."

"Your staff are on active duty, Sir. Doesn't that change things?"

"Probably. I'm not clear on the law. But I suspect the real fear is that if we do step in, someone'll go running to the press. You can imagine the headlines if that happens. NAVY MUZZLES WOUNDED VETS! Wouldn't the antiwar people love that?"

Caleb shook his head in disgust. "Those jerks aren't going to stop the war. They're the reason it's still going on."

"I don't follow you."

"Hell, Sir, as early as 1966 we were already picking up NVA propaganda leaflets. They'd reprint pictures from our own newspapers showing the demonstrators in front of the Capitol, and the message was 'we don't have to win this thing, comrades, all we got to do is hang in there until our peace-loving American friends force their war mongering leaders to bring the troops home.'" He paused, shaking his head. "That seems to be pretty much the way it's playing itself out, doesn't it, Sir?"

As they talked, Wee Willie was manipulating Caleb's fingers which stuck out from the end of the cast like three swollen sausages all in a line. "Feel anything?" he asked

"Not much, Sir."

"Shut your eyes and tell me which finger I'm holding."

"Middle one, Sir." He grinned. "But I guess it's not the middle one any more!"

"Nope, it isn't. Going to be your new thumb."

"How am I going to pick my nose, Sir?"

"Left-handed! But seriously, Gunny, you really think the NVA would have hung it up if it weren't for these demonstrations? We've been hammering them for five years already and they're still at it."

"Read *Peoples' War, Peoples' Army*, Sir. That's their bible and what is says is that in the face of overwhelming force, the peoples' army fades into the woodwork and waits for a better time. We were that overwhelming force, Sir, or we would have been if..."

Short arrived, leaning nonchalantly against the door. Miss Reardon stood behind him.

"Get in here! Both of you." Wee Willie pointed to the blood-sodden cast. "How do you explain that, Lieutenant?"

"Like Nancy told you....."

"You mean Miss Reardon don't you, Lieutenant?"

"Like Miss Reardon told you, Captain, the cast room was booked solid."

"*Bullshit*! I can forgive her for covering for you, but coming from you, that's a bald-faced lie. I was down there myself and the place has been pretty much empty all day."

"Then there must have been some misunderstanding." Short turned to Miss Reardon. "Didn't I ask you to..."

"Don't try to pass the buck. You're senior. You're responsible, and you're on call every night for the next week. Got it?"

Short nodded sullenly. "Can I go now? I've got patients to look after."

"I'll tell you when you're dismissed, Lieutenant. And I'd be one hell of a lot more impressed with your concern for your patients if I weren't looking at this cruddy cast." Wee Willie sat down on the Vulture's stool. "You two better make yourselves comfortable," he rasped. "We got some talking to do." He waited, drumming his fingers impatiently.

There was only one chair. Caleb saw the problem. Protocol gave it to Short as the senior officer. Manners gave it to the nurse. He watched as the two of them jockeyed uncertainly.

Sit, goddamnit!" thundered Wee Willie.

Short took the chair. Seeing no other option, Miss Reardon perched on the edge of Caleb's bed. "May I?" she asked him apologetically. He nodded, not at all sorry to have here there.

"Now that you got that worked out," grunted Wee Willie, "I got another problem for you. The Gunny here's been telling me it's on account of these peace marches of yours that the North Vietnamese are still hanging on. He's saying they're hoping to wait it out until you've turned the rest of the American public against the war. How do you answer him, Lieutenant?"

"By telling him he's not making any sense. I mean, what kind of Orwellian logic does it take to think you prolong a war by trying to stop it?"

"Same logic as you just heard."

Short looked impatiently at his watch. "I don't buy it."

"No? So what *do* you say to the kid today who comes back a cripple to this Alice-in-Wonderland world where the draft card burner is the hero and he's the baby killer?"

Short didn't hesitate. "I can't help it that he was made to fight a war we had no business getting involved in," he said hotly. "But I can tell him he can still hold his head high if he faces up to that fact and takes a stand to keep other kids from suffering as he has."

"You think that's going to be enough to carry him through his crippled life?"

"Damn right it is! Because someday he's going to be able to say to his own kids that because of him and others like him, there's a lot more men who might have lost arms and legs but didn't."

"Which brings us back to Gunny Caleb's original point, doesn't it? If he's right, you're the ones who are responsible for more lost arms and legs. Not less."

"Trouble is he isn't right."

"Maybe he isn't. But you still haven't told me why." Wee Willie swiveled around on his stool to face Miss Reardon. "How about you, Miss? What do you tell that kid?"

Caleb felt her start. "I... I don't tell him anything, Sir. I..." She stopped, swallowing hard. "I just try to make him feel like he's.... he's... still the boy he was before... before this stupid war *ruined* him, Sir."

The giant Captain's face softened. "He's only ruined if he thinks he is, Miss, so the way I see it, you do a damn sight more to heal those kids than I do." He stood up to go. "Lieutenant?"

"Yes?"

"You made your case well enough that I'm going to shorten your nights on call to two."

Short started for the door.

"One more thing before you go."

"Yes?"

"Try to sprinkle in a few more Sirs when you're talking to a senior officer. OK?"

"Yes. . . Sir."

The two doctors left the room. Miss Reardon stayed behind, turning instinctively to tidy things up before she left. Her eyes were sparkling. "Godzilla has a heart!" she laughed as she almost skipped out the door.

Alone again, Caleb fought his usual losing battle against sleep.

*****

He was a child again, lying in the little ship's bunk his father had made for him. Outside his open window the lobster boats were swinging to their moorings and on the ceiling above him danced the shadows from the blowing curtains. He watched those shadows grow shorter as the sun rose and, when they had grown much too short, he got up to go look for his mother. He tiptoed down the hall to her room. Her door was half shut. He peeked around it and saw she was not in her bed. So he ran around the house calling for her and when finally he did find her she was collapsed in the bathtub with a bloody towel between her legs and blood still trickling down the drain.

He tugged at her frantically, trying to wake her up, but somehow his right arm would not work and then it was him who was awake lying in a pool of his own blood and they were sewing him up yet again.

*****

"Freud liked to quote an old proverb," began the Vulture, settling himself awkwardly on his stool the following afternoon. "'*Tell me your dreams for a time*' is the way it went, '*and I'll tell you what you are within.*'" He paused to wiggle himself into a more comfortable position and continued. "If he'd written that proverb himself, I suspect he might have said instead '*Tell me your dreams for a time, and I'll tell you what torments you have within.*'"

He was interrupted by angry voices from the hallway followed by the sounds of a scuffle. The Vulture started to his feet, thought better of it, and sat back down. "Oh well," he said, "I guess they'll call me if they need me." He rearranged his notes. "So where were we?" he asked guilelessly. "Oh yes, we were talking about dreams!"

"You were, Sir," Caleb corrected. "I wasn't."

"Quite right. But with the inducement I've just provided you from Doctor Freud, I wonder if you'd be willing to tell me anything about last night's resurfacing of the demons?"

Caleb's defenses were down. The confrontation with Short and all that followed it had so drained him of what little energy he had left that he just shook his head.

"The watchers at the gate," murmured the Vulture.

"Sir?"

"Another quote, Gunny, even if not entirely apropos. This one from the German poet, Schiller. '*In the case of the creative mind,*' he tells us, '*intellect withdraws its watchers at the gate, the ideas rush in pell mell and only then does it review and inspect the multitude.*'"

"Which has what to do with me, Sir?"

"Only that I was hoping you might relieve those watchmen from duty and, in the pell mell rush of thoughts which followed, we would perhaps flush out the demons." He smiled. "But that's not going to happen, is it?"

Caleb blamed the dope on what he said next. "It was about my mom, Sir," he blurted. "The dream was about my mom. About when I found her after she died."

"You found her dead? Good Lord! How old were you then?"

"I was only three, Sir. My dad was off fighting in the Pacific and afterwards I went to live with my aunt."

"Would it be too painful to tell me how she died?"

"She bled to death, Sir. A hemorrhage.

"That had to be a terrible shock for a small boy, Gunny. For anyone really. And then you say you went to live with your aunt. For how long was that?"

"Two years. She had a farm in Middleborough, not far from where we lived on the Cape."

"You were happy there?"

"Yes Sir, I was. I stayed there until my dad came home."

"And then?"

"And then we moved back into our old house in Woods Hole. It was just the two of us." Caleb thought a minute and then corrected himself. "The two of us and the memory of my mom."

"How did that work out?"

"How? We were close. When I was a kid, Dad and I did everything together."

The Vulture checked his notes. "His name was Everett, wasn't it? That's a good New England name. Could you describe a typical day in the life of Everett Caleb and his young son, Johnny? Perhaps not a typical day, but one which stands out in your mind."

CHAPTER FOUR

They got underway before daylight. "No point both of us staying on deck, Johnny," his dad told him, "I'll drive. You go below and take a nap." So he climbed into his bunk and was soon lulled to sleep by the steady throb of the engine. When he woke up again it was already full daylight. He climbed up on deck, squinting into the sunlight and saw Gay Head at the end of Martha's Vineyard already behind them.

He loved jigging for cod. When he'd been hardly tall enough to see over the rail, Everett had rigged him a jig with a single hook and put a little cleat on the coaming for him to snub his line around when he hooked a fish bigger than he could handle. Back then, most of them were too big for him to handle. But no longer now that he was ten. He still couldn't keep up with his father but he could give him a run for it.

They came up on Southwest Ledge and began catching fish as fast as they could haul them off the bottom. Then, when they'd drift off the school, they'd stop and gut the ones they'd caught. He had seen other fishermen slice open still struggling fish, but his dad would never do that. Everett always stunned his fish with a wooden club before ripping them, and when he'd asked him why, he said simply, "So we won't hurt them anymore than we have to." It had never occurred to the boy that a fish might feel pain, and when that thought did register he asked with the logic of a ten year-old, "If we don't want to hurt them, then why do we catch them, Dad?"

"Because we have to eat, same as a fish does, Johnny. The people you see buying fish in the market count on us to do their killing for them, but I've always thought if you're willing to eat an animal, you should be willing to kill it." Everett looked up at his son, his hands and apron covered with gurry. "I hope you'll never get to where you like to kill just for the sake of killing." He handed Johnny the fish he'd just gutted. "Here, I'll rip 'em. You ice 'em down."

They cleared the deck of fish. Everett put them back on the school and they started in all over again. By mid afternoon Johnny's arms felt like they were coming out of their sockets and their boat, the *Sarah B.*, was down at the stern with the load they'd put on her.

The sun set with the boat so heavy with cod that her scuppers were under and she was leaving a slick of fish oil behind her. Johnny pulled in the first dogfish. Everett looked at it, grinned, and said, "Well, that's that. Once you start catching dogfish, that's all you're going to catch. You crank her up, Johnny, and I'll rip the rest of them."

He steered for the loom of the Gay Head light. His father iced down the last of the cod and came to stand beside him at the wheel. His dad's face shown red in the reflected light of the compass.

"You look like a devil," he laughed. "A good devil."

It was a magic night. Water hissed by the bow and boiled away into the darkness. The old Lathrop engine rumbled along. A tiny sliver of a moon laid right over on its back hung in the western sky.

"Planter's moon," Everett said. "That's what your Indian ancestors would have called it. Cupped like it is now, they said it held water and they took that as a sign it was time to plant."

"You believe that, Dad?"

"I think there's something to it. They'd plant things like corn—whatever yielded above the ground—when the moon was getting bigger and they'd put in root crops like potatoes when it was waning."

Johnny laughed. "Why's a potato care what the moon's doing?"

"All I know is that it does. It's a mistake not to believe something just because we can't explain it. The Indians knew that better than we do."

"We're part Indian, aren't we, Dad? Everyone at school says I look like an Indian."

"You'd have to go back some to find the Indian in us!" Everett laughed. "You got even less than me. No Indian on your mother's side, that's for sure. Druid maybe. But no Indian. She was born in Scotland." They went on a ways in silence.

"Good night for stars, Johnny. Funny to think that some of the stars we're looking at actually died out millions of years ago and we can still see them now."

"How can we still see them if they're not there?"

"Because the light they left behind has to travel thousands of years to get here. Be the same for anyone living up there and looking back at us. They'd be seeing the earth still crawling with dinosaurs." He laughed at the thought. "Let's get a rocket of our own, Johnny. We'll ride it out far enough to see the dinosaurs ourselves. Then we'll turn around and ride it back until we see you and me and your mother all back together again."

Johnny didn't see how they could be in one place and looking at themselves in another. But he thought back to a time when he was living with his aunt. They'd been coming in from milking in the early dark of winter when she'd stopped by the barn gate. She'd looked pretty that night, the toll taken by sun and sorrow erased in the soft light of the moon.

"Our day's near over," she'd said softly, "but somewhere far away on the other side of the world your dad's day is just beginning. So let's pray that he has a safe one." Johnny hadn't understood how it could be evening for him and morning for his dimly remembered dad, but it occurred to him now that the two ideas might be connected. If it could be day in one place and night in another, then maybe a rocket really could zip back and forth towing time behind it.

He liked that idea because it meant his mother was still somewhere out there. Which made him glad, because ever since they'd moved back into their old house he'd been trying to conjure her up from the blur of images that some cue would send flashing unexpectedly across his mind. He'd look at her sewing box and see her hands drawing thread through a button. The instant would be so real to him that he could even feel the tickle of her hair on his neck as he sat on her lap watching her sew. He knew from her photographs what she looked like, but he wanted desperately to recapture more of those times they'd had together.

He looked up at his father. "She said 'boot'. I remember her telling me you were away on a 'boot'."

"Boot? Oh, yes, boat. That was her Scottish accent."

"You miss her, don't you, Dad?"

"Sure I do. Always will. But she gave me five wonderful years and I got you in the bargain! So I'm not complaining."

They rounded Gay Head, ran up along the Vineyard Shore and put in at Menemsha, where they tied up alongside the fish pier for what little was left of the night before selling their catch the next morning.

*****

"Fascinating!" the Vulture exclaimed, leaning back precariously on his stool. "You've introduced me to a world I know nothing about and also to a man I would have liked to meet. So it would seem that to the extent that one could have an idyllic childhood while growing up without a mother, you did. Or am I wrong about that?"

Caleb lay silent. "Yes," he said finally. "You are."

"Oh? Why?"

"I had the best dad in the world," Caleb began tentatively. "Sometimes I'd come downstairs late at night to take a piss or whatever —I never could go near that upstairs bathroom after I'd found my mom there—and dad would be asleep in his chair holding my mom's picture in his hand. I'd stand there watching him and I'd think I'm all he's got now." He paused again. "I guess in a way I was happy about that. I saw myself as his link to her. I felt he needed me. And then one day, I found out that I had that all wrong."

"How so, Gunny?"

*****

He'd come home from school one spring day to find their next door neighbor, Ruth Fowler, in their kitchen shelling peas. This was no surprise. Ruth and Donny Fowler were his dad's best friends and Ruth often came over to fix them dinner. "Peas come in early this year,

Johnny," she told him. "Everything's early. Looks like it's shapin' up to be a hot summer."

"Not everything's early," he said. " One of my aunt's ewes just lambed. It's pretty late for that."

"Well" she laughed, "you were a mite late coming yourself. Your mom didn't have an easy time carryin' you. That's for damn sure."

Hid ears pricked up. Maybe here was another piece of the puzzle.

"You were an enormous big baby, Johnny."

He shot a pea at her.

"Quit that nonsense!" she said, not breaking stride. "I remember the day you were born. Valentine's Day it was in 1940. Started off unusual warm, but then 'round mid day a Nor'easter come on could've blown hell up by the roots!"

There were footsteps on the back porch. Donny Fowler came stomping in still wearing his boots. "Thought you might be here, Ruthie," he boomed. "Johnny around?"

He's sittin' right here in front o' me, Donny. You goin' blind?"

"You weren't big as a barn, I might've been able to see him!" Donny dropped into a fighter's crouch. Johnny jumped laughing out of his chair and the two of them flailed around the kitchen until Ruth called a halt. "Knock it off!" she commanded. "This place is mess enough without you two makin' it worse."

Donny grinned sheepishly. "Reason I come, Johnny, is I seen your dad down behind Gay Head. He says to tell you he's runnin' late. Should be in around dark."

Donny left, leaving Ruth to her peas and her story. "How it did snow that day, Johnny! Frannie Potter came by my house around two o'clock to tell me your mom was getting' near her time, and by the time we'd got to your place there must've been near a foot already on the ground. And you know what we found when we got there? That fool father o' yours was carryin' Sarah out to his car, intendin' to drive her all the way to the Tobey Hospital acrost the bridge in Wareham!

"Everett," I said, "you take that girl back inside an' call the ambulance." But your dad's never been much for askin' for help. "I'll be hallway there before the ambulance can get here," he says an' off they went into the storm."

She paused to sweep the pea pods off the table. "You can cook these too," she said. "Shame to waste 'em, but I don't imagine you or your dad'll ever get around to doin' anything with them."

Johnny wasn't interested in pea pods. "What happened when they drove to Wareham?" he demanded.

"They *started* to Wareham," she corrected. "I'd have gone with them but they were driving a little Model A roadster an' there weren't no room in it for me."

He grinned and she read his mind. "Wiseacre!" she said. "I weren't so big back then. But anyway, somewhere just t'other side o' the bridge they fetched up in a snowdrift and by then you'd got stuck too. Ev wrapped that poor slip of a girl in his coat and left her to go lookin' for help. That Model A didn't have no heater either.

"Your dad walked with no coat near two miles through that blizzard, an' by the time he got back ridin' on the Wareham snowplow with the doctor, it was almost too late. They got you out by some miracle, but your mom was all tore up inside. She never did heal up right, Johnny. You were just too big for her. You were near a ten pound baby."

She took the peas over to the sink to rinse them. "These'll hardly need cookin' at all. Just pour a little sugar in with 'em and bring 'em to a boil."

Johnny just sat there. She turned around to face him. "Cat got your tongue?"

He nodded dumbly but she was too busy to notice. "You got some potatoes here too, although it looks like these 'uns are as old as Adam." She plunked them down in front of him. "Pare 'em and cut 'em in quarters," she ordered. "I brung you a roast but I'm going to slice off a chunk of it for Donny an' me."

Johnny started in mechanically to peel the potatoes. Ruth bustled about the kitchen. "Everett ain't much on housekeepin'" she muttered, "but he does keep a sharp knife." She came back to the table. "Land sakes, Johnny, you still not done with those potatoes? Well, I got to run along. You get a fire goin' in the stove an' start them potatoes to boilin.'

She glanced at the clock. "Five thirty already. Lord, where does the time go?" She rushed out the back door, calling over her shoulder that she'd see about getting them more ice for the icebox.

Johnny laid a fire in the stove, starting with birch so it would catch easily, and then putting oak on top of that because those potatoes were going to need a long time cooking. Then he filled their iron pot with water and put the newly peeled potatoes in it. He put the peas in a sieve. His dad could steam them over the boiling water. The meat he left in the frying pan. Then he ran away.

He went down to their dock, climbed into the skiff his dad had built for him and rowed out into the harbor. Fog was rolling in thick on the south wind. He could hear the bell on the entrance buoy but he couldn't see it. The tide was ebbing to the west, but he didn't dare ride it through the fast running Woods Hole passage in fog too thick to see the eddies. Instead he rowed across the harbor, keeping the wind on the right side of his face. His plan was to fetch up on the neck of land that separated the harbor from the bay beyond and then ride the current around the point and into the bay. He didn't know where he'd go after that. Just somewhere far away.

He rowed steadily into the fog, still numb with the knowledge of what he'd done. His dad's words swirled around in his head. "Sarah used to look like that too." "Sarah didn't like spinach either." "Your mom had the same knack with twine as you do. She'd knit two bait bags to my one."

And all the while he hadn't known he'd been the one who'd taken her from him. He didn't think he could look his father in the eye ever again.

He rowed on into the gathering dusk, stopping often to get his bearings. At one point he heard the unmistakable sound of the *Sarah B.* coming through the Hole and he felt his face wet with tears. Then later, when he was beginning to think he might have missed the point altogether, the skiff's bow grounded on rocks. He climbed out and pulled her up on the beach. Beyond the rocky shore where there should have been lawn and houses there was only thick brush. He had a moment of disoriented panic and then realized that he'd fetched up on the small island that lay in the middle of the harbor.

He was getting cold. The wind was picking up and he felt a few heavy drops of rain. He pulled the skiff further up onto the rocks and started along the beach looking for shelter. Not far from where he'd landed he found what he thought was an animal path disappearing under a thick mat of tangled branches. He followed it on hands and knees and came unexpectedly to a clearing someone obviously not an animal had hollowed out of the brush. There was a wooden table and a chair and a ramshackle hut built from whatever driftwood had floated up onto the beach. Life rings and lobster floats hung from its weathered walls.

He tried the door, which was not locked. Then he crawled back to the beach and started walking his boat around the island looking for a place to hide it. He was wading along, holding the skiff against the tug of the current when suddenly the Woods Hole fire whistle started to sound. Startled, he let go of the boat and before he could grab her again the current caught her and she went spinning off into the night.

He walked back to the path, too cold and scared now to worry about anything more than just getting out of the rain. He made his way back to the hut and was just opening the door when he heard something or someone coming up from the beach. He tiptoed into the shadow of the brush and hid there with his heart pounding so hard he felt as if something inside him was about to shake loose.

Whoever it was on the path was talking to himself and pushing something heavy along in front of him as he came. Johnny could just make him out as he stood up and walked over to the hut. "Fucking hell!" he heard him say. "Someone's been here."

Johnny crawled deeper into the brush and made himself a nest of sorts in a hollow near the water. He was too miserable to sleep. All that foggy night he could hear boats coming and going through the channel. He recognized most of them from the sound of their engines. Donny Fowler came through headed west not long after he'd settled into his hollow. *Sarah B.* came and went all through the night. Several times he heard his dad shut down and call his name. It was all he could do not to answer.

As dawn broke the wind went northwest and the fog cleared. He heard Donny Fowler's boat again and looked out through the branches in time to see her coming through the Hole towing his skiff. By then he was shivering uncontrollably from the cold and no longer cared what happened to him. He staggered back to the hut and fell onto the porch. The door opened and there stood the town vagabond known only as Mr. Wesley.

He knew Mr. Wesley only because his father was one of the few people in town who would give him the time of day. They'd fed him a few times at their house and got to know him well enough to learn his story. He claimed to be an ex-patriot Englishman and a once well known artist brought low by bad luck and a vindictive wife who'd stolen his fortune. Nobody who'd heard this tale knew whether to believe it, but Mr. Wesley did have an accent you could cut with a knife and he did sell an occasional painting to the summer people.

"Jesus Christ, Johnny," he said now, all trace of his accent gone. "What the hell are you doing here?"

Johnny teeth were chattering so hard he couldn't answer. Mr. Wesley wrapped him in his coat and carried him into the hut. He made him a cup of tee laced with whisky and had to hold him while he drank it. Johnny felt the warmth spread through him. He decided he'd tell Mr. Wesley he'd been out rowing and got lost in the fog.

"It was thick," agreed Mr. Wesley. "I wasn't sure I'd find my way out here myself. Problem now is how to get you home without giving away my little hideout." He sucked his cheek thinking. "Well," he said finally, "we'll just have to risk it. So here's what we're going to do. You wait here until it's six. Then walk down to the beach facing the point. I'll be on the other shore setting up my easel. I'll pretend to spot you and go for help. That way nobody will have to know I was out here myself, OK?"

Johnny nodded.

"Good. I'm going to have to hurry before it gets any lighter. There's some cornbread on the table. Help yourself." Johnny watched him as he gathered up his things. Mr. Wesley's normally sallow face was flushed with excitement. He grinned as he tied up his easel, already relishing his role as heroic rescuer. "That should do it," he said shouldering his load. "Remember. Six o'clock down at the beach."

It all went as planned. His dad picked him up on the island an hour later. "Donny found your skiff," he said. "You'd stowed your oars so I figured you had to be ashore somewhere. Still, you gave us one hell of a night." He looked at his son and grinned. "Doesn't look like yours was any too pleasant either." Johnny couldn't look him back.

They landed at the town pier. Quite a crowd had gathered. Mr. Wesley was there, jaunty in his beret. His accent was back. "Oh yes," he was saying to a local newspaper reporter. "I was just setting up my easel intending to capture the sunrise. The light, you know, is really quite exquisite this time of year." He smiled a big yellow toothed smile. "Lost the sunrise but found the boy. Fair exchange, I'd say. What?"

Johnny slept all that day, only waking up long enough for dinner before going to sleep again. That night he dreamed that he was walking alone on a deserted beach. Far ahead of him he could make out something moving and as he drew closer he saw that it was a dog worrying a dead seal that still rolled back and forth in the surf. And then somehow he was that dog, ripping and tearing at the seal until the sand was red with blood and its entrails spilled out of the gash he'd torn in its stomach.

His father woke him up and held him tight until his shaking subsided. "I'm sorry for what I did, Dad," he sobbed. I didn't..." Everett cut him off. "It's OK son," he said. If I had a dime for every time I've got lost in a fog I'd be a rich man." He checked his watch. "Damn near five," he said. "Too late to go back to sleep. Let's go watch the sun come up."

Johnny pulled on his clothes and followed his father out into the night. They went down to the pier and untied the skiff. "I'll row this time" his dad grinned, and they set out across the Hole to a little east facing cove on the other side and there they went ashore. The sky turned from grey to pink as they sat on the sand. Then a sliver of light broke the dark line of the eastern horizon. The low clouds above burst into a riot of soft pinks and grays which faded to white as the sun rose seemingly right out of the water.

"I never get tired of sunrises," his dad began. "Your mother loved them too." He put his arm around Johnny's shoulder. "You weren't just out rowing, were you Son? I'm guessing there was something else going on. Right?"

Johnny broke into tears. "Mom…" he began but could go no further. They sat in silence. The sun climbed higher and Johnny's sobs subsided to an occasional snuffle.

"I know it's hard growing up without your mother, Johnny," his Dad said finally. "Not having Sarah's hard for me too. But you help me and I'll help you and we'll get through it just fine. OK?"

Johnny nodded, still too choked up to speak. And after that morning, both father and son each kept his pain to himself. Which, given who they were, was the only way they knew to help one another.

*****

"How did this Yankee reticence play out in your daily lives, Gunny?"

Caleb shrugged. "I dunno, Sir. I guess we just steered clear of painful subjects. I remember, I came home from school one day not long after I'd run away and Dad had moved all my mother's stuff up to the attic. He never mentioned it and neither did I. But sometimes when I'd find him asleep with her picture I'd want to shout, 'It's not my fault, Dad! It's not my fault!'

"Of course if I had, he wouldn't have known what the hell I was shouting about. Dad would never even have thought to blame me for how she died. But I blamed myself."

'That's a terrible thing to live with. How did you manage to do it?"

Caleb shrugged. "I don't know, Sir. I just did.

"You'll have to do better than that, Gunny. In my trade we use the term 'coping mechanisms.' And evidently you did cope. You just said as much. So what were your coping mechanisms?"

"If you hadn't told me different, Sir," Caleb laughed, "I'd have thought a coping mechanism was some power tool from a carpenter shop." He paused, staring at his good hand. "Yeah," he muttered after a long silence. "That does fit." He looked up.

"Coping's a good word for it, Sir. The way I coped was by working harder. That's the only way I knew how to make it up to my dad for what I'd done."

"By working harder? You mean at school?"

"No Sir. *After* school. When all the other kids were out playing ball, I'd be home overhauling gear or knitting bait bags or doing whatever else needed doing. Dad was the one who was always pushing me to spend more time with kids my own age. He pretty near *made* me go out for football." He paused again and then added, "I almost wish he hadn't."

"Why do you say almost?"

"Because I loved playing football. Not just football. Boxing and track too."

"Is there something wrong with that?"

You're the wizard, Sir," Caleb said bitterly. You figure it out."

"That's not my job, Gunny. I'm supposed to help you figure it out."

"Well, don't bother, Sir, because I already have. I had to choose between sports and my dad and I chose sports. I guess you could even say I got hooked on sports."

"I don't understand why it had to be one or the other. Surely there must have been room in your life for both."

"No Sir. Not when competition turns into an addiction as it did for me. I wasn't driven so much to compete against other kids. I mean I liked that too. But mainly I had to compete against myself, which was a lot harder. Running, pull-ups—whatever it was—I'd go as fast and as far as I could and then I'd make myself go further. Not because it was fun. It wasn't. But I couldn't help myself." He paused, gathering his thoughts. "So you see, Sir, I *was* an addict and pain was my drug." He smiled mirthlessly. "Or so I thought until I got here."

The Vulture nodded. "We wizards have a name for that compulsion, Gunny, and a neat clinical explanation for what drives men to it. But in your case it doesn't quite seem to fit. And even if it did, I still don't see why this addiction you speak of had to get in the way of your relationship with your father? *You* saw it as a choice between being the son you thought you should be or else going off to play football. But how do you know your father's pride in your athletic accomplishments didn't mean more to him than having your help on the boat?"

"That's not the point, Sir. Don't you see? I wasn't doing it for him. I was doing it for *me*." He paused again, and then went on uncertainly. "Funny thing is that the more my life grew apart from my Dad's, the more my mother's death haunted me." He paused, trying to make sense of that thought.

"Go on, please."

"On school days, Dad and I'd have breakfast together and then I'd walk down with him to the water. He'd always get underway before dawn. I'd watch him row off into the darkness and I'd hear that Lathrop engine crank up and I'd have to stop myself from hollering at him to come back so I could go with him and... and try to make things right."

"Yet you didn't. Why not?"

Caleb grinned. "Guilt might have been pulling me one way, Sir, but girls and sports were pulling harder in the other."

"Which strikes me as perfectly normal for a seventeen year old. Yet if I read your record correctly, you left it all behind." The Vulture checked his notes. "Yes, I *am* right. You never finished high school." It was more a question than a statement.

"My aunt died, Sir. That was in the fall of my senior year. She was like a second mother to me, so... so that made two down."

The Vulture's pen hovered over his notebook. He looked up expectantly.

"It hit my dad just as hard. So after we'd buried her and he got asked to sail as relief skipper on a research ship, we sort of reversed our roles. I was the one pushing him to go, and he thought he should stay home with me. But this time I won out. We drove up to Portland together to meet the ship and I came home alone to try to go back to school.

"I couldn't do it, Sir. I knew I was letting him down again, but I couldn't do it. I drove down to Hyannis and enlisted in the Marines. End of story."

"Not quite. You haven't told me what your father thought of that decision."

"He never said anything outright. But I knew him well enough to know he was disappointed." Caleb's voice caught. "He did come down when I graduated from boot camp. He'd been his company's honor man when he went through Parris Island and I was for mine so I think—I hope—it made him proud."

"He never said so?"

"He wouldn't have. That wasn't his way. That day we watched the sunrise was about as close as he ever came to opening up." He corrected himself. "No, there was also that time we went after cod."

The Vulture smiled. "Like father like son! So then what?"

"I never saw him again. I went on to the Infantry Training Regiment and then to the Second Division, but I never took leave. The Marine Corps became for me what athletics had been in high school. Everything about it...." He stopped there.

The Vulture looked at him quizzically. "Certainly not everything?"

"Just about. It sounds corny when I try to describe it. Stuff like the bark of the sergeants when we were forming up in the field at dawn, and the high I'd get when we'd come in hollering out the cadence after a hard hike." He shrugged. "Kind of dumb, I guess, but I got off on all that. I mean it *was* dumb when you think about it. There I was, a PFC who couldn't even leave the base without a liberty card and I still felt I had more freedom than I'd ever had at home. How do you explain that?"

"I think you just have, Gunny." The Vulture bent over his notebook writing, and when he looked up again his patient was asleep.

*****

It was a very vivid dream. He and his dad were caught out in a storm and were running off before a steep following sea. Everett was at the wheel having to work to keep *Sarah B.* from broaching and he was standing beside him, hanging onto the davit to keep his balance.

"She seem down at the stern to you, Johnny?" his dad hollered over the shriek of the wind. So he went aft, crawling on his hands and knees as the spray cascaded over him. He pried up the hatch to find the bilge awash and a geyser of water coming off the top of the rudder post.

Even in his dream he could feel the weight of the wrench in his right hand as he tightened down on the packing gland until the leak was reduced to a drip. Then he waited for long enough to make sure the electric bilge pump was gaining on the water in the bilge before starting forward again, working his way hand over hand along the side deck.

He saw the giant wave before his dad did. "Watch out, Dad!" he called. "Big one coming." *Sarah B*'s bow went under green water. She started to slew around broadside to the seas as Everett spun the wheel hard and jogged the throttle to catch her. He made a desperate dive for the davit, missed it, and would have gone overboard if his dad hadn't caught him by the belt and hauled him back aboard.

He woke up wet with sweat. It was a puzzling dream but not a bad one. Recalling it as he watched the sunrise from his window, he decided there was no risk in sharing it with the Vulture. *We'll see what he can make of this one*, he thought, grinning inwardly. *He'll conjure up something deep and hidden about that wave and I'll string him along just to see where he goes with it.*

To his disappointment, the Vulture took another tack. "Odd," he remarked. "The theme so far has been you abandoning your father. So how does *he* saving *you* fit in with that?" He smiled. "Any thoughts?"

"None, Sir." And then suddenly in his mind's eye he saw again the breaking seas and felt the *Sarah B.* becoming sluggish. He saw his Dad, one hand on the wheel and the other on the throttle, fighting desperately to keep her from broaching as her stern settled until her deck was awash and she would no longer answer the helm. He felt her slewing around broadside to the seas and it seemed so real to him that he instinctively tried to shift his weight to the high side. But it was too late. He watched as she rolled her rail under and saw his Dad thrown from the wheel as their old *Sarah B.* went down. The Vulture was looking at him strangely. "Are you all right, Gunny?"

"It's how he drowned, Sir. I see that now. That boat could take you through just about anything if you handled her right. But you had to steer her. If you left her on her own with any kind of a sea running, she'd want to broach."

"I'm afraid you've lost me."

"That's what happened to Dad. Something let go. He couldn't leave the wheel to fix it. Or maybe he did leave the wheel to fix it. Either way, he'd loose her." He rubbed his hands over his eyes, trying to banish the image. "Oh Christ! If only I...." He didn't finish the sentence.

The Vulture finished it for him. "If only you had been there. You could have saved the day. That's what you're thinking, isn't it?"

Caleb nodded.

His doctor snapped his notebook closed in barely concealed exasperation. "I take it then that you'd be feeling better about yourself now if you were still living at home and still playing second fiddle to your father? Yes?"

Caleb smiled despite himself. "The way things have turned out, Sir, I probably would."

"I doubt it, Gunny." The Vulture paused, fingers tented together, staring idly at his notes. "What if we approach it this way?" he said looking up over his glasses. "You *did* leave the nest. That's a given. So what if your father had drowned yesterday instead of fifteen years ago? Would you *still* blame yourself?"

The question caught Caleb by surprise. "No, I guess not," he conceded. "I guess even if I'd stayed on to finish school, I'd have... I mean dad would have wanted me to, don't you think?"

"Wanted you to do what, Gunny?"

"To... to have my own life, Sir."

"Of course he would."

The room was silent. "It's funny," Caleb said finally. "I know it's not my fault that they're both dead. But there's no arguing the fact that if I hadn't been too big a baby, my mother would still be alive. And if I'd stayed home to fish with my Dad, odds are he'd still be alive too. So where the hell does that leave me, Sir?"

The Vulture wrote something in his notes, crossed it out, and leaned back again precariously on his stool. "I'm afraid you'll have to work that one out on your own, Gunny. But perhaps the better question is why you insist on pleading guilty when even the most brilliant prosecutor couldn't make a case for holding you responsible for the death of either one of your parents?"

Caleb didn't hesitate. "There's no logic to guilt, Sir."

"There isn't. But the corollary to that truth is that if you have the courage to examine guilt logically, you may be able to get the monster off your back." The Vulture started packing up his things. "Before I go, can I tell you a scary bedtime story that may be instructive?

"It's a short one," he began leaning back in his chair with his hands clasped behind his head. "Once long ago, at a time and place immaterial to this story, I was still a young man practicing my trade rather than teaching it. One day I was summoned to a clandestine meeting with a prominent cleric. He was a bishop, and his pretext was that he wanted to consult with me about one of his priests who had an unnatural attraction to boys. However it came out soon enough that *he* was the priest in question and that he needed my services to help cast doubt on the mental stability and hence the veracity of the young man he'd raped and whose parent were now threatening to expose him.

"Having of necessity let me into his secret world, this powerful and arrogant man then seemed to find it necessary to bring me further into his confidence."

The Vulture paused. "I'm still not sure why he did that. Perhaps it was to so bind me to his depraved world that the awful thing he was asking me to do would seem less monstrous in that context. 'They are being unreasonable,' he complained of the aggrieved parents, speaking as if he were the one being imposed upon. 'Most of my flock are flattered by my attentions to their children.'

"'What of the child?' I asked.

He shrugged. 'He is young, it will pass.' He did not say what 'it' was.

"Feigning ignorance, I asked him what his church's teaching was on such matters. 'Pah!' he answered. 'What does it matter? That is for the little people.'"

"Jesus!" said Caleb.

"Jesus had long since left the picture. 'I answer only to my needs,' this Bishop boasted, 'and if in moments of weakness I feel myself drawn towards the confessional, I sin again just to prove I am who I know myself to be.' But as we talked, I began to realize that the man's new god was guilt. He hated himself for what he was, and he used that self-loathing as a justification for his depravity. It was almost as if he were saying, 'You see the man I am. How can you expect me to act any differently than I do?'

"He was accustomed to being obeyed, and it never occurred to him that I might not do as he asked. To my own shame, I did not refuse him directly. To have done so would almost certainly have cost me my career and perhaps my liberty as well. So I prevaricated, saying I would need time to investigate the case and would report back once I had done so. To my enormous relief, he called me a few days later to say that the problem had been taken care of and he would no longer need my services. The parents had capitulated."

The Vulture stood up to go. "That's pretty much the end of the story. I was still a believer in those days, so I went to my own rabbi to ask for guidance. He advised that I remain silent. At that time and place, the word of a deformed Jew would have stood no chance against that of a Prince of the Church. The Bishop knew this. That's why he had chosen me to confide in."

"What happened to the kid, Sir?"

"As I heard it, he grew up to abuse children himself. His parents received a cash settlement in exchange for their silence, and the Bishop himself was promoted to a sinecure in Rome, where upon his death he was eulogized as a great and good man."

The Vulture smiled. "So endeth the lesson."

Caleb was genuinely puzzled. "I don't see it, Sir. What's any of that got to do with... with *me*?"

"Maybe nothing. Possibly everything. I'll leave you to ponder the question." The little doctor snapped closed the heavy brass latch on his briefcase with a satisfying clunk. "Goodnight, Gunny."

*****

"Any progress?" Wee Willie had run into the Vulture on the elevator.

"Some. He's opening up about his family. That's one wall breached."

"How's that going save his arm?"

"We're all of a piece, Will. All the threads in the fabric are connected."

The elevator overran its stop and jerked hard as it reversed direction. The Vulture did an awkward shuffle trying to keep his balance. "I'm practicing," he grinned. "We also do dance therapy!"

"Sweet Jesus!" laughed Wee Willie as he lumbered off to his ward.

*****

When the Vulture next returned to his bedside, Caleb had his watchmen back firmly at their posts.

"No more pell-mell rush of thoughts today, Gunny?" said the Vulture after trying in vain to elicit more than monosyllables from his patient. "Well then, let's get on with your story. As I recall, you'd just landed at... at... Where was it they sent you?" He checked his notes. "Yes, a place called Chu Lai."

CHAPTER FIVE

The chopper that had flown him from Da Nang to Chu Lai set down in a cloud of blowing sand. The crew chief gave him the thumbs up and he jumped out the door, crouching to stay clear of the still spinning rotor. His first impression was of sand and pine trees, reminding him of North Carolina and the years he'd spent at Camp LeJeune.

He flagged down a passing jeep and asked directions to the Second Battalion, Fourth Marines headquarters area. The driver nodded towards a collection of tents next to the airstrip. "Over there, Corporal," he said, "and welcome to paradise!"

2/4's S-1 assigned him to Echo Company and Echo Company assigned him to the first platoon, which he found bivouacked behind the beach. He reported to the gunny, who sent one of his messengers to find the man Caleb would be relieving as squad leader.

Five minutes later the messenger was back with a tall corporal shambling along behind him.

"This here's Corporal Hummer," began the gunny.

"Hume," interrupted this scarecrow. "My name is *Hume,* Gunny, not Hummer. Hume as in broom. Shortened by the good folks at Ellis Island from Huminski. Would you like me to spell it? H-U-M-E."

"Whatever!" laughed the Gunny. "Anyway, this here's Corporal Caleb who's gonna be taking over your squad. Caleb's just been busted from E-5 so he's senior to you."

"*Sic Transit Gloria*!" said Corporal Hume. He grinned at Caleb. "I guess that now applies to both of us, doesn't it?"

"College puke!" growled the gunny. He turned to Caleb and shrugged. "He ain't a bad Marine. Just shows you can never tell. Right?"

Corporal Hume held out his hand. "My real name's Jacob but for reasons unknown I'm called Hummer or, by my most intimate friends, simply Hum." He bowed deeply. "And now, if you'll be good enough to accompany me, Sir, I'll show you to our quarters."

He led Caleb over to the platoon area, giving him a rundown on the platoon as they went. "Lieutenant Boyle's OK. Knows he doesn't know shit, which is why he's OK. The Gunny's a pro, but he's only got a month to go on thirty and he's taken his pack off."

"How about the other two squad leaders?"

"Sergeant Wisniewski's got the first squad and Sergeant Union has the second. Ski's good people and I'll let you make up your own mind about Union. My squad, sorry, I mean your squad, is still pretty green but we're going to be OK. Turk Turekian and Carl Jurgens and, of course, yours truly here are your fire team leaders and we're all three of us highly trained killers."

"I bet! Any fuckups?"

"Nope. Not really. We've got one other college puke in the squad. Name's George Blandon. He washed out of Officer Candidates School. Still bitter about it. Says he's going to write a book about our outfit and make us all famous."

Caleb made a mental note to keep an eye on Blandon.

*****

In the weeks that followed, his new squad grew to respect him as a good field Marine. He being the Indian, they began referring to themselves as the Tribe. The Indian's judgment went unquestioned on tactical matters, but on any issue unrelated to the Marine Corps, Corporal Hume remained the final authority.

He and Caleb were crouched together one afternoon in a stifling hot bunker, assigned to watch for an enemy they knew was smart enough not to show himself in daylight. "How much time we got left, GL?" Hume asked. He'd nicknamed Caleb "Glorious Leader" which he'd then shortened to GL.

Caleb checked his watch. "Christ, Hum, we just got here! We still got two hours, forty- seven minutes to go."

"Two rats in a shit hole," Hume laughed. "Not exactly the heroic role I'd envisioned when I went to see the recruiter."

"Why the hell *did* you go see the recruiter? I mean, couldn't you be swinging a bigger stick? You know, designing moon rockets or curing cancer? That kind of stuff."

"I've come to these far shores in the defense of freedom," Hume intoned. "Isn't that the highest calling of all?"

Caleb could never tell when his friend was being serious. "Yeah," he said skeptically. "Although it's hard to see how we're doing much of that right now."

Hume yawned expansively. "Mine is a long story, GL."

"Shoot. Time's one thing we got plenty of."

"Yeah, you got that right. Then let me begin with a question. Have you ever been to Brooklyn and seen strange looking black suited men with funny hats and scraggly little curlicues of hair hanging down in front of their ears?"

"Nope. Never even been to New York except to go through it on the train."

"No? Well, I was one of those guys. I was raised an Orthodox Jew and, believe me, we were orthodox! We did every damn thing by the Book—how we dressed, what we ate—you name it, we had some ritual attached to it."

Caleb laughed. "Good training for the Marines! You must've breezed right through boot camp."

"Actually, I didn't. But that's another story. The truth is that I nearly broke my parents' hearts when I left the fold. They wanted me to be a rabbi, but the trouble was—the trouble still is—that I couldn't reconcile the God I was raised to believe in with the world I saw around me."

He wiped the sweat off his face. "Damn, it's hot! Will you write me up for being out of uniform if I bare my manly chest?"

"Bet your ass! I'll go right to the Lieutenant and tell him you started ripping off your clothes and making lewd and lascivious advances."

Hume whistled. "Lewd and Lascivious! Where'd you learn that?"

Caleb shrugged. “Heard it somewhere. Kind of words you want to use when you’re talking to an officer.”

“It wouldn’t work. Even with those fancy phrases, the Lieutenant would never believe you. He knows my tastes are too refined to make probable your scurrilous allegations.”

“What the hell are you talking about?”

“Only that if I were a flamer, which thank God I’m not because being Jewish is trouble enough—but say I were, I can assure you that I would be of too fastidious a nature to even conceive of a great, sweaty, evil-smelling oaf like yourself as an object of desire.” He shucked off his jacket, threw his cartridge belt into a corner, and leaned back luxuriously against the sandbags. “Wake me up at 1600, will you?”

“Court martial offense, Hum. Sleeping on watch.”

“If we had anything to watch, I wouldn’t do it. But I know you won’t rat me out. You’ve showed your hand, GL. The rugged individualist is at heart an anarchist!”

“Don’t push that theory too far,” Caleb grunted, and went back to scanning the perimeter. They were silent for a while. “It really shouldn’t make any difference, should it?” Hume said from his corner.

“What shouldn’t?”

“Whether or not a guy’s queer. I mean, as long as he doesn’t bring it to work with him, who cares?”

“I dunno,” Caleb shrugged. He was uncomfortable with the subject.

Hume wouldn’t let it drop. “You take any all-male society—the military and the Catholic priesthood for examples—and common sense will tell that you’re going to find men drawn to these callings if for no other reason then to escape facing up to that side of their nature. Right?”

“Maybe. But like you said, who gives a shit? As long as they’re not lewd and lascivious, who’s to know? But weren’t you talking about God before you got onto queers?

“To be more specific, I was talking about how I lost my faith *in* God. But I suspect that too is a subject you are not likely to find of much interest.”

“Try me.”

"OK, I will. It all started when my uncle was dying from Lou Gehrig's disease. So I asked myself, how could I square a merciful God with that? Answer: I couldn't. I decided a God who lets a good man die so horribly has got to be a prick. Either that, or else, as is more likely, the whole religion thing's just a crock of shit." He paused to swat at a fly. "Heard enough?"

"No, go on."

"Well, religion having failed me, I turned to science as a better path to truth. I shed my black suit, shitcanned that fool hat, cut off those curlicues, and off I went to Cal Tech, where quarks became more real to me than God. But all the while that I was chasing atoms, something was bugging me. The Freedom Marches were in full swing at the time, and I couldn't understand what would make a liberal white guy go down to Mississippi to get the crap kicked out of him marching for a cause he personally didn't stand to benefit from at all.

"So I went down there myself to find out. I did get the crap beat out of me, but for the first time in my life I felt like I was part of something that was actually changing a tiny little bit of the universe. I wasn't just learning how the damn thing works. I was changing how it works!" He took another futile swipe at the fly. Caleb reached up, caught it out of the air, and squashed it against Hume's bare back.

"Brute!"

"Like hell. I just sent him on to a better world."

"Maybe. But my hope was—still is—to make *this* world a better one. Which is what I thought I was doing in Mississippi. It was like I'd found a way to rearrange the hate and happiness atoms for the better. And strange to say, that's the revelation which led me back to God. Or to sort of a God. Not to the personal God of my childhood, but to a kind of Cosmic Force for Good." He grinned wistfully. "It's something anyway. But I still wish I had a God I could talk to."

Caleb was looking through the binoculars. Hume poked him with his foot. "You listening?"

"Hanging onto your every word, Hum. But there are two guys out there who've been standing in the same place for the last fifteen minutes just watching me watch them. I wonder what they're up to."

"They're probably wondering the same thing about us. Would you like me to shoot them?"

"Wise Ass! Just keep talking. That is unless you can rearrange the time atoms to make it 1600. We've still got more'n an hour to go."

"My, how time flies when you're having fun! Well, the rest of my tale is quickly told. When I got back from Mississippi I dropped out of grad school to join up with a bunch of campus radicals—people who it seemed were also trying to move around the atoms for the better. But I guess I still thought too much like a scientist to put up with all the contradictions I found there. I'd be sitting around with a bunch of bearded guys wearing peace symbols on their shirts while they plotted violent revolution and I'd be thinking, there's got to be something wrong with this picture!

"I got tired of that kind of sloppy thinking. I missed the rigor of physics, but I didn't miss it enough to return to my studies. Instead I went looking for an organization that would provide me with both rigor and certainty. And here I am!"

*****

Pain was pulling Caleb back from his reverie. Outside his half open door, he saw the head nurse go by carrying a tray of small white paper cups and he knew that the ward's never ending background noise of tormented cries and manic laughter would soon fade as the pills she carried did their work. A nurse came in with a syringe. Caleb felt the pain flowing away. His eyes shut briefly, then opened half way. He could hear himself talking again, but it was as if his voice was again coming from a great distance. He was vaguely aware that the Vulture was still at his side. But he was far away now, far from the sterile reality of his hospital room, and it was his best friend, not his doctor who was sitting next to him.

*****

They were half in the bag, sitting at the bar in a seedy nightclub called The Golden Dragon. "Gotta go wee wee," Hume announced solemnly and disappeared. Fifteen minutes went by and he didn't come back. Caleb didn't find him in the head or anywhere along the main drag. So he started looking along unlit back streets which he knew were bad places for an American to be. He wandered around, alert to every shadow, until he came to a construction site lit up by rows of naked light bulbs hanging from a cobweb of wires. A huge crane loomed up into the darkness, and from the top of the boom came a deep bass voice singing "*Nearer My God to Thee, Nearer to Theeeeeee.*"

"Hum," he hollered. "Get your ass down from there! Double Time!"

"Not comin' down! You come up. *'Yet in my dreams I'd beeeeee, Nearer my God to Theeeeeee!'*"

Caleb climbed up the boom. Hume was hanging on just below the sheave. "Nice up here," he said, letting go with one hand to point. "See the lanterns on the sampans? Pretty! But we're gonna fuck it up! Wait an' see, Glorious Leader! We're gonna fuck it up for 'em!" He swayed out into space.

"Hang on for chrissake! Both hands!"

"*'Or if on joyful wing, Upwards I fly, Still all my songs shall be, Nearer to Theeeee!'* Like my song?"

"Come on, goddammit! MPs'll be along any minute."

"Gotta puke first. Soon as I puke, we'll go down. 'Kay?"

"Not with me underneath you, you don't. Down first. Then puke. Come on!"

"So by my woes to beeeee Nearer My God to Thee!" He'd started climbing down. "Fu-uck! This is hard. Always harder going down. I know all about that. Promise! That's what they said I had, Glorious Leader. Promise. My father said I had promise. The rabbis said I had promise. My professors said I had promise. *Fuck 'em! Fuck 'em aaaaalllll*!"

He stopped.

"Keep moving, goddammit."

"Something I gotta tell you. Did I ever tell you I'd been born again? That's right! Ol' Hummer was born again. *Hallelujah Brother! I was booorn again*! But it didn't stick... Nothing sticks."

Caleb led him weeping drunken tears back to the base.

"When I'm drunk," Hume confessed the next day, "I feel sorry for myself, and when I'm sober I think self pity is the most contemptible of emotions."

"So what was that shit about being born again?"

"Detour. Short detour I took between my orthodox phase and my physics phase. I joined an African Baptist Church over on Ocean Avenue. Only white guy there, and I wish I could tell you, Glorious Leader, how badly I wanted to buy into the kind of pure, unquestioning faith I found in that little church.

"I couldn't do it. I couldn't just believe. I had to understand. That's the curse of the Western mind. We have to understand before we can believe. That's why I took up physics."

*****

Night had fallen and the lights of the Philadelphia skyline shown bright outside Caleb's window. He shook his head, trying to clear away the morphine fog. "You still here, Sir?" he said as his vision cleared. "Sorry. I guess I was just rambling."

"I am still here," said the Vulture, and Caleb slipped off again.

*****

He, Hume and Blandon were sitting with their backs against a sand dune with the sea breeze blowing cool against their bare skin. Their platoon had rotated off perimeter security and they'd spent this last afternoon of their twenty-four hour respite from dust and boredom down at the beach swimming. They'd been 'in country' nearly a month now. They'd learned not to duck at the sound of distant firing, and they'd even on occasion been fired on themselves, but mostly they'd just waited in their bunkers, trying to stay alert for the attack that never came.

On this particular afternoon, though, they had no complaints. Blandon cracked open a beer and chugged it down.

"Want another, Hum?"

"Later."

"You, Indian?"

Caleb had just come running up the beach after a long swim. "Let me catch my breath first," he panted. "Hell of a current. Must've carried me a good half-mile down the beach."

"An allegory on the grunt's condition," laughed Hume. "Small pawns swept along by mighty currents. That's us!'

They lay in the still warm sand as dusk fell over the South China Sea. Blandon broke the silence. "Hey, Indian," he said, "you ever going to tell us how you got busted? There's all kinds of rumors floating around."

"Pick the one you like, George."

"Sodomy," said Hume. "Word is they caught him buggering a dog."

"You sure it wasn't a water buffalo?" laughed Blandon. "Be more to scale."

"Fuck you guys!" said Caleb. But sun, exercise and beer were all conspiring against his taciturn nature, and so the story of his run-in with the Ice Man came out.

"Just like an officer," Blandon snorted. "He'll tell you war is hell and all that shit, but he knows fucking well 'Nam's his big chance."

"George," sighed Hume resignedly, "as usual you've missed the point."

"What point?"

"The Colonel took as his text the question 'Can morality exist in warfare?' and he argued with unassailable logic that it cannot. Indeed, he went so far as to say that it is immoral to be moral since the end result of gentlemanly behavior is inevitably to prolong the war and hence the suffering." He turned to Caleb. "That is the issue, isn't it?"

Caleb nodded.

"Moral or immoral, who gives a shit?" said Blandon. "Far as I'm concerned, those two words ceased to exist when we crossed this beach.

Only thing I'm going to worry about for the next twelve months is keeping my head down."

A sand crab crawled out of its burrow, saw them and froze. Hume lobbed a pebble at it. "Incoming!" he laughed. The crab scuttled back into its hole.

"*Ooo-Ra*!" grinned Blandon. "A grunt crab. Knows when to duck."

"Keeps his head down," grunted Caleb. "Kindred spirit, George."

"Whoa," laughed Hume. "For the sake of harmony, gentlemen, let's not go there. But the point is an interesting one. How kindred are we to that crab? What does differentiate us humans from the lower orders?" His voice took on a mock professorial tone. "We'll start with you, George."

"Brains, obviously. What a stupid fucking question."

"You agree, GL?"

"Agree that it's a stupid fucking question?"

"No, knucklehead! I'm asking if you agree that the only thing we got going for us more than that crab is a bigger brain?"

"Yeah, I guess I'd go along with that."

"Well, you're both wrong. We may be smarter than that crab but the difference is only one of degree. So no, you numbnuts, superior intelligence is not what makes us human."

It was fully dark now except for the clouds over the base that glowed incandescent in the reflected light from the airfield. Hume began absentmindedly opening a C-Ration with the can opener hung from his dog tags. Caleb watched his friend's fumbling efforts for as long as he could stand it. "Here," he said finally, "give me that damn thing." He grabbed the can and opened it. "Want it hot?"

"Hot ham and limas? Oh joy unspeakable."

Caleb built a ring of rocks as a stove, lit a heat tab and set the can on top of it. They silently watched the thin plume of acrid white smoke twist its way skyward. "Am I the only one dining?" Hume asked.

"I pass," said Caleb.

"Me too," Blandon echoed. "I'd sooner starve than eat that shit."

Caleb used two sticks to pick up the hot can. Hume grinned. "Wonderful thing, the opposable thumb if you know how to use it." He scooped some of the green tinted ham onto his finger and transferred it to his mouth. “Hot!” he said.

“What the fuck did you expect?” Blandon opened another beer. “Last one. Any takers?”

Caleb shook his head.

“Not I,” Hume grinned. “Not when one is experiencing the deep, rich flavor of impeccably prepared ham paired, if you will, with the ineffable delight of the robust bean. Warm beer could only detract.” He scooped up another finger full and licked at it noisily. Green paste dribbled down his chin.

“Chrissake, Hum,” Blandon laughed. “Put that shit in your mouth, not your ear.”

“Slovenly behavior is often a mark of genius, my ignorant friends. You may take Adam Smith and me as cases in point. But, gentlemen, if I may return to my thesis in hope of no further interruptions, I will propose to you that what make us uniquely human is our capacity for feelings.”

He paused to wipe his mouth on the back of his hand. “We love. We hate. We have a sense of fair play, we differentiate between good and evil, between right and wrong. These are the things that make us what we are.”

They saw that he was serious now. The mock professor had turned into a real one. “If you’ll permit me a little theology,” Hume continued, “I’ll also suggest that God gave us these attributes precisely because He knows too well the pitfalls into which intelligence unchecked by conscience can lead us. He saw the monster He’d created by allowing us too big a brain and He gave us Heart as a check on runaway Head.”

Caleb saw where this had been leading. “You’re talking about the Ice Man, aren’t you, Hum? Saying he’s a runaway Head?”

“Exactly, Glorious Leader! If to stop evil we become evil ourselves, then what have we gained?”

“All well and good,” said Blandon. “But I’ll let the Man decide what’s evil and what’s not. If he says burn the village, I’ll burn the village. Anybody doesn’t like it, they can take it up with him, not me.”

“You can’t get off that easy, George. That defense didn’t work at Nuremberg. It won’t work for you.”

It was getting late. The heat tab had gone out, leaving behind an acrid stink. Caleb yawned. "I don't know about you guys," he said, "but I'm going to pack it in."

*****

The Vulture looked up from his notes, saw that his patient's head was slumped onto his chest, and tiptoed out the door. Randall tiptoed in to take his place.

*****

Wee Willie and the Vulture had fallen into the habit of meeting for coffee. This to the amusement of the younger staff who'd taken to calling them Mutt and Jeff.

"We're running out of time," said Wee Willie to the man he was not yet quite willing to accept as a friend. "If I can't get that arm into traction soon, it's going to have to come off. I'll do one more debriding. There's still a big chunk of shrapnel near the radial nerve I want to get out, but that's it."

The Vulture's own arm suddenly shot up, sending his mug clattering across the table. Wee Willie jumped nimbly out of the way of the stream of coffee heading in his direction and then sat back down, catching the other man's hand that was now jerking about uncontrollably. A nurse from the next table wiped up the spilled coffee. For a long, awkward moment the cafeteria was silent and then slowly the noise level rose again to normal.

The Vulture's paroxysms subsided. He nodded at Wee Willie's hands that still held his own and grinned. "I often wonder how you do the work you do with those huge paws of yours."

Wee Willie's face brightened. "Scissors are the worst. Beats me why they make the holes in the handles so goddamn small. But I do OK. The hotshots may have better pedigrees but I'm the better craftsman."

"Yes. I doubt anyone would argue that. But you can let go of me now, Will. The crisis has passed."

"Were it me," said Wee Willie, "I'd go see a neurologist."

They sat in embarrassed silence. The Vulture picked up his now empty cup and experimented absentmindedly with different ways to hold it. "Bit of a nuisance, these tremors. I tried to put on my watch this morning and instead hurled it across the room. Sad to say, it broke."

"What kind is it?"

"Excuse me?"

"The watch. Who made it?"

"I really don't know. Some obscure French firm I think. It's quite old. Belonged to my father."

"Stem wound?"

"I wind it every morning. Or did until today. But why this interrogation, Will? Why this sudden interest in my father's old watch?"

"Because I can probably fix it."

"You? A watch-smith? Blacksmith, maybe, but I'd never have thought a watch-smith."

Wee Willie's face clouded. "You making fun of me, doctor?"

"Good Lord, no! It's only that for one who even in the best of times has trouble buttoning his own shirt, the watchmaker's art verges on the miraculous." The Vulture glanced at his wrist before remembering that his watch was no longer there.

"1320," said Wee Willie.

"Which if I've done the math correctly translates to twenty minutes after one. Be easier if you'd just said so!"

"Jesus! What's the Navy come to?" Wee Willie heaved himself ponderously to his feet. "No rest for the weary. Bring me that watch, OK?"

*****

"They got you down for the OR again today, Gunny," said Randall as he emptied Caleb's piss pot. "Gonna pull more metal outa your arm." He grinned broadly. "Been me, I'd have sold you for scrap!"

Another corpsman wearing green operating room scrubs came pushing a gurney into the room. They loaded him onto it and wheeled him back down to the OR where Wee Willie set to work removing the last large piece of shrapnel left in his arm. "Sometimes you can do more damage digging this stuff out than it'll do if you just leave it where it's at," the giant doctor lectured Short, who was assisting him that day. He grinned under his mask, "In surgery less is often more, which is something you hotshots want to remember.

"Got it!" he said, holding up a dull green chunk of steel. He examined the piece more closely. "Ours," he grunted before handing it to the head nurse. "Don't let me leave here without taking this with me." He turned back to his patient who was beginning to mutter.

"That's the sodium pentothal talking," said the anesthesiologist.

"Anybody make out what he's saying?"

"Something about a man on a stretcher, wasn't it?" Short asked.

"Something about *shooting* a man on a stretcher," Wee Willie corrected. He nodded to Short. "Your turn, Lieutenant. Go ahead and sew him up. Stitches are the exception. Less is never more!"

*****

Caleb fought his way back to consciousness to find Wee Willie looming over him. "You were talking up a regular storm while we had you under, Gunny."

"What was I saying, Sir?"

"Mostly we don't pay much mind. But there was something about shooting a man on a stretcher. That got our attention. We medical types like to think that kind of thing doesn't happen."

"Yes, Sir," said Caleb.

That night he again pulled out his stitches.

*****

"Here we go again," said Wee Willie

"Was his a coherent recitation of events?" asked the Vulture. "Or was he just rambling?"

"You'd have to call it rambling. He was talking to himself about whether to risk the shot. Lot of garbled mumbling about losing the light and such. But from what we could make out, it seems pretty clear his target was a wounded man."

"Maybe it was. Maybe it wasn't. Either way, I wish you hadn't been so judgmental. I blame this last nightmare on you."

"Yeah, you may be right. But it pissed me off. At any event, we're back to square one. I'm thinking I'll try a little juju of my own."

"Please don't, Will. Let's each of us stay in our own bailiwick."

Wee Willie just grunted. He started to stand up, sat back down and reached into his pocket. "Keep forgetting to give you this," he said pulling out the Vulture's watch. "Broken main spring. Probably would have happened even if you hadn't dropped it. But it's running fine now."

"Much obliged, Will. Can I at least pay for the parts?"

"Nope. Might jeopardize my amateur status."

*****

Wee Willie was leaning over Caleb's arm with Miss Reardon by his side. "Nurse!" he barked.

"Yes, Sir?"

"Say you were the triage nurse in a field hospital. You've just been swamped with more wounded men than you can handle and you've got to sort 'em out. In what category would you have put the Gunny here—would you have said he's beyond help; would you think he needed immediate attention without which you'd lose him; or would you have decided he could wait until you'd worked through your more critical cases?"

She didn't hesitate. "Depends on whether the people in the field had been able to control his bleeding, Sir. If they had, I'd just do pain management until we had the more life threatening wounds out of the way."

"Good girl! But still, with triage you gotta be careful. I remember back at Chosin I had a kid with half his chest blown away. Big goddamn gaping hole. I knew he didn't have a snowball's chance in hell so I shot him up with morphine and moved on to the next guy. Figured I'd come back to bag him up later." He paused. "We got any zinc?"

"Yes, Sir."

"Gimme it."

"Far as I'm concerned, zinc's a hell of a lot better than those antibiotic creams they got out now," he mumbled, slathering the white cream over red meat. "But to get back to my story, we had a lot of Marines hit that day so I never did go back for that boy. Went looking for him before we moved out the next morning, but it was snowing to beat Jesus and I couldn't find him."

He looked over at Caleb. "Be glad you've never had to fight in deep snow, Gunny. It's hell." As he talked, he was spreading gauze pads like tiles over the open wound. "So there I was poking at every snow drift that might have had a man under it when I heard this kind of whistling sound." He closed up the cast and swiveled around on his stool to face his nurse. "You know what that whistling was, Miss?"

"The man you were looking for, Sir?"

"Right. Tough son of a bitch had made it through the night. I was hearing the air whistling in and out of that hole in his chest."

Wee Willie heaved himself to his feet. "Poor bastard died on the operating table. I still wake up nights thinking of that kid lying there alone all those hours, slowly freezing to death." He shook his massive head as if trying to rid himself of that memory. "That was my introduction to triage and I screwed up. You can't just look at the wound. You have to look at the man." He grinned. "I expect that's a subject you know something about."

"Yes, Sir," she said levelly. "It's a hobby of mine."

"Use that skill then. If the day ever comes when you've got to decide who to help and who not to, pick the fighter. Even if he's the worse hurt, pick the guy who won't quit."

Doctor and nurse gathered up their tools and departed, leaving Caleb to wonder if that story had been intended for him. He decided it had, and the point of it was that he, Gunny Caleb, the great war hero, with all his nightmares and thrashing about had been found wanting in comparison with that indomitable man in the snow drift.

*****

His next nightmare unwound like a movie. It began with Blandon on the radio telling the Medevac Helicopter pilot that the LZ wasn't hot. Then the camera panned across to where he—Caleb—was sitting, with his arms wrapped tightly around his knees as he stared vacantly into space. Hume was kneeling beside him "You're gonna be OK, GL," he was saying. "Three hots and a flop back at base, and you'll be good to go again." But even in his stupor, Caleb could see the disappointment in his friend's eyes.

The chopper came in low over the trees and bounced down in a cloud of dust. A little man jumped out the door carrying a briefcase and Caleb recognized him as the Vulture.

"What's wrong with your man?" the Vulture asked Blandon.

"Not a scratch on him, Sir. He liked to play the tough guy, but when push came to shove, he just couldn't hack it."

The camera scanned back to Hume who was leading him by the arm to the chopper. But he was resisting, trying desperately to break free. "No! No!" he was shouting, "I'm OK!" But he was sobbing uncontrollably as they lifted him struggling in the door.

Caleb woke up with his cast soaked in blood and his pillow soaked in tears.

*****

The Vulture was spitting fire, and with his rage had returned his accent. "You vill immediately stop meddling with my patient, do you hear me? You haf set my verk back perhaps irretrievably and I vill not have it!"

Wee Willie also lost his temper. "Oh, quit the bullshit, Ernie! You know damn well all he's got to do is just suck it up and stop all this wallowing in guilt or self pity or whatever the fuck it is that ails him. Chrissake, he's not the only combat vet who's done something he wishes later he hadn't. Happens a lot. Like I told him, he's just got to put it behind him."

The Vulture made an enormous effort to calm down. "I vish... *wish* it were that easy! But why not just put him in traction? Even if he does tear everything apart, we won't be any the worse off than we are right now."

"Triage. Same as I was trying to tell him. I got too many kids needing surgery to tie up both me and an O.R. for half a day on a procedure that isn't going to work." He pushed back from the table and flexed his knees. "Hear 'em?"

"Hear what?"

"My knees. Goddamn things creak like old barn doors. Halfway thinking about getting a pair of those artificial ones I been reading about." He snorted. "Shit, way things are going, it won't be long before we're all just glorified mechanics. Part fails, just yank it out and plug in a new one."

"Yes," agreed the Vulture. "I see the same trend towards the mechanical in my field too. Brain's not running right, just adjust the fuel mix."

"Better watch out, Juju Man! They're taking a lot of the voodoo out of your work."

The Vulture didn't try to hide his annoyance. "No," he said sharply, "they'll never do that. Even if I concede the role of chemical determinants to behavior, I'll still give at least equal weight to the impact of experience on who we are. That's my realm, Will. I untangle the way the subconscious processes the experiences we go through. So until someone can prove to me that the subconscious doesn't play at least as big a part in driving the engine as does the fuel mix, I'll stick to being a Juju Man."

"Juju doesn't seem to be doing a helluva lot for Caleb."

"It takes time. Caleb's isn't a fuel mix problem. His subconscious has churned around all the awful things he's been through and made its own connections between them. He's tough, Will. He can keep the lid on when he's awake, but it all comes welling up in his dreams. You can't blame him for that, can you?"

"Guess not. So what if we just zonked him out bigtime? I got him on ten milligrams every four hours. I could crank that up some if you think it'd help."

"I doubt it would. I had a professor at Heidelberg, a brilliant man and later a high ranking Nazi. He used to make the analogy to bringing a second generator on line in an electric plant. I never quite understood the physics, but the idea was that the second generator had to get up to the same output as the one that was running before you could run them in parallel. His point was that it's much the same with the conscious and the unconscious minds. You've got to parallel the two up."

"Fine. But why's it have to take so christly long? Someone with your training's going to be able to see where that process is headed long before your patient does. Why not just lead him by the nose to where he has to go?"

"For one thing, the destination's rarely that obvious, and for another, the patient has got to get there himself. When he does, it can be quite dramatic. Heroic even, that moment when he faces down his own demons. What you're seeing then is the mind adjusting its own fuel mix. For me that's the great reward. Helping to make that happen."

"I'm shooting for a lot less," said Wee Willie. "Be enough for me just to see our man walk out of this hospital with a half way functioning right hand."

"If we work together, maybe he will."

"OK. I can give you another week. Then that arm comes off."

*****

Now into his second month at PNH, Caleb had settled into the routine on Ward Nine. He'd grown used to the sounds of the wingnuts. He'd learned how to tune out the terrified shrieks and the bellowed profanity. And how to calibrate almost to the minute the four hour wait for the morphine which he now craved more than ever.

He'd also established the boundaries that with varying degrees of success he tried to keep the Vulture from crossing. Protocol had become his first line of defense, and on the day following the movie nightmare, he hunkered down behind it. "Good afternoon, Sir," he said formally when his doctor came in the door.

The Vulture didn't answer right away. Instead his face took on the impish look Caleb knew foretold a zinger. He stood looking like a cheerful gnome, silently counting on his fingers, and then looked up delightedly. "Parroting his prior pleas," he grinned, "the sagacious shrink says sternly to the supine sergeant, stop saying sir! That's three p's and nine s's all in one sentence. Match that if you can."

Caleb was in no mood for word games. "I can't, Commander," he said sourly. "Two c's. Best I can do, Sir!"

"A very feeble effort! But I sense the walls are up again today." The Vulture was no longer smiling. "Why are you playing these games, Gunny? Haven't we been at this for long enough now that you can risk a bit more candor?"

Caleb took the easy way out. "You're wearing oak leaves, Sir," he said. "I'm wearing stripes. You can call it a wall, but the way I see it I'm just sticking to the rules."

"Rules? What rules?"

"You know what I'm talking about, Sir. The rules we all learn in boot camp."

"No, I'm afraid I don't. You have to remember that I'm still very new to your world. So perhaps you could elaborate?"

"It's pretty basic, Sir." But having said that, Caleb hit a roadblock. He'd so taken for granted the conventions governing relations between officers and enlisted that now, called on to explain them, he found himself wishing he were still a Drill Instructor. If he were, he could have barked "We do it this way, Shitbirds, because we've always done it this way!" But that line wasn't going to fly with the Vulture. So he tried to put into words what before he'd simply accepted as the way his world worked.

"We're both parts of a pyramid. . ." he began haltingly. "It's a pyramid with every brick in it important in its own way. The general on top can't do shit without his troops and the troops at the bottom are just a mob without the general to steer them all in the same direction. Point being, Sir, that we've each of us got our own role to play."

He paused, marshaling his thoughts, and then went on, growing more sure of himself as he went along. "I'm proud of my place in that pyramid, Sir. A platoon sergeant is as critical to holding the damn thing up as any other brick in it, officer or enlisted. But I also know that the chain of command is the cement that holds the whole works together. That's why it's OK with me to take orders from some wet-behind-the-ears second lieutenant. All I ask is that he understands his place in the pyramid same as I understand mine."

"The proud yeoman happy in his station," muttered the Vulture, scribbling something in his notes.

"Sir?"

"Just thinking out loud Gunny. Bad habit of mine. You've reminded me of one of the many utopias I've read about. This one conceived by an Englishman whose ideal was a society in which everyone from top to bottom recognized their place in the social order and cheerfully accepted the positions they'd been born into."

Caleb thought about that for a moment and then shook his head. "That wouldn't work in real life, Sir."

"Why? Haven't you just been telling me that's very much how things operate in the military?"

"Yes Sir, the difference being that as soon as we shed our green suits, the general and I meet as equals. We both know the chain of command is only a temporary hierarchy and we live by it because it's the only way the military can do its job." Caleb grinned. "Some officers forget that. The worst mistake an officer can make is to start thinking his shit doesn't stink!" He corrected himself. "No, that's the second worst mistake an officer can make. The worst is to try to get too friendly with his men."

"Oh? What's wrong with that?"

"What is wrong is that you can't be good buddies with a guy one moment and ordering him into harm's way the next. Those rules you're asking about are there to... to keep relationships between the ranks professional and not personal." That last, along with a couple of other phrases he'd called into service were bits and pieces he'd remembered from a leadership class at NCO School. They hadn't exactly rolled off his tongue but they had made his point.

"I see," said the Vulture. "An excellent elucidation of a system I'm still struggling to understand. But let's say I were a general practitioner who happened to be a Commander and you were a Gunnery Sergeant who happened to be constipated. Would these niceties you've enlightened me about stop you from candidly describing your condition?"

"That's different, Sir."

"Nonsense! We both know you're hiding behind your wall for reasons other than a punctilious adherence to protocol. You don't have to tell me what those reasons are. Just admit to them. That would be progress of a sort, would it not?"

Caleb didn't answer and the Vulture plowed ahead. "You know very well I'm a doctor first and a Commander a very distant second, and you know equally well that the customs and traditions governing relationships between officers and enlisted have no applicability whatsoever here in this room." He looked straight at his patient with eyes that showed more steel than humor. "I'm here to help you and you're not letting me do it. So it seems I'm wasting my time." He started packing up his briefcase.

Caleb felt suddenly like a little boy, caught out in a fib, and he remembered what his dad would tell him at such times. "A reputation for honesty is like credit at the bank. It's easy to lose and damned hard to get back." That injunction didn't quite fit the case here, but he did feel that he was somehow using up his credit. "You are helping, Sir," he stammered. "It's... it's the best part of my day. . . the only good part of my day. It's. . . it's fun, Sir, when you're here, and God knows I'd almost forgotten what fun was."

"I suppose that's something," conceded the Vulture, continuing with his packing, "although I had hoped to provide more than entertainment." He stood unsteadily up to leave.

The head nurse poked her head in the door and Caleb used the diversion to furtively scratch his balls. He'd developed jock rot which he'd been frantic to scratch, something which the same protocol he'd been hiding behind wouldn't let him do in front of an officer. He saw the irony in that.

"Sorry to interrupt, Sir," apologized the nurse, "but the CO's office just called. Today's Department Heads meeting is canceled."

"Alleluia!" grinned the Vulture. "A reprieve! After a fruitless hour here with you, Gunny, I wasn't looking forward to a further waste of time listening to our beloved leader spouting inanities. So it's home early for me tonight." He paused. "That is unless you'd like to go on with our fun and games?"

Caleb felt as if he too had been given a reprieve. "I'd like to, Sir. But I don't want to screw up your evening."

The Vulture sat back down. "You won't. So let's return to business." He flipped through his notes—another ritual that Caleb suspected was more theater than necessity. "Yes, here we are," he said, adjusting his glasses. "The last we talked before Captain Williamson hauled you away to the operating room, you were telling me about that afternoon on the beach with your friend Corporal Hume.

"Interesting fellow, your friend Hume," he muttered. "I can't bring myself to call him Hummer. But he does have a way with words, doesn't he? That along with the gift for reducing fundamental questions to simple terms. As a pedagogue, I admire both those talents."

"You got that right, Sir" Caleb laughed. "I remember once he had was telling us about some top secret government lab he'd worked at where they were studying captured space aliens."

"You believed *that*?"

"We sure did. Hum could throw in enough real science to make most anything believable and he really had us going that time. We were asking him all kinds of questions about what those aliens looked like and whatnot, and he was snowing us with fancy sounding technical bullshit and it wasn't until he was telling how they screwed using their tails that we caught on that he was pulling our chain."

The Vulture looked up smiling. "What did you do then?"

"Ski jumped him. The rest of us piled on, and we ended up wrestling around in the dirt like a bunch of kids."

Which really is what you all were, the Vulture thought sadly. He felt a lump form in his throat and had to wait a long moment before going on. "But back to that day on the beach," he said finally. "As I recall,

Corporal Hume had you examining what you might call the opposing ends of the behavioral spectrum. He used the word Head to describe one end and Heart the other. Have I got that right?"

Caleb nodded.

"So let's say you had to pick just one word to describe the man anchoring the Head end of that spectrum. What would it be?"

Caleb was still feeling like a chastened schoolboy. "Ruthless maybe?" he said, half ashamed at being so anxious to please.

"Well chosen, Gunny! Our man *would* be ruthless. He'd be someone who approaches every issue simply as a mathematical problem whose solution is the one that aligns best with his own interests. Moral consideration wouldn't factor into his thinking at all." The Vulture cocked his head quizzically. "Can you add anything to that?"

"No Sir. I'd say that covers it."

"So now on to the Heart end. What's your one word for the man anchoring that pole?"

Caleb grinned. "How about muddleheaded?"

"I'm not sure that's a noun. But we'll use it if we can define a muddleheaded as someone so entirely ruled by his emotions that neither logic nor common sense would enter into his thinking at all. Is that what Corporal Hume had in mind?"

"I think so. Hum didn't go any easier on the flower children than he did on the Ice Man 'They don't think,' he'd say, 'they feel. That's why you get peaceniks blowing up college laboratories.'"

The Vulture smiled. "A point well taken. Then can I assume that if your friend saw problems with both ends of the spectrum, he would look for some ideal middle ground, some balance between Head and Heart?"

"I guess so, Sir," Caleb said warily. "We never got into it that far."

"That's too bad. I'd like to know how he resolved that question, because it really is a crucial one. How in the real world do we find the right balance? Or, for that matter, can there even be a single right balance? Is it a fixed point or does it shift with circumstance? What do you think?"

The watchers were creeping back. "I'd say there's no formula, Sir. You've just got to trust your gut."

The Vulture glanced up from his notes. "It sounds to me like you've just made a better case for Heart than Head. But doesn't that put you at odds with the Ice Man?"

Caleb was suddenly angry, a reaction that took him as much by surprise as it did his doctor. "I see where you're headed with this, Sir," he found himself saying, "and it's bullshit. We were in a fucking *war*, OK? So until you've been there yourself, don't give me this theoretical crap about balances. In a war there *is* no right balance!" He paused to catch his breath. "And even if there was, how the hell do you expect a bunch of eighteen year old kids to know how to find it?"

The Vulture was only momentarily taken aback. "Am I seeing a breach in the wall, Gunny?" he asked quietly. "I ask you that as one for whom what you call 'that crap about balances' is not entirely theoretical. You see, it wasn't just my parents who were in the concentration camps. Towards the end of the war, I ended up in one myself. So I too have had to walk a moral tight rope and, if I hadn't kept my balance, I wouldn't be here talking with you today."

Caleb's head snapped around, itch and anger forgotten. "Jesus! You too, Sir? Because you're Jewish? I mean that's why they. . ." His voice trailed off.

"No, the ones who rounded me up weren't so much concerned with religion. Their fear was that I and others like me might contaminate their gene pool. Hitler's plan was to breed good blue-eyed Aryan stock just as he would prize cattle. And he stuck with it, even as his world was collapsing all around him.

"Dumb bastard! You'd have thought if he was going down that road, he'd have bred for brains."

"He did, but only if those brains came packaged with blue eyes and blond hair. I didn't fit that mold, so the guardians of the super race took the necessary medical steps to make sure my sort would pose no threat to Aryan womanhood."

It took Caleb a moment for what he'd just heard to sink in. When it did, all he could do was shake his head. "My God," he said. "How low could those bastards sink?"

"How low can any of us sink, Gunny? I wish I could believe there were limits beyond which no sane man could be persuaded to go. But I doubt there are."

CHAPTER SIX

The following afternoon found Caleb rambling semi-coherently about his early days "in country." The Vulture sat quietly at his side, annoyed that a change in his schedule had put him out of synch with his patient's more lucid intervals. But he was learning to make sense of Caleb's slurred recollections, which he transcribed as best he could into his notes. *War begins to heat up for him in May '65*, he wrote. *Washington still telling press US role strictly defensive, but Marines begin moving further out from their bases ...*

*****

The rain came, not the monsoons but a drizzly mist the French had called *le crachin*, and they slogged along days at a time soaking wet. Hume produced a quote to describe their condition: "*No arts; no letters; no society; and which is worst of all, continual fear and danger of violent death; and the life of man, solitary, poor, nasty, brutish, and short.*"

He proposed an onion as the metaphor for their lives. Every act of kindness or generosity or compassion added skins to the onion. Acts of cruelty, or of greed, or of hatred shucked skins off and brought men closer to the poor, nasty brute at the center. "We onions spend our lives expanding and contracting," he maintained. "We are each one of us works in progress."

He extended the concept to music. "Dvorak," he announced. "Great big onion there. Johnny Cash too. He's another big one."

"How about the Stones?" someone asked.

"Who?"

"The Stones, you asshole. The Rolling Stones."

"Those turkeys? Shit, man, if howling was music they'd rank right up there with Beethoven. As it is, they don't even rate as *scallions*!"

He got no argument on Dvorak since nobody had ever heard of him. But he did face vehement opposition about the Stones.

Some other issues he was called on to arbitrate:

"Hey Hum, Shit for Brains here wants me to trade him my turkey loaf for his ham and limas. I get a skin if I give it to him?"

"I hesitate to say, Ski. As a good Jewish boy, I can't rule on transactions involving ham."

Or:

"Whaddaya say I make out an allotment to my church, Hum? Send 'em a couple o' bucks each month, sorta like an insurance policy? That way I'll have bought me enough skins by the time I get home, I can screw every girl in town and still go straight to Heaven, right?"

"Good idea, George, but not an original one. It used to be if, say, you were thinking to cheat on your wife, you'd go see your priest, tell him what you had in mind, and he'd tell you what you'd have to pay him to buy a pardon in advance. That way you could make a cost benefit analysis and go from there."

"No shit? The Pope know that stuff was goin' on?"

"Hell yes! It was probably his idea."

But sometimes it got more serious:

"She's pregnant, Hum. I ain't seen her in more'n a year and she's got herself knocked up."

"She your wife or your girl, Lou?"

"My wife. She says she still loves me. Says it was a mistake. But she wants to keep the kid. So what am I supposed to do? Be his fuckin' dad?"

"I guess the first question is whether you still love his fuckin' mom?"

"Love her? Christ yes! She's... she's all I got."

"Well, there's your answer. As to the kid, you won't be the first stepdad in the world, You'll get to love him too."

"You think so, Hum? Yeah, I bet you're right! Won't be long before he's tellin' other kids his Dad's a badass Marine."

"Or that she's telling other kids her Dad's a badass Marine."

"A girl? I never thought of that."

"You're a good man, kid. A real big onion!"

*****

After a couple of weeks in the field, the Tribe got pretty close to the center of that onion. Animal senses grew sharper, everything else duller. Something as simple as a pair of dry socks could make their whole day. Most of the time they went without dry socks, and it was on one such waterlogged day that Hume developed his theory about adjusting to the unbearable.

"Say you walk into the shit house when Turk's in there taking a dump," he explained. "Stink'll damn near knock you on your ass. But you squat down beside him and pretty soon you got it tuned out. The stink's still there, but you're not smelling it. Right?

There were skeptical nods from his audience.

"So it's got to be the same way when your feet always hurt or you're always wet or always hot, doesn't it? After a while you ought to be able to tune that out too."

"Horse shit," they said.

"OK," Hume conceded, grinning under his dripping helmet, "but you can tune it *down*!"

They did the same thing with their feelings. In a world where death and injury were to become everyday events, they all just shut down, some more than others. And some shut down completely. Turk had a PFC in his fire team who they called the Bread Man because he'd once been a baker. As their deployments in the field stretched out from days to weeks, Bread Man appeared to shrink more and more inside himself until the day came when he tuned out entirely.

They were bivouacked next to a rice paddy. Turk called Caleb over to where the Bread Man sat with his arms around his knees, rocking back and forth like a metronome. Caleb looked into a pair of vacant eyes and called the chopper. Fifteen minutes later they heard the "*whup whup whup*" of the approaching bird. Turk took Bread Man by the hand and led him like a child over to the LZ. The Huey bounced down in a cloud of dust. Bread Man climbed aboard. They closed their eyes against flying grit, and when they opened them again the man who had been a part of their strange world since it had begun was gone from their lives forever.

Most of the time they just went along, dead to everything beyond the demands of the moment. Check out that tree line, lift that base plate, look, smell and listen for the unusual—all the things that becomes second nature to a grunt in the field. Then they'd make contact and everything, every nerve ending, suddenly came alive. Colors became sharper, noises louder and time slower. They flew on adrenaline, right on the knife edge of hysteria. It was narcotic. It was also dangerous. The most valuable man in a firefight was the one who could keep his head.

Caleb learned to watch out for adrenaline. Whenever he'd feel that rush coming on, he'd recite under his breath the old airborne chant "*Stand up, hook up, shuffle to the door. Jump right out and count to four.*" He'd keep repeating it until he got himself back under control. Hume called it his mantra.

*****

He found himself mumbling that same mantra as the morphine fog began to lift. Beside his bed, the Vulture was scribbling furiously. The little doctor, looked up, saw his patient had returned to the present, and smiled. "I wish I knew shorthand," he said, shaking the kinks out of his hand. "Then maybe I could keep up with your story."

He checked his watch. "Oh Lord, it's that time again. What do you think, Gunny? Could I come up with a mantra of my own to help me curb my tongue when captive at our own Glorious Leader's interminable staff meetings?" He tried to stand up, fell back heavily onto his stool, and staggered back to his feet. "Clumsy of me! We'll have to call it a day, Gunny. I'm already late to one of those miserable things!"

*****

"I've got something here you might find interesting," began the Vulture when they met again. He withdrew a pamphlet from his briefcase and held it up for inspection. "It's a follow-up study done by a colleague of mine on Holocaust survivors. Rather a good piece of work actually, even if he didn't see fit to include me in it. But it does contradict many of my assumptions."

"How so, Sir?"

"Because the men and women who adopted what should have been the least effective coping mechanism to deal with the horrors they'd experienced seem to be doing better than the ones I'd have put my money on."

He waited, hoping Caleb would bite, and when he didn't, continued. "The people studied split rather neatly down the middle. If you're interested, I'll describe the two groups to you and see if you do better than I did at picking which one ended up the more successful. I'll even put fifty cents on a bet that you can't."

Caleb grinned. "Even odds. I'll take the bet."

"Then here goes. The men and women in the first group did everything they could to put the whole nightmare of the camps behind them. They wouldn't talk about them or even associate with others who were there with them. Their goal was to stay so compulsively engaged with the present that the past would never again have the chance to rear its ugly head. Or so they hoped."

He looked up quizzically. "Clear enough?"

Caleb nodded.

"Then on to Group Two. They did just the reverse. For them the Holocaust would always remain the defining experience of their lives. Their memories from that time had become so much a part of who they were that they kept them alive every bit as compulsively as the first group tried to suppress them. Everything they did—their professional lives, their personal relations—everything—were all in one way or another colored somehow by those memories.

He put down the report. "So there you have it, Gunny. And now, with fifty cents riding on your answer, which of the two groups do you think the authors found to be the better adjusted in later life?"

"I'd say that's a no brainer, Sir. You're always better off looking forward than back."

The Vulture bent forward on his stool, risking disaster to simulate a bow. "I salute you, Sir! You see, I would have thought the Group Twos who were venting the steam would have done better than the Group Ones who were holding it in. But the study indicated quite the reverse. You have the Group Ones today out there running businesses and the Group Twos stuck in therapy.

"How do the Group Ones do it? I can only surmise it's through relentless mental discipline. God knows, their demons aren't banished. At best they're only held at bay, and I have to admire the strength of will it must take to keep them there."

He checked his watch, muttered "Damn!" as he always did, and set methodically about repacking his battered briefcase. He snapped its heavy brass latch shut and held it up. "My father's," he said. "Or did I already tell you that? Had he survived, I don't doubt he would have fallen into Group One. And you, Gunny? Where would you have landed?"

"I'd hope in the first one too, Sir. I'd hope I'd be able to do what they did."

"Yes, and I expect you'd be able to. But there is a price. One which I think my colleague overlooked."

"What price? Didn't you say those Group One's were doing fine?"

"Outwardly, they are. But my guess is that their success comes at a cost. I doubt if you'll find many musicians or poets among the Group Ones. Much love either. They're running businesses and married perhaps to trophy wives. But beyond that, I suspect their lives are pretty much empty."

Caleb grinned. "If it comes with a high paid job and a trophy wife, I guess I'll settle for the empty life!"

"You'd be making a deal with the devil if you did. Because that firewall you'd build to lock out the demons would keep a lot that's worthwhile locked out as well." He got up to go. "I'll leave you with that to think about."

"You forgot my fifty cents, Sir."

"So I did!" The Vulture groped around in his pocket and came up empty. Then tried his briefcase with the same results. He pulled out the

Holocaust study and tossed it on the bed. "I'll have to leave you this as collateral. You might like to read it, Gunny."

Caleb shook his head. "I can't, Sir. I used to read everything I could get my hands on, but now the words just swim around. It's the dope. At least I hope it is."

"I expect it is. But no matter. If nothing else, the document is redeemable for fifty cents tomorrow. Good night, Gunny."

Alone again, Caleb made a desultory effort to read, but his mind drifted back to Viet Nam. He tried to steer it elsewhere—back to happy times with his aunt or father—but his life before the Marine Corps no longer seemed real to him.

So it was that his thoughts returned again to his memories of the war.

*****

They were a small cog in a large operation and now, having spent a day hacking their way through nearly impenetrable jungle, his platoon was dug in along a cloud-covered ridge line, two to a fighting hole, and very much on edge due to a rumor that VC infiltrators were sneaking catlike behind their lines to kill silently with knives.

It was 0200 and the Indian was checking on his tribe. He'd run communication wire between positions to help him find his way in the pitch dark; and as he left each foxhole, he'd tug three times on the wire to make sure the next two men along the line would know it was him and not Charley crawling up behind them.

Hume and Blandon were sharing a fighting hole. Caleb dropped silently in behind them. Blandon was asleep. Hume had the watch. "Something's out there," he whispered. "Listen."

Caleb heard nothing but the usual night noises. But Hume either had better ears or else was imagining things. He squeezed Caleb's arm. "There! Hear?"

"Where?"

"Right in front of us. There it is again!"

They waited silently. Ten minutes went by without Hume hearing anything more. "I guess it was a false alarm," he whispered.

"Yeah, probably. Well, I better get along. Wake George up if you hear it again."

"Better to let him sleep. Nighttimes, George gets a little nervous in the service. The curse of the overactive imagination!"

"Your call, Hum. If Charley is out there, use a grenade. If there's others with him, they won't know where it's coming from." Caleb slipped out of the foxhole, tugged three times on the wire, and disappeared into the night. He finished his rounds and was headed back to the hole he shared with his grenadier when he saw the flash. A split second later came the unmistakable *crump* of a grenade.

He froze, waiting for rifle fire. But there was only silence. It started to rain. "False alarm," he said to himself as he crawled on back to his hole. "What was that?" whispered the grenadier.

"Hum winging grenades at shadows," Caleb whispered back. "You get some sleep. I'll watch the shop."

First light found him back at Hume's foxhole. He and his friend watched the jungle landscape emerge out of the gloom. Caleb was the first to spot the blood stained black clad scarecrow, spread-eagled grotesquely over a log not thirty feet from their position.

"Looks like you weren't hearing things, Hum. You got one."

"Holy Mother!"

Blandon yawned from his corner of the foxhole. "What's going on, you guys?"

"Not a whole lot," Caleb grinned. "Hum greased a gook. That's all."

Blandon jumped up for a look. "Damn! I didn't hear anything."

"Well, now that you are up and about, George, how about you chop on back and report this to the Lieutenant."

"Will do, Boss!" said Blandon, leaving at a run.

"I'd like to be there when he tells the story," Hume laughed.

"Yeah, he'll probably come back with a medal! You want to check out that Gook or shall I?"

The reaction had set in. Hume was beginning to shake. "Sort of dumb, I'll admit, but I'd hoped I could get through my time here without killing anybody. You do it, OK? I don't want to look at him from any closer than I am now."

"Sure. But keep an eye out. He may not have been the only one out there." Caleb wormed his way over the sandbags and ran at a crouch to the dead VC. He rifled quickly through the man's pockets and came back carrying a Russian-built carbine along with his own M-14.

"Here," he said, tossing Hume a packet of photographs he'd taken off the body. "These'll cheer you up."

The pictures were all pornographic. "Sure as hell not his mom and dad," said Hume, riffling through them. "At least I hope not." He handed them back to Caleb. "Hooray for me!" he said, trying to smile. "I've just made the world safer for democracy." He reached out absentmindedly to block the path of a big black beetle climbing a leaf in front of him. The bug turned this way and that trying to find a way past his finger and finally climbed onto it. Hume inspected it carefully. "I could kill you too, Mister Beetle," he told it. "There wouldn't be any broken beetle hearts if I squashed you, right? No Mama Beetles or Papa Beetles to cry for you? So that's good. Because we higher orders aren't so clever. We mourn our dead, which means I probably just broke a few hearts in some little Vietnamese village out there somewhere. But other than that, Mister Beetle, if I kill you or kill that poor kid, what the fuck's the difference?"

He was talking too fast. "Of course if that kid had got me instead of me him, there'd be a lot more fuss. They'd ship me home and plant me at Arlington with full military honors. There'd be a bugle and important mucky mucks who didn't know me from Adam putting on long faces and... and..." he paused to catch his breath before rushing on, "and a sermon by some horse's ass about how I'd died to protect freedom, but you and I know that's just horse shit, don't we, Mister Beetle? Nobody—not one fucking soul—is going to be any more or less free whether Ol' Hum here's alive or dead. Same as with you, Little Guy. Truth of it is, in the big scheme of things, neither one of us counts for shit!"

The beetle had crawled around under his hand and was hanging there upside down. Hume maneuvered it back into his palm and, when he turned to face Caleb, tears were streaming down his face. "Maybe you know the answer, Glorious Leader. You tell me what's the difference between killing this Vietnamese beetle or that Vietnamese kid?"

He didn't wait for an answer. "Stupid question," he went on, stumbling over his words. "Really fucking stupid! Of course there's a difference. But how the hell do you measure it? I mean, look at it this way, GL. Say I wanted to build a bridge, and I knew from having built other bridges that I'd probably lose four of my workers building this one. So how do I do the math? How do I weigh those four lives against the value of a fucking bridge?"

"Beats me," said Caleb. "So just slow down, kid. What I do know is that if you hadn't got that Gook, he'd have gotten you. For me, that kind of simplifies the equation."

"I guess it does." Hume laughed mirthlessly "It's easier to think of him as some hard ass killer instead of as a poor kid sneaking away to pull out his porno pictures and whack off! Which I bet is closer to the truth."

"If it is, you saved him from sin. So shut up and help me bale out this shit hole. George must have been sleeping with a snorkel in his mouth!" They sloshed water out of the foxhole with their hardhats. "My trick is just to keep busy doing this kind of shit," Caleb grunted. "That way I don't have time for those kind of thoughts."

"I wish I had the gift, GL. I think too damn much."

They worked in silence. "Fucking lake you got in here, Hum. You'll be growing gills if you stay in this hole much longer."

"Could happen," said Hume absentmindedly. "I just thought of a better example than that bridge. Want to hear it?"

"Looks like I'm going to."

"You are. It seems that just before D-Day in World War Two, the British told one of their agents in France, one of their best men, that the landing was going to be at Calais which, of course, it wasn't. Then they set it up so that their guy would be caught by the Gestapo.

"You can guess what happened. The Gestapo tortured the guy until he cracked. He told them that the invasion was going to land at Calais. He'd tried so hard not to tell them that the goons who were crushing his nuts were convinced that he was telling the truth. Because even the nut crushers couldn't believe that anyone would do to anybody what the Brits had done to this guy. That was the genius of the scheme."

Caleb wiped the sweat off his face, leaving a muddy streak on his cheek. "Yeah? So what's that bit of history got to do with two grunts standing ankle deep in a goddamn cesspool?"

"Don't you see? It's the same problem as with my bridge. I mean, was it right, what they did?"

"Fucking A, it was right. Four lives weighed against a bridge. You may have a case there. But one life to save thousands? Shit, you can't argue with that math!"

"Yes, you can, Glorious Leader. I'm not sure how, but you can. You have to."

Blandon was back. "Lieutenant's on the way. He called battalion and they want the Gook brought in."

"What the fuck for?" Hume demanded.

Blandon shrugged. "Add him to the body count, I guess. Show him to the press. At least with him they'll have a real body."

*****

A week later the Tribe was on patrol, headed out to set up a night ambush. It was late afternoon, still blazing hot and, as they passed by the farmers who would become their enemies that night, Caleb was thinking that they should already have been in position if they were going to fool those little men who watched them impassively from under their straw hats.

Hume's fire team was in the lead and he was taking his turn on point, questing back and forth like a hound dog with his huge beak of a nose. They were on a trail crossing the last rice paddy before starting up into the hills when Hume gave the signal to hold up and beckoned Caleb forward.

"See how those footprints ahead on the trail just seem to stop?" he whispered. "Then there's a place that's been raked, and then the prints start up again? Something for sure wrong there."

Caleb thought it was probably a deadfall. But somehow it seemed too amateur. The VC were artists at disguising their spike-filled pits. So maybe they'd just raked the trail smooth to check for new footprints. Or maybe it was a trick intended to make whoever spotted it all bunch up for a look. If it was, it hadn't worked. His fire team leaders had their men well spread out, lying prone and facing outboard. He looked around, trying to spot where the VC could have set up an ambush without being up to their necks in water.

"Maybe that little rise over there to the left?" suggested Hume, reading his mind. "But shit, if I was setting up an ambush, I sure as hell could find a better spot than here."

"Right. So I guess we just go around that raked spot and keep moving."

"Makes sense. I'll check out the edge of the trail." Hume grinned. "Hope George's taking notes for his book. 'Once more into the breach went the Hummer!' Good start for a chapter."

Caleb watched his friend move off the dike to the left of the raked area. He saw the ground give way beneath him, and heard him cry out as bamboo spikes ripped deep into his legs and stomach.

The men who'd dug that pit hadn't figured on someone so tall. Hume went in only up to his waist. He wrenched himself around. "Stay back!" he yelled pointing. "Wires over there! The... trail's... "Blood gushed out of his mouth. He raised his arm in a mock salute and slowly slumped forward until his face settled into the mud.

Blandon came charging up. Caleb grabbed him. "Get down, goddammit!"

"Fuck you, Indian! We gotta get him outa there."

Caleb slammed him down and a second later they were both nearly buried in the geyser of dirt that erupted from the mined trail ahead of them. Caleb sat up, choking in the dust, in time to see a black-clad figure sloshing through the water towards that little rise Hume had pointed out. He aimed for a spot between the little man's shoulder blades and dropped him into the water.

His squad forgot everything. Twelve men crowded around, gawking. Hume somehow was still alive. The blast had flipped him onto his back. Blood gurgled in his throat. He moaned once as Blandon tugged futilely at the spike-filled logs.

Caleb shoved Blandon away so savagely he sent him sprawling into the paddy. Hume reached out to him, Caleb knelt beside him and took his hand and watched him die.

Then he remembered his job. "Spread out, you assholes! Turk and Carl, get your people back where they belong. George, you got the first team now. Leave Hum where he's at and get your people spread out!"

He looked around, realizing that if the man he'd shot hadn't panicked and triggered his mine too soon, he might have got the entire squad. The little rise was too far from the trail for a night ambush but it would have to do. He beckoned the fire team leaders to him. "OK, we're going to get the cock-suckers that got Hum."

"Yeah? How we gonna do that?" Turk asked.

"Good chance they'll be back tonight. Hum'll be the bait. We'll leave him right where he's at. They won't be expecting that, so I'm betting they'll all bunch up and gawk just like we did.

"Set up on that little hill over there. You'll probably want to use aiming stakes. I'll wait in that same weed patch where that guy who set off the mine was hiding. When I pop the illumination, let the bastards have it. Turk, you're in charge. Pick up the Gook's rifle on your way across. Any questions?"

Blandon was still shaking. "Jesus, Indian, we can't leave Hum there."

"We're going to. Anything else? OK get moving!"

It was a long night. He waited where the Gook had waited, waist deep in water, choking back tears. He had been the amateur, not the VC.

He thought back to another time in Da Nang when he'd managed to persuade his friend to come along on one of his long walks through the old city. "I don't believe it!" he remembered Hum bitching. "This guy's idea of a good time is a goddamn twenty mile hike!"

They'd found a very European sidewalk café and later, sleepy from beer, flopped down on the grass in a shady little park which must also have been a legacy from the French. Hume went noisily to sleep and he lay there, half asleep himself, until the sound of gongs and cymbals made them both sit up in time to see a procession of orange-robed Buddhists passing by the square.

"You ever have a Buddhist phase, Hum?"

"Nope. But I'll tell you, GL, I've tried damn near everything else."

The sounds of the parade faded away and evening fell over that ancient part of the world. "We physicists postulate something we call the Four Forces," Hume told him as they started back for the base. "Ever heard of those?"

He shook his head. "I'm not a college puke."

"Well, all you need to know about those four forces is that they seem to suggest a universe that comes right around to meet itself. Sort of like a closed loop. No beginning. No end. No way out. A prison.

"But you know what occurred to me this afternoon, Glorious Leader? We physicists, we arrogant bastards, we just assume God is trapped by these four forces just as we are. But why should He be? Why shouldn't the realm of God be beyond time and space?

"I bet there's a Fifth Force out there. I bet God doesn't want us to understand it. He's telling us 'Look, you assholes, you can't prove I'm out here, but if you want what I've got, you've just got to believe I exist. So take it or leave it, you silly prisoners of reason! It's your choice!'"

They just made it back at the helo pad. The chopper making the mail run back to Chu Lai was already turning up on the runway. "Know what I can't wait to do?" Hume hollered to him over the sound of the engine. "I can't wait to tell my dad he's right. His God's the one I've been looking for all along. So thanks, GL. What a great day!"

Remembering that great day, Caleb broke down. He crouched sobbing, waist deep in foul water, waiting out the long dark night. Then, around 0200, when he thought he could stand his memories no longer, he heard movement on the trail. Nothing happened for several minutes and then there was a dim light and singsong voices from over by the pit. He gave them another thirty seconds to bunch up and popped the grenade. Turk was on the job. Fire erupted from the ridge, and when it was over they'd got six VC. One of them was a woman. They also bagged two M-1s, three carbines and an old French 7.5mm army rifle.

At first light that morning the Tribe carried their wise man back to the base in his poncho with the flies already thick around him. Blandon passed Caleb on the trail. "Bastard," he muttered and kept walking.

*****

"I'm sorry Gunny," said the Vulture. "I rather suspected from the way you spoke of him that he'd been killed, but I thought it better not to ask." He paused, tapping his pencil on his notebook, weighing the risk of rubbing new salt into an old wound. He made up his mind, snapped closed the notebook and asked, "Here again, Gunny aren't we seeing the same unhealthy penchant for taking more on your shoulders than the facts warrant? Is guilt once again rearing its ugly head?"

Caleb didn't answer.

"No thoughts on that? Well then, I'll rephrase the question. With the wisdom of hindsight, what might you have done differently?"

"Don't think I haven't asked myself the same thing a million times, Sir. We took a chance staying on the trail. I knew that. But the book says the mission comes first, so what choice was there? We'd never have gotten to our objective in time if we'd had to wade waist deep in water to get there."

Nine stories below, an ambulance raced down Broad Street, its wailing siren audible even through the closed window. Caleb nodded towards the sound. "I was like those guys, Sir. "So locked on to doing the job that nothing else counted."

"Not even the safety of your men?"

"Not even that, Sir. You can't lead men in combat if you make that your priority."

The Vulture looked up from his notes. "Do you see things any differently now?"

"I don't know, Sir. We lost one guy. They lost six. Seven if you count the one I shot. So in the body count business we came out ahead. But maybe Hum had it right. For all the difference it made, maybe that day might just as well never have happened."

"That's not true, Gunny. Not true for Corporal Hume's parents. Not true for the parents, wives and children of the Vietnamese who died that day. Not true for you. You say nothing changed? Of course it did.

Whatever happens, no matter how seemingly insignificant, it changes all that follows."

"Maybe," said Caleb. "But not often so you'd notice."

"Perhaps the connections aren't immediately obvious. But your friend's death didn't occur in a vacuum. Much was changed because of it. Much more may yet be. For good and for bad."

"Good? What the hell good came from that day, Sir? To Hum? To me? To anyone?" Caleb's voice caught. "He was the best friend I ever had. The best friend I ever will have. And because I let those bastards outsmart me, he was killed." He wiped angrily at his eyes. "When that happens, Sir, and you're in my line of work, you don't ever again want to let anyone else get as close to you as he was to me. Because it can happen again. It *will* happen again and once is enough for that kind of pain."

The Vulture nodded. "I understand that. It may even be that my own choice of profession was motivated by the same fear of letting others get too close. We freaks live in constant fear of rejection. So you see, in more ways than one, we're kindred spirits."

He smiled. "Apologies, Gunny. These digressions of mine are quite unprofessional. Please go on."

CHAPTER SEVEN

Caleb wasn't going to lose another man to a booby trap if he could help it. He learned to look out for the branch that just happened to be lying across a trail or the leaves that were wilted when they shouldn't have been. He developed a sixth sense for situations that just somehow seemed wrong. Obstacles with too easy a way around them, birds suddenly silent, villagers where villagers shouldn't have been, no villagers where villagers should have been, all were tip-offs to trouble.

Their lieutenant made him the platoon's training NCO. His job was to teach new men how to stay alive long enough to learn their own lessons. They listened because they knew he knew his stuff. But they were scared of him. A Marine couldn't spend five minutes in Echo Company without learning that he was the ruthless bastard who had used his best friend's body to bait an ambush. For his part, he had become harder and more withdrawn. He had no friends, never went on liberty with his men, and spent his own free time driving himself to exhaustion on long runs or swims along the beach. Although technically he was the junior squad leader by virtue of having been busted to corporal, everyone from the lieutenant on down deferred to his superior competence. The Tribe might not have liked him, but even Blandon would not have wanted to see him replaced. They knew that with him as their leader they had a better chance of staying alive. They were good because he was good.

His squad became the experts at prisoner snatches. Regiment was beginning to get intelligence that regular NVA troops were moving into Quang Tin province. So when the order came down from battalion to bring in an NVA prisoner, they got the job. For a couple of days before they left on patrol, they made themselves unpopular around the company area by snatching any Marine who let down his guard on the way to the mess tent or latrine. This went on until Turk's team bagged the Lieutenant who called an end to the game.

Caleb asked the chopper pilot who was to lift them into the mountains to touch down in four or five different places to confuse any NVA within hearing about their destination. They went out the door on the third stop without making contact with anything worse than giant leeches. On the first day they moved several miles cross country through thick jungle and set up a patrol base by a stream a couple of hundred yards from a well traveled trail. That night he left Turk's and Blandon's fire teams at the base and took Carl's with him down to the trail to wait for the their quarry.

He was counting on the fact that NVA troops were well enough trained to move properly spread out, and his plan was to take the last man in the column. He and Carl would make the snatch. He doubted if the enemy would put out flank security at night, and was counting on them moving single file.

"You sure this is going to work?" Carl whispered as they lay in wait.

"Nope," he whispered back. "But they're no different from us. Dark like it is, each man's going to be worrying a lot more about not losing touch with the guy ahead than he is about what's going on behind him."

They waited all that night. NVA were all around them. At one point they heard voices, but nobody came down the trail and at dawn they crawled stiffly back to their base. The next night was Turk's team's turn in the barrel and the one following was Blandon's. Both times they again struck out. On the morning of the third day Caleb had to decide whether to abort the mission or to hold off the chopper which was on deck to pull them out. They had nothing left to eat but peanut butter and cheese spread.

He decided to hang in one more night. Blandon wanted to stake out another location. He was against it. The odds were as good where they were as anywhere else, and the spot he'd picked for the snatch was perfect. The trail took a sharp turn just ahead of where they'd waited which meant that the rest of the NVA column would be around the bend before the last man got to it.

They stayed put. It was Turk's fire team's turn again. They moved back into position at dusk and Caleb began what was to be his fourth night awake. He tried every trick he knew to stay alert, but by 0300 he was starting to nod off when Turk jabbed him in the ribs. "Movement on the trail."

They watched a whole NVA company file past them, and Caleb suddenly realized he had no way of knowing which man would be the last in line. What saved him was their perfect spacing. He started counting. One, two, three, Gook. One, two, three, Gook. After a while this got so hypnotic that he was already up to the count of five before he realized he'd come to the end of the column. He poked the Turk. "Let's go!"

They moved silently onto the trail. The last man was already disappearing around the bend. They followed, Caleb first with Turk right behind him. It was dark as pitch. Caleb heard their man before he saw him. He grabbed him in a choke hold and slapped a hand hard over his mouth. Turk got hold of his feet and they carried him squirming like a fish back around the bend and into the trees. They'd just finished tying and gagging him when one of their lookouts tapped him on the arm. "Shit, Indian!" the man whispered, "Fuckers are coming back!"

He threw himself on top of the prisoner with his knife against his throat. Footsteps passed not two feet from where they lay. The prisoner grunted through his gag. Caleb jammed his face down into the mud. He started to struggle.

Caleb cut his throat. Warm blood spurted all over his hands. The little NVA soldier's dying gurgle was indistinguishable enough from the other sounds of the jungle night that the squad which had come back to look for him went on by, disappearing down the trail in the direction they had first come from. Turk came crawling up.

"I had to shut this guy up," Caleb whispered. "We'll have to grab another one when they come back."

"Jesus Christ!"

Fifteen minutes later the NVA returned. Their spacing was still perfect. He tried a different way of counting. *One, two, three Gook. Two two, three, Gook. Three two three, Gook.* He counted twelve men before he got to *thirteen, two, three, no Gook.*

He and Turk did a repeat performance. The NVA patrol didn't come back a second time.

He knew that come daylight the enemy would comb over the whole area and he wanted to be as far away as possible before that happened. They waded, sometimes waist-deep, up the mountain stream, counting on the sound of rushing water to cover their own noise. They slipped and stumbled over moss covered rocks and tried not to get separated in the inky darkness. Every five minutes or so, he held up the column and waited, frantic with impatience, for a head count to come up from the rear. They carried their prisoner slung by his hands and feet from a cut sapling with Turk at one end and Caleb at the other. Those three hours before dawn broke were as hard as any he could remember.

When finally he began to make out the shape of the trees, he turned left out of the stream bed and headed up one of the many deep gorges cut by the smaller streams that fed into the main one. The Tribe traveled another mile into the growing light and then collapsed, exhausted, under a hole in the jungle canopy where the underbrush had grown thick enough to hide them.

He let everyone rest for fifteen minutes. Then he called over the fire team leaders to assign the watches they would maintain during the day. Turk, Carl and Blandon hunkered down around him, swaying from exhaustion, but still game. For a moment he felt very close to this filthy, bearded, red-eyed crew of his. But they were staring at him with the same mix of awe and horror he'd seen in their eyes on the day he'd used his friend's body for bait. He looked down at his jacket that even after all those hours in the water was still stiff with the blood of the man whose throat he'd cut.

He couldn't sleep. He'd never killed with a knife before and he'd cut deeper than he had to. His hand still felt the knife grating against bone. His ears rang with the singsong, gurgling the NVA soldier had made trying to draw in air through a severed windpipe. Turk snapped him out of this nightmare reverie. "Hey Indian, you better come check on our Gook."

"Jesus! I'd almost forgotten all about him."

The little soldier was moaning softly through his gag. His wrists and ankles were horribly swollen around the ropes that bound them.

Caleb dropped to his knees. "Quick Turk, untie his feet. I'll get his hands."

"You sure you want to do this?"

"Look at his feet, for chrissake. He's not going anywhere." Caleb knelt beside his prisoner, rubbing his swollen hands. The man writhed in new agony as the circulation began returning, and in that moment he was no longer an enemy but simply a fellow human in awful pain.

All during the long hours they waited for the fog to clear enough for the chopper to get in to pull them out, Caleb stayed beside his prisoner, trying as best he could to make the man comfortable and hoping by this simple act of humanity to erase the sing song gurgling sound that still rang in his ears.

At some point during that interminable day, Blandon came by. "Who'd have thought it?" he laughed. "Jack the Ripper one moment, Saint Francis the next!" Whatever he said next was drowned out by the *whup, whup, whup* of the arriving Sea Knight.

Once back at the base, they turned their prisoner over to battalion for interrogation, and nobody ever heard what happened to him after that. As for Caleb himself, he was promoted back to Sergeant and awarded the first of his Bronze Stars. George Blandon rechristened him K-Bar, and so he became.

*****

The Vulture had an office that he seldom used. But he happened to be at his desk when Wee Willie came lumbering in without bothering to knock. "So OK," he admitted. "Maybe I did fuck up, pissing in your backyard like I did. Let's do it, Ernie. I'll wire him up and we'll see what happens."

Later that same day, Wee Willie stuck his head in Caleb's door. "No food or liquids after 1800 tonight, Gunny. Gotta get you back down to the OR tomorrow so I can drive a spike through your wrist!"

"I can hardly wait, Sir."

"It's going to mean going back more heavily on the dope for a couple of days. Your leg's going to hurt worse than your arm when you wake up."

"My leg, Sir?"

"I'll need a slice of your femur for the graft and you'll need to hold still until it takes. Go back to thrashing around and you'll fuck things up for fair!"

Caleb slept well that night and the next morning they wheeled him down to the OR and left him to wait his turn, parked next to a glass cabinet filled with the kind of instruments a carpenter would have recognized. There were saws and awls and pliers, all of shiny stainless steel, and all, he realized groggily, soon to be used on him.

He felt the gurney jerk. A masked green figure was behind him pushing. He could hear the hum of rubber wheels on linoleum and he felt himself sway as his invisible driver maneuvered him around corners. Then he was stopped again in a room bright with huge overhead lights. A masked Wee Willie loomed up beside him. Nurses in the background busied themselves with instruments. They tipped him off the gurney onto the operating table where a too cheerful anesthesiologist plugged a needle into his IV. He fought his usual losing battle against the sodium pentothal and descended into blackness.

There he stayed for the next 48 hours, and when at last he did fight his way back up to partial consciousness whatever images had roiled through his subconscious during that period were lost in the murk. He woke up more fully to find a pin through his wrist to which they'd fastened the wire that suspended his arm.

Wee Willie was right. His leg did hurt like hell, but he was by now a connoisseur of pain and he knew that this was a variety he could handle.

*****

Another week went by. Caleb learned to live with his arm suspended above his head. He re-mastered the humiliating routine of the bedpan and became more adept at eating with his left hand. Brushing his teeth proved a particular challenge. He slept fitfully but had no nightmares violent enough to damage the still fragile bone bridge.

"Still got them caged?" asked the Vulture.

"What caged, Sir?"

"The demons."

Caleb grinned. "Maybe it's this sling, Sir. Goddamn thing won't let me sleep well enough to have nightmares!"

The Vulture secured the watch he'd stationed at Caleb's bedside during his sleeping hours and Wee Willie began tapering off on the dope. For Caleb, now more alert to his surroundings, the months during which he would have to remain a prisoner in his bed stretched out interminably before him.

*****

When he next returned, the Vulture found his patient staring blankly into space. "Do I see a mind relentlessly focused on weighty issues?" he asked. "Or a man asleep?"

Caleb jumped. He saw it as evidence of his enfeebled state that he hadn't heard the door open. "You see a mind relentlessly focused on escape, Sir," he said. "This damned rig they got me strung up in is like being on the rack."

"I brought you a radio," said the Vulture. "I thought it might offer some diversion." He found an outlet but couldn't manage to plug in the cord. Randall materialized to do it for him.

"My shadow," grinned The Vulture.

Randall put the radio in reach of Caleb's left hand. "Try turnin' it on, Gunny. You got to push this button here."

"Actually, I thought we might wait on that," said the Vulture.

"No Suh. Best he try it out now. He can't work this thing himself, he gonna be callin' one of us all the time to do it for him."

The Vulture shrugged resignedly. Caleb tried but only succeeded in shoving the radio out of reach. “Just like I thought,” said Randall. He secured the radio to the table with adhesive tape. “Try it now.”

Caleb tried again and this time the table rolled away. “Fucking hell!” he muttered. With every day that passed, it rankled him more to be so totally dependent on others. He maneuvered the table to jam its wheels against the bed frame and punched angrily at the button again. An explosion of androgynous wailing filled the room. Randall reached quickly across and turned it off. “Them be the Stones,” he grinned. “Mick Jagger howling like a ‘coon dog got his balls hung up in barbed wire!”

“Thank you Randall,” smiled the Vulture. “A most graphic image.” A grinning Randall left the room, closing the door behind him. The little doctor started to wiggle his way onto his stool, felt his legs give way, and fell heavily across the bed. “I’m sorry, Gunny! Did I hurt you?”

“No, Sir,” Caleb lied.

“Sorry. Happens to me now and again. But don’t tell anybody. You’d be giving more ammunition to the people who don’t think I belong in the Navy.”

“How’d you get *in* the Navy?” Caleb saw the awkwardness of that question as soon as he’d asked it. “Sorry, Sir,” he said quickly. “It’s none of my business.”

“No feelings hurt, Gunny.” As he spoke, the Vulture was clumsily trying to get settled. “There!” he said finally, “That’s better!” He looked up, grinning like a child who’d just done something clever and Caleb couldn’t help grinning back.

“To answer your question,” said the Vulture, “in real life I’m a professor at the University of Pennsylvania Medical School. I’d been coming down here for some years as a consultant to the psychiatric staff, and when the war started heating up, they asked me to come on full time as a civilian staff member. I told them I’d only do it if they let me wear a blue suit. So they commissioned me a Commander.”

“Just like that, Sir? No basic training or anything?”

“Six weeks in Newport with a group of other doctors and chaplains mostly. I did quite well actually. Led my class in physical fitness.”

Caleb's expression betrayed his doubt.

"I really did. You probably won't believe it but I was once a passably good acrobat. I put myself through medical school working in a circus."

"No shit, Sir?"

"God's truth. Watch!" The Vulture tipped awkwardly head first off his stool and landed standing on his hands where he remained for a long shaky moment before collapsing in a heap. "Damn!" he said. "Can't do it anymore. I used to be able to do that one handed."

"Sonofabitch!" said an astonished Caleb. "But they sure as hell didn't commission you an O-5 to do handstands. They must have wanted you pretty bad."

"They did. I've made my career studying the after effects of traumatic stress, and the Medical Corps was seeing a lot of that among you returning Marines."

Caleb had seen men crack. First the Breadman. Then others.They'd been taken away, sometimes crying hysterically, sometimes helpless as little children, usually without a scratch on them. He'd felt some pity for those broken men but more contempt. His nightmare in which he'd dreamed he was such a man himself had been one of his most horrible, and now it seemed he was being treated as if he were.

"I'm not…" he began.

The Vulture held up his hand. "I've got the floor, Gunny. Odd thing is that I've grown to love the Navy. I'm only a Reserve, serving 'at the pleasure of' someone—the Congress or the President, I can't remember which—but I hope whoever that someone is doesn't throw me out once this war's over."

"You'd be making a lot more on the outside, wouldn't you?"

"Yes, but I've found a home here. Before, I'd always felt myself an outsider. That comes with being deformed. But here, in this odd uniformed subculture that I've stumbled into, I put on my blue suit and I'm part of the fraternity.

"Telling you any of this is quite unprofessional," he admitted. "But I hope I've revealed enough that you'll perhaps grant me at least conditional membership in your armed brotherhood. I grant you, I'm applying for the wrong reasons. *Honor, duty, country*—all those remain abstract concepts for me. It's the *'we few, we happy few, we band of brothers'* that appeals to me. That's what I, the freak outsider, want so much to be a part of.

"I suppose the question is why?" the Vulture continued. "I know why for me—I've just told you that—but why for you Spartans? Why for you, Gunny? What draws you to the military life?"

Caleb grinned. "If you want the short answer, Sir, it's this." He held up the magazine he'd been thumbing through. It was LIFE's *Year in Pictures* which gave prominent billing to the Woodstock concert of the previous summer. "Look at those shitbirds!" he demanded, pointing to one of the photographs. "Christ, Sir, when I was at Parris Island, MacNamara was sending us recruits with IQ's lower than the temperature in this room and I'd still take those kids over the spoiled self-satisfied stoned shitheels in this picture!" His grin widened." In case you didn't notice, Sir, that's five s's in a row."

"Well done, even if the sentiment expressed might be a bit extreme. But to return to my question, are you telling me that yours was the simple choice of order over anarchy? That's why you chose the Marines as a career?"

Caleb shook his head. "If by order, you mean high standards, OK. But if you're suggesting the kind of order which attracts men who don't want to make their own decisions, that's crap!" He tapped irritably at the offending picture with his good hand. "There are eighteen year old Lance Corporals in Viet Nam right now who will make more life and death decisions this afternoon than most of these deferment-chasing shitbirds will make in a lifetime."

"Peace, Brother!" smiled the Vulture. "But your eloquently expressed sentiments remind me of a poem. Let's see if I can remember it. "*'In the battlefields of life...'*" he began. "No, that's not right." He sat silently for a long moment, gazing at the ceiling. "Yes, here's how it goes! *'In the world's broad fields of battle, In the bivouac of life, Be not like dumb, driven cattle! Be a hero in the strife!'*

"That's your American poet Longfellow exhorting us all to be like your lance corporal. He's no dumb driven beast—I'm talking about the lance corporal now, not Longfellow—but still he makes his choices within boundaries. Even in war there are conventions that say 'thus far and no further.' So his options are limited. He stays on safe ground as long as he remains within the boundaries. Yes?"

Caleb had learned to be wary of that 'Yes?' "Sure," he said. "But so what?"

"Simply that we need those boundaries. If you'll permit me a parable, imagine a traveler who comes upon a crossroads, but instead of being confronted with only four roads to choose from, he finds an infinite number, all heading off in different directions. What's he going to do?"

"Close his eyes, spin around three times and point!"

"Maybe, but for the sake of my parable let's say that he stands there, paralyzed by indecision, until he is joined by his parents who point to some of the roads and tell him he'll get a spanking if he follows them. Then along comes a priest who points out more roads, a great many of them for that matter, and warns him that hell awaits him at the other end should he travel down any one of these.

"Now our man's choice is made somewhat easier. But a lot of roads still remain open to him. He's still trying to decide which one to travel when he's joined by a policeman. 'Stay off of those,' advises the policeman, pointing out yet other roads. 'Some will lead you to the lockup and some even to the noose.' So now our traveler is much relieved to finally have his choices reduced to a manageable number, and he resumes his journey.

"Now let's travel with him to the next crossroads and there we find awaiting him your Colonel Kant who tells him that at this particular intersection all roads are open. There are no parents, no priests, no policemen or anyone else to provide guidance. Anything goes. So what will he do then?"

The room fell uncomfortably silent. "No thoughts on that dilemma?" the Vulture prodded.

"None, Sir."

"Then we've come to a crossroads of our own, haven't we? You've vanquished your nightmares, which I suppose means that my job here is over. Shall I do as that Vermont senator is advising we do in Viet Nam?

Just declare victory and go home? Or do I still have a role helping you to lower the pressure in the boiler?"

"I think I've got that under control, Sir."

"Perhaps. But from the bits and pieces I've picked up along the way, I'd venture that, like the Group Ones, you're still holding the lid on a lot of steam. You've got the nightmares on hold for the moment, but whatever was behind them must still be lurking somewhere. On top of that, we have the man on the stretcher and, of course, that odd business about the chicken. It all adds up, Gunny. At some point, the steam will have to vent."

For Caleb, this was all happening too fast. Up until this moment his status as a wingnut had been an involuntary one. But now it seemed he was being asked if he wanted to maintain that status by choice. The Vulture sensed his indecision. "It's nothing you need to decide right now," he said kindly. "You've taught me enough about the culture you come from to make me sympathetic to your dilemma. If you do decide that the war hero is not necessarily unmanned by talking to a wizard, I'd be very pleased. If not, my job is done." He turned towards the door, lost his balance, and just barely managed to catch hold of the knob to stop himself from falling.

Caleb watched this brave struggle and felt a wave of affection for his indomitable doctor. "Thank you, Sir," he said. "You did a lot for me."

The Vulture turned back from the door. "That 'did' sounds rather final. I take it then you've decided to go it alone?"

He had. What went on inside his head was his own affair. It was the only independence he had left. "Yes, Sir," he said. "I guess I have."

"Goodbye then, Gunny. If you'll allow me, I'll check in with you from time to time. Just to see how you're doing?"

"I'd like that, Sir."

Caleb lay back, not at all certain he'd made the right choice. He decided to try the radio again and, after a lot of left handed fumbling, managed to tune in Philadelphia's classical music station. Hume had put him onto that. Ever since the Vulture had brought him the radio, he'd been hoping to hear something by Dvorak, but this night the only composer whose name he recognized was Beethoven and that only because of an argument he'd once overheard in a train station. Two old men had been debating whether Beethoven might have become a Nazi had he been born to a later age. One of the two had been scandalized at the thought. "To write such music," he'd said, "a man must have something of God in him."

"Sure," said the other, "but that still leaves a lot of room for the Devil!"

He went from that thought to imagining all of humanity lined up in one of the Vulture's spectrums with the Devil anchoring one end and God the other. He wondered where he'd fall along that line. If good intentions were the measure, he'd probably find himself more or less in the middle. But if he were judged by where those good intentions had led him, he decided he'd be standing a whole lot closer to the Devil.

That got him to wondering if he would have become a Nazi. Had he grown up as a young man in pre-war Germany, he decided he probably would have. "My country right or wrong!" He hadn't questioned that sentiment as an American headed for Viet Nam. Why would he have done so as a German marching into Poland? And why wouldn't he have felt the same shiver go up his spine hearing Wagner at Nuremberg as he did even now when they played the Marine Corps Hymn? He didn't doubt that Storm Trooper Caleb would later have regretted his choice of party. With Caleb the Nazi, just as with Caleb himself, things would have ended up looking quite different in hindsight than they had at the time.

He was interrupted from these thoughts by a light knock at his door. Nurse Reardon came in, closing the door behind her. He was surprised to see her alone. She seemed taller without Wee Willie by her side.

"Hi, Gunny," she smiled. "I was up here on Nine and thought I'd drop in. How're you doing?"

"I'm doing OK, thanks, Ma'am. Except for being strung up in this damn straightjacket."

"Ma'am!" she laughed. "I'm younger than you are. Try calling me Nancy."

"Yes, Ma'am."

She came over next to his bed. "I could give you a back rub? It's part of our job."

"Don't know how you'd do it. I can't roll over."

"But you can sit up a little. Come on, try!"

He found that he could. She had strong hands and she worked from behind him with her head so close that he could feel her warm breath on his neck. It seemed to him that her breathing was coming faster and, for his part, he was having trouble hiding what was going on under his sheet. But he needn't have bothered. She pulled the sheet away and laughed softly. "My goodness! There's one piece of you that's still working properly!"

She bit her lip thoughtfully. "Darn!" she said, noticing the bandage on his thigh. "I'd forgotten about that bone graft. Now how are we going to do this?"

Caleb figured he had to be dreaming. "Do what, Ma'am?" he asked dumbly. She hiked up her skirt, revealing long, athletic legs and the fact that she wore nothing underneath. "This," she said, climbing carefully up on the bed to straddle him.

"Where there's a will, there's a way," she grinned as she lowered herself onto him. And then she spoke no more until she collapsed, spent, with her head lying lightly on his good shoulder. He could feel her heart beating hard against his chest. She'd tied her raven hair up tight behind her head and he ran his fingers through it, working it loose. "Don't," she said, her voice muffled. "They'll guess what we've been up to."

"Nobody'd believe me even if I told them,' he laughed. She reared back on her haunches, smiling. "Beats a back rub, doesn't it?"

"First time in my life it ever felt good being screwed by an officer!"

"You gave your body to this damn war," she said. "This is how I give mine." And then she was sobbing. "They just keep coming, Gunny! Four more on the ward today. Beautiful men! I can see them as they must have been, and now they're all just... just ruined." She wiped her eyes on the corner of his sheet and smiled through her tears. "I'd fuck every last one of them if I could figure out a way to do it!"

"That'd be a tall order." Caleb started to say Ma'am but recognized that now the rules had changed. "There's lots of shot up Marines in this hospital."

"Yes," she grinned. "But not all of them have their own room!"

*****

Randall came by the next morning to wheel him, bed and all, down to the Bone Ward. He didn't say anything, just piled Caleb's few possessions on the bed, and pushed him silently out into the passageway.

"You forgot the radio," Caleb said.

"Radio belongs to the Vulture."

In the hall, the morning routine was in full swing. A corpsmen was swabbing down the decks, nurses moved busily from room to room and Ward Nine's ambulatory patients padded about in their slippers and bathrobes, most of them looking like vacant-faced zombies. Randall maneuvered his unwieldy cargo skillfully through this confusion and stopped in front of the elevator.

"Seems you've got the rag on today, Doc," Caleb said. "What's wrong?"

"What's wrong!" Randall exploded. "Vulture, he start workin' every day at 0600. He goes the whole damn day without stopping and by the time he get to you, he's hurtin' so bad he can't hardly even walk no more. But he come anyway, and he stay longer with you then with any of the rest, trying to help your fucked up head."

"Watch your mouth, Doc!"

"Fuck you, Gunny! 'Cuz that's what you done to him. He be tryin' to help you an' you be tellin' him to fuck off."

Caleb bit his tongue and watched the green lit numbers above the door record the elevator's progress down from the twelfth floor. Randall was watching the same thing. "That one's coming down from Officer's Country," he muttered. "Best let it go by."

They waited in silence. "I'll be on a ward full of grunts, Doc," said Caleb finally. He had visions of himself baring his soul to the Vulture with a thousand curious ears tuned in to what they were saying.

"Nuthin' say we can't move you somewhere else, same as I'm movin' you now. An' don't you be tellin' me your head ain't fucked up either. I be sittin' there lot o' nights now, listenin' to the stuff you been sayin' in your sleep. Some of them things I tell the Vulture. Some I don't 'cuz they be so fucked up."

"Those are things I've got to work out on my own, Doc."

"Vulture helped me a lot. Same way's he can help you."

"Helped you? How?"

"Helped me with my fightin.' I'd be fightin' anybody who even *looked* at me funny before I met the Vulture."

The elevator door hissed open. Randall rolled him into it. They were alone. "OK, we'll try it, Doc," said Caleb. "But I'm counting on you guys not to let the whole ward know I'm a wingnut. Fair enough?"

"Yassuh," grinned Randall. "We'll tell 'em we be takin' you off so you can get laid by some pretty nurse!"

Caleb's head jerked up.

"Just kiddin,' Gunny. I be just' kiddin.'" They stopped on the ground floor. Randall rolled Caleb out into the bustle of the hospital lobby. He looked around him curiously. Cars came and went outside the main entrance. He didn't recognize some of them, reminding him that between Viet Nam and the hospital he'd missed the last model year. He spotted a flower shop occupying temporary plywood quarters against one wall and a more permanent looking news stand against the other. But most of all, he noticed the noise. Cars, voices, a distant bus accelerating away from the curb; it all sounded as foreign to him now as had Da Nang when he'd first gone there on liberty.

They pushed their way through a mix of civilians and sailors with Caleb feeling self-conscious until he realized that in that setting gaunt looking men being wheeled around on beds were too common a sight for anyone to spare him more than a cursory glance.

Randall wheeled him down a long sloping corridor and into Wee Willie's fiefdom. They rolled down the length of that seemingly endless bed-lined ward past men, some in traction as he was, some with one or both sleeves empty, and some with sheets lying flat where legs should have been. But Caleb sensed spirit in the place. Marines laughed and joked and hollered back and forth. He closed his eyes and imagined himself back in barracks.

The far end of the ward was curtained off to make a Staff Noncommissioned Officers' Quarters. Randall parked him in an empty slot. Caleb wasn't sure how to react when Miss Reardon came through the curtain but she was all business, making sure the wire from his wrist ran free through its pulley and hanging a fresh piss pot from the bed frame.

"Comfortable?" she asked, and Caleb thought he detected the ghost of a grin.

"Yes, Ma'am."

"You've got the buzzer if you need anything." She and Randall departed through the curtain.

Caleb looked around him and concluded that for the moment at least the NVA weren't bagging too many staff NCOs. The only other man on the ward gave him a thumbs up. His jaw was wired shut and above his legs the sheets were tented up over a wire frame. He scribbled on a pad and held it up. *Mike O'Malley, E-6*, Caleb read. *G Company, Second Battalion, 5th Marines. APC I was riding hit a mine, Ba Ren. You?*

"Lima Company, Three Seven," said Caleb.

Name? scribbled O'Malley.

"Caleb. John Caleb."

Heard about you, O'Malley wrote. And then, picking up the pad again, *Glad they got you tied down*! He saw Caleb's expression and wrote in big letters, *JOKE!*

*****

"Thanks for asking me back, Gunny," said the Vulture. They were meeting in an examination room adjacent to the bone ward.

"Thank Randall, not me, Sir," said Caleb. "He shamed me into it." Which was pretty much the truth. Now back again among his Marines, he'd found himself wishing more than once that he had stuck with that original decision to go it alone.

"I have a great deal to thank Randall for," the Vulture was saying. "That chair too." He pointed to an upholstered armchair in the corner. "I don't know where he got it from."

"You probably don't want to know, Sir."

"Yes, I probably don't!" The little doctor settled himself comfortably into his new chair, pulled out his notebook, and looked up smiling. "Well," he said happily, "here we are. Now what'll we do?"

"Isn't that for you to tell me, Sir?"

"Technically, it isn't. It's your role to talk, and mine mainly to listen."

Caleb grinned. "Pretty soft job you got, Sir. How can I get to be a wizard?"

"About fifteen years of school should get you started. But I did say'mainly to listen.' My contribution, if you'll allow me to make it, is to occasionally suggest interpretations to the things you tell me, which, according to the script, may over time lead you to an alternative reality which is both closer to the truth and easier to live with than the one that confronts you now." The Vulture grinned sheepishly. "I suppose you could call that my stump speech."

"I don't buy it, Sir. What's done is done. Facts are facts. You can wish like hell for your 'alternate reality' but that won't change a damn thing."

"No? For a very long time the accepted reality had it that the world was flat. Then along came someone who looked at the same set of facts that had always been there for everyone to see and came up with an 'alternative reality' that just happened to be the correct one. My job is to suggest to you different ways of looking at the same events. But I can't tell you which interpretation is ultimately correct. That's up to you."

"As my dad used to say, Sir, 'When you hear the thunder of hooves, why suspect you're hearing zebras?'"

The Vulture looked momentarily puzzled. "Oh, I see," he said finally. "The point being that the beasts in question are most likely to be of a more common variety. But I fail to see the relevance."

"What I'm saying, Sir, is why go looking for these alternative realities of yours when the one right in front of your nose makes perfectly good sense?"

"Good sense only if you accept the assumptions which underlie it. What you overlook, Gunny, is the very human penchant for adjusting facts to square with what makes us most comfortable."

Caleb looked skeptical.

"You don't believe me? If you're willing to sit through yet another parable, let me give you an example. Let's say that Smith, who is basically quite a decent fellow, one day loses his temper and strikes Jones. The attack is entirely unprovoked. Smith regrets it immediately. But it's too late. The blow is struck. And there is only one completely true telling of the event. Smith struck an innocent man. Period.

"But for Smith this is an uncomfortable truth. So he starts to bend it so as to make it easier to live with. He comes up with rationales for what he did—Jones is evil; Jones provoked him; etc., etc., etc. Eventually that version of the event becomes his reality. And it escalates from there. If Jones happens to be of a different religion or perhaps of a different race, then all who are of that religion or of that race become villains as well.

"But what of Jones? His jaw hurts and so does his pride. Even so, he can more easily get on with his life. He can put the whole unhappy business behind him, because it's easier to forgive one's attacker than it is for the attacker to admit he's in the wrong.

"So Smith remains captive to the alternate reality he has created. But this is not a psychologically healthy state to be in. Somewhere deep in his subconscious he knows he's living a lie, which of course leads to inner turmoil, and that ultimately leads him to the wizard."

The Vulture took off his glasses, polished them carefully, and then set about methodically rearranging his notes. Caleb began to grow uncomfortable with the silence. The little man at last seemed to have everything organized to his satisfaction. "Now, Gunny," he said, "put yourself in my shoes. Let's say you are the wizard and Smith, however reluctantly, is before you with this problem. What would you tell him?"

"I'd tell him he's fucked up, Sir. That he's the bad guy, not Jones."

"But you can't do that. For one thing, too much of his self image is by now tied up in the version of reality he has created to be able to accept so blunt a truth. And for another, it's not a wizard's job to tell him anything. You can help but he has to get where he's going on his own."

"Be a damn sight easier just to flat out tell him he'd screwed up, wouldn't it?"

"It would. But for him to believe it, he's got to figure that out for himself."

For a long moment, neither man spoke. The only sound was of distant voices from the other side of the door. Caleb finally broke the silence. "OK, Sir," he said, "I'm not sure where this train's headed, but I guess I'm along for the ride."

"I'm very glad, Gunny. Then if you'll let me, I'll be the conductor. All I ask as you take this train ride we've embarked on is that you look inward with clear eyes. We can't change what's in our past but we can learn from it and in the process perhaps loosen the grip it holds us in."

"Maybe," Caleb said skeptically. "But for now all I'm saying is that I'll ride the train."

"I'll settle for that. But if we're to change where that train is headed, we'll have to start with where it's been. So on with your story, Gunny. When we left off, you'd just found it necessary to cut a man's throat."

"Are you going to tell me that was wrong, Sir?

"I'm not going to tell you anything. But why don't you tell me what happened next?"

CHAPTER EIGHT

Not long after his squad got back from the prisoner snatch, he got called up to the battalion CP.

His old company commander, the Wop, now a Lieutenant Colonel, was CO of 2/4. In the years since Caleb had last served with him, his close-cropped curly hair had gone salt and pepper gray, but he was still the same irreverent old mustang he'd always been.

"At ease," he grinned when Caleb reported. "Find somewhere to park your ass. Ammo box over there you can use." He nodded towards another figure behind him. "Colonel Kant here, he's been asking me about you. I tell him you're a hot shit, so don't embarrass me, OK?"

Caleb had walked into the CP tent right out of the sun. As his eyes adjusted he made out the Ice Man and a Major he didn't recognize sitting in the shadows. The Colonel noticed his surprise. The corners of his mouth turned up slightly in what could have been a smile. "Hello, Sergeant Caleb. I take it you haven't been beating up any more of our brothers in arms?"

"No, Sir." Caleb noticed the Ice Man now wore eagles. "Congratulations, Sir."

The colonel nodded acknowledgment. "They've kicked me upstairs. I'm Fourth Marines' new XO. Major Price here is our intelligence officer. He'll tell you why we're here."

Major Price was a chart and pointer man, the opposite end of the spectrum from the Wop. "We're fighting a new kind of war," he began. "It's a war in which cultural and political considerations often trump military ones. I imagine you've run into such situations yourself?"

"Yes Sir. We sometimes take fire from Buddhist temples and we're not allowed to return it." He paused. "It's kind of hard on morale."

"Morale, shit!" exploded the Wop. "Caleb, you know damn well the VC'd like nothing better than to have us shoot up one of their temples. We'd win all kinds of Hearts and Minds doing that!"

The major nodded agreement. "The reason you're here, Sergeant, is because we've got ourselves a situation that's giving us more problems than all those temples put together. There's a village called Ba Hom which is home to a District Chief named Nguyen Van Mung who's got friends in high places. He's been able to turn that village into such a showplace that it's become a must see for every one of our Congressmen who fly in here to see all the good things we're doing for our Vietnamese allies.

"So the puzzle has been why, when Ba Hom has become I Corps' favorite model village, have the VC never touched the place. Wouldn't you think that for the same reasons we're showing off Ba Hom, Charley would want to show us he could knock it off any time he felt like it?"

He paused, evidently expecting an answer. "Yes, Sir," Caleb agreed, taking his cue. "That makes sense."

"The reason Nguyen's village has been immune to attack," Major Price continued, "is because he's been playing both sides of the fence. I can't tell you how we know this, but I can say that due to his influence a lot more medical and military supplies have been funneling through Ba Hom than his local defense forces could use up in a hundred years. We think it's all going to the VC."

"We *know* it's all going to the VC," interrupted the Ice Man, "but we can't shut down that pipeline because, for reasons the Major will explain, Nguyen's untouchable."

"He is," said the Major. "He's Saigon's number one hero, so much so that if this were Japan, he'd have been designated a National Treasure. He made his reputation fighting first the Japs and then the French, but he apparently never had any use for the Communists. When the country was partitioned, he stayed here, where, like Cincinnatus in Rome, he's gone back to his village to live simply without any of the perks his fame could have earned him. His wife died last year. Before that, he lost one son to the Japs and his second to the French."

"He sounds like someone we'd want on our side, Sir," Caleb ventured.

"We would, but he isn't. We don't know why he's changed sides. Maybe he's been a sleeper all along, left behind when the Commies went North. Or maybe he's just walking a tightrope trying to keep his people safe from both sides. Either way, he's doing us a lot of damage."

Major Price looked inquiringly at Colonel Kant. Caleb saw the Ice Man nod and the Major turned back to him. "That's where you come in, Sergeant. We'd like to see Nguyen turn up dead. We'd like to make it look like the VC did it."

Caleb didn't have to say no. They read it on his face.

All eyes turned to the Colonel. There was a long silence. "Has it occurred to you, Sergeant," he began finally, "that we may not be winning this war?"

It had not. Caleb, like most Americans in Viet Nam in 1965, never even considered that possibility. But as he listened to Colonel Kant go on about how they were engaged in what was shaping up to be the most inept application of superior force in the history of warfare, he found himself thinking of the enemy who was always still out there despite the body counts; MACV passed on to the press like football scores, and of all the sweeps they'd made only to have the VC come filtering back into the areas they'd declared pacified. He saw again Hume up there on the crane saying how we were going to ruin the country we'd come to save, and he had to force that image from his mind.

"Hanoi's learned how to do a lot with a little," the Ice Man was saying. "We've got to learn to do the same. We've got to develop the tactics that will let us go after the enemy with a scalpel instead of the sledgehammer we're using now."

It was stifling hot in the tent and the Colonel wiped the steam from his glasses before continuing with what sounded to Caleb like a lecture he had given many times before. "My contention is that our current tactical organization is ill suited to our mission here. I'm equally convinced that our over-reliance on supporting arms alienates the very people we need to win over to our side."

He paused again. "I'm asking you to be my scalpel, Sergeant Caleb. I hope to use you to show the gentlemen who are running this war that a relatively small number of highly skilled men such as yourself, capable of operating alone or in small teams, can inflict more real and psychological damage to the enemy than we can with our large clumsy conventional operations."

Major Price was looking uneasy. "We should make something clear," he said. "However it turns out, none of what we're discussing here can ever be officially acknowledged. If for some reason it blows up in our faces, the party line will be that it was a rogue operation gone sour."

"Where's that leave me, Sir?" Caleb asked. "If I go out and shoot everybody's favorite district chief, am I acting on orders or aren't I?"

"You'll be acting on my orders," said the Wop. "The Colonel and the Major still have their careers to think about. Mine's just about over." He grinned wolfishly at Caleb. "So there you have it, kid! Seems the only thing's gonna stop us from fuckin' up this war is if you and me put our asses on the line."

"OK, Sir," said Caleb. "If you're in, I am too."

"Good!" said the Ice Man. "We'll meet here tomorrow to go over the details." He and the Major got up and left.

Caleb stood there, dazed. "Why all the speeches, Sir?" he asked the Wop. "I'm just an E-5. The colonel doesn't have to convince me we're fighting this war all wrong."

"Beats the shit outa me," grinned the Wop. "Been me, I'd have just found someone who can shoot straight and told him to go ding that two-faced cock-sucker. But the Ice Man says he wants you for the job. Says it's because you beat up that ARVN lieutenant. Don't ask me what that's got to do with the price of eggs, but what do I know? I'm just a dumb wop!"

*****

"Did you ever ask yourself what that did have to do with the price of eggs," asked the Vulture.

His question caught Caleb by surprise. "No, Sir," he said finally. "I guess I just figured he thought I could do the job he needed done. That's all."

"I think he was smarter than that. He could have recruited some unfeeling psychopath. You might even think that that would have been his first choice. But no, he realized that if he could convince you that in the skewed morality of war killing innocent people was not only necessary but right, then he'd have found himself, as he put it, a far better scalpel than he would if he were to rely on someone who killed for money or for thrills or even for darker motives. Does that make sense?"

"I guess I was the proof of that, wasn't I?" said Caleb bitterly, and once again wished he'd held his tongue.

"You were in good company, Gunny. The Crusaders, the Inquisitors, the Stalinists, even the Nazis who killed my parents—all of history's most dedicated executioners—all of them were convinced they were acting in the service of some higher good."

The Vulture paused to wipe his glasses. "But forgive me. I can't seem to keep myself from interrupting. What happened next?"

*****

Major Price had brought a map. He and Caleb bent over it, leaning on their elbows, while the two Colonels sat and watched.

"Here's Ba Hom," said the Major, tapping on the terrain features with his pencil as he pointed them out.

"You can see how the Song Lo River turns to pass about 150 yards to the west of the village. Over here's the road which runs out to Highway Six, and over here's an unusual piece of real estate you may find useful as a vantage point for scoping out the village. See this hill here, just south of the village? We call it the Rock Pile. You can see from the contour lines that it rises almost vertically out of the coastal plain. I'm not even sure you could climb it. But if you could, you'd be able to look right down into Ba Hom. You could even shoot right down into Ba Hom if you had a scope. Problem is everyone would know where the shot had come from. By the time you climbed back down, they'd have a reception committee for you at the bottom. And if we picked you up by chopper, then there'd be no doubt whose side you were on."

"We don't want that," said the Ice Man. "If we can make it look like the VC killed Nguyen because he was in bed with us, his people will be unhappy with the VC for bumping off their sugar daddy."

Major Price nodded, unrolling his next chart. "What we've got here is a sketch of the village itself. By their standards, they've done a pretty good job on their defenses. You can see there's an outer perimeter of wire and sharpened stakes. Then you come to this moat, which is also filled with Punji stakes. Inboard of the moat, right here, there's a roughly square palisade running right around the village. The Regional Forces platoon garrisoned inside the village mans these block houses at each corner."

"How about mines or flares in the wire, Sir?" Caleb asked.

"Aren't any. Nguyen won't allow it. He says he's worried the children would set them off. The guy loves kids. This building you can see here just beyond the main gate is a home he's set up for war orphans."

"What about that RF platoon? How does he keep them fooled?"

"We don't think he does. We think the platoon itself is pretty heavily infiltrated by VC. That's another reason why Charley hasn't ever hit Ba Hom."

"And Nguyen himself, Sir? Do we know any more about him than what you've already told me?"

"He's about sixty years old and, as we said, a widower with no surviving children. He graduated from Hai Phoung University with a degree in engineering. As far as we know, he's never been out of the country. Never to Paris or Moscow or Peking. We know very little about his personal life. He lives alone in the same kind of simple grass hut the other villagers live in. He's not at all like most Vietnamese of similar rank. When he's not sitting in the square with the village elders, he's home reading, or else looking after his orphans. He rarely goes outside the main gate. He does on occasion bring one of the orphans to spend the night with him. We'd hoped that might give us a handle on him, but it appears to be perfectly innocent. Just a night at Grandpa's house. That's all there is to it."

Major Price rolled up his charts and stuck out his hand. "Good luck, Sergeant. From here on you're on your own."

"What about my squad, Sir?"

"We'd rather you work alone. You OK with that?"

"Yes, Sir, that'd be my choice too."

*****

Turk took over the Tribe and Caleb moved over to Headquarters and Service Company. Colonel Riccio saw to it that he bunked with the battalion armorer. On paper, his job was chief scout in the S-2's office. It was an E-6 billet and the Wop somehow got around his broken time to put him in for another stripe.

He tagged along on a daylight patrol that passed close by Major Price's Rock Pile. Then he flew over it in a chopper. The major was right. It wouldn't be easy to climb, especially at night and carrying all he'd need to stay up there for any length of time. But it was the only plan he could come up with. If he could get up to the top with a spotter scope, he might be able to find Nguyen's Achilles heel.

Water was going to be the limiting factor. There was only some scrub for cover on the summit. It was already October, but the monsoons were late in coming and it was still blisteringly hot. Caleb didn't much like the idea of four or five days roasting on a hot rock with only the water he could lug up that cliff himself.

Colonel Riccio solved that problem. He sent his reconnaissance platoon out to the Rock Pile to practice rappelling, and had their lieutenant leave extra water and a climbing rope on the summit, supposedly stashed there for other climbers. He even cleared the exercise with Nguyen. "If nothing else," he said, "sending recon out there will get Nguyen's people used to having us screwing around in their backyard."

Recon's platoon commander was Lieutenant "Bull" Best, who'd been an All-American tackle for Michigan State. The Bull was the only black officer in the battalion, but his outsized personality and enormous physical strength had done much to allay the latent racism that was still very much a part of Marine Corps culture at that time. He hiked his platoon out to the Rock Pile, returning the following afternoon with a stack of Polaroid pictures with which to show Caleb the best way to the top.

His first picture was of an enormous boulder shaped like a shark's tooth at the base of an easily climbed chimney ending in a smooth rock face about half way up the Rock Pile. He'd marked with a pen the route he had taken to traverse that rock face and circled the pitons he'd driven in as hand and foot holds. Caleb asked him how he was going to find those pitons in the dark.

"Maybe you won't," laughed the Bull. "But I marked 'em for you with pieces of my last white skivvy shirt which I tore up on your behalf. If there's any light at all in the sky, they should show up well enough. Once you find the first one, the rest'll be easy. They aren't that far apart."

He pointed to his next picture. "This one shows where you're going to be when you reach the last piton." The line he'd drawn now ran up a second more vertical chimney which went on up to the top. "You shouldn't have much trouble climbing that one either, if you're careful and take your time."

That evening, Caleb followed a patrol through the wire and then dropped off into the bushes without anybody even knowing he'd been behind them. The Marines he'd been tailing disappeared into the night. He waited until all he could hear was the clicking of insects and then set off for the Rock Pile ten miles away. It was 2130 and he had four hours to get there with time enough left to make the climb before daybreak.

He had the world all to himself. The rice farmers had gone back to their hamlets, and the fields and paddies, which during daylight would have been impossible to pass through unnoticed, now lay empty before him. Or so he hoped. Now and again the moon would break through low broken clouds to send him ducking into the shadows. But most of the time it was just dark enough that he could see without worrying too much about being seen. The night breeze off the South China Sea rustled through the bushes, masking what little noise he did make walking on dew-soaked grass.

He was carrying two canteens, his poncho, a week's rations, the spotting scope he'd checked out from the battalion armorer, and his rifle. Sixty pounds all told, which was a manageable load, thanks to the NVA pack he was carrying it in. It burned him up that the enemy were being issued a better engineered piece of equipment than the World War One vintage packs the Marines still used to carry their gear.

He swung along, glad to be on his own. He'd planned to intercept the Song Lo a mile or so east of Ba Dom. Then he'd head upriver to the Rock Pile, and after that he'd work his way along its base until he found the Bull's shark-tooth rock. He used his compass, moving from landmark to landmark along his azimuth, but soon found himself navigating more or less by dead reckoning.

There was no way to travel in a beeline across the coastal plain. But even as he twisted and turned among the dikes and paddies, the orientation of the stars and the feel of the night breeze on his neck kept him headed towards his destination. So after four or five times glancing down to find the north arrow still swinging reassuringly right under the luminous line he'd set to the course, he stowed the compass and went on without it.

He reached the Song Lo far enough ahead of schedule to take a break. He crawled into a bamboo thicket and opened up a can of peanut butter. The river ran low at that time of year just before the monsoons broke. He waited there, listening to the water gurgling along four feet below the muddy bank, not thinking about much of anything. Then suddenly he knew he was not alone.

He listened for a good minute and heard nothing. Convinced that he was just imagining things, he'd started back in on his peanut butter when that internal alarm went off again. This time there was no mistake. From somewhere down river came a faint, rhythmic splashing. He waited motionless, eyes straining into the darkness as the splashing grew louder.

It was a boat of some kind. Several boats. The first one passed by, very close from the sound of it, but invisible, for clouds now covered the moon. There was a pause, more splashing, and he heard a second one go by. The sounds of paddling grew fainter as the two boats continued on up the river. He waited fifteen minutes, hearing only silence, and then continued on his way. Half an hour later the moon broke through again to reveal the Rock Pile looming up on his left, and he turned away from the river.

The Bull's shark-tooth rock was just as he'd described it. Caleb felt his way around it, counterclockwise, towards the cliff that disappeared up into the darkness above him. The route to the top was closer to vertical than it had seemed in the pictures.

He started up the chimney, cursing under his breath each time he sent a chunk of loose rock crashing down, and no longer so happy about his NVA pack, which seemed to want to pull him off the mountain. The easy part of the climb took him almost an hour. He was breathing hard by the time he reached the top of that first chimney and gave himself five minutes to rest before starting to look to his left for the pitons.

He couldn't find them. He tried to get higher but couldn't. Then he dropped down ten feet and started working his way back up again, searching as he went. Still nothing. The night was fading, and he had visions of still being stuck there in plain sight when the farmers arrived in the fields below. He had to do something quickly. If he couldn't go up, he'd have to go down and hole up somewhere until the following night.

The moon broke through the scudding clouds, just for a second, but long enough for him to catch a flash of white cloth. He then spent another long minute trying to orient himself on whether this first piton he'd found was a handhold or a foothold. It was a foothold. The second row of pitons was above it. Gingerly he started across. The rock face he was traversing leaned out beyond the vertical. He hung out over space, most of his weight on his arms as he inched along in the dark, feeling his way from piton to piton. The sharp edges of those square steel pins cut into his palms, and his rifle swung awkwardly around behind him, adding to the weight trying to pull him off the mountain.

There was nothing for it but to keep going, which he did until finally, when he was beginning to wonder how much longer his hands were going to hold out, he got to the last piton and found the second chimney.

The rest of the climb was no easier. At one point he kicked loose a small avalanche of rocks, which went bouncing off into the darkness, loud enough, it seemed, to wake up anyone within earshot. He reached the top just as the eastern sky exploded into pink, and dragged himself over the lip where he lay without moving next to the climbing rope, three canteens, and one melted Hershey Bar that the Recon Platoon had left there for him.

He fell asleep after eating the Hershey Bar, and when he woke up three hours later he was already dehydrated enough from the heat of the morning sun to know he was in trouble. Even the water in his canteen was too hot to drink. He managed to get some down by holding it in his mouth until it was cool enough to swallow. He tried to stand up but his legs wouldn't hold him.

He knew he had to do something fast. He figured all the water in the world wouldn't be of much use to him if he passed out from heat stroke. So he opened two of the lieutenant's canteens and poured both of them over his head. He was bone dry again in minutes, but the evaporation of the water was enough to cool him down. He crawled towards the center of the Rock Pile, burning his hands on the hot stone and trying to figure out how to rig himself some shade.

The few thorny scrub bushes that had established a foothold in the cracks between the rocks were too low and too far apart to be much use. He wasted half an hour trying to use their branches to rig a tent out of his poncho, and by the time he figured out that this wasn't going to work, his head was spinning again. He started to get confused.

When he came to it was evening. The third canteen was empty. He didn't know if he'd drunk it or poured it over his head. The sun dropped below the horizon. He used what daylight remained to make a proper reconnaissance of his small rock-bound world. Over on the west side, overlooking the village and made to order for his purposes, he found a small ravine, narrow enough across the top that he could stretch his poncho across it and wide enough at the bottom that he could lie comfortably behind his scope and look down on everything that lay below. He anchored the four corners of the poncho with rocks, crawled into the ravine beneath it and went back to sleep.

He woke up to the sound of roosters crowing. His watch read 0430. He had a pounding headache but was otherwise none the worse for wear. One C-Ration can of cold turkey loaf, mixed with cheese, spiced up with Tabasco and washed down with a quarter of the canteen he'd brought with him, cured his headache. It was still too dark for the scope.

Ba Hom lay sleeping below him. As dawn broke, voices began floating up out of the fading darkness. He could smell cooking fires. Then as the eastern sky exploded into pink, he saw a yawning man step out his door and look around, checking the weather just as other farmers and fishermen were doing the world over. It reminded him of home.

The only thing that seemed out of place in this timeless scene was the Regional Forces platoon in their khaki uniforms. At 0545 he watched another ritual he knew better. A squad of troops came straggling out of the incongruous looking Quonset hut RF barracks and formed up sleepily on the parade ground in front of it. He could hear the high pitched commands of the corporal falling in his men. "*Phan-doi! Vao Hang!*"

The corporal took his post. The sergeant of the guard came strutting out of the barracks to inspect the detail. Caleb put the scope right on him and watched as one by one the guard came to inspection arms with M-1 rifles that in some cases were almost as tall as the men who held them. But he had to hand it to the Sergeant. He ran a good inspection, even sending one man back to the barracks. The rest of the detail waited grinning until the fuck-up returned, and then the corporal faced them right and marched them off to relieve the guard. Caleb watched the sentries coming off post turn over their ammunition and the relieving men lock and load. All in all he thought, it was a pretty good show.

By 0700 the sun was high enough to remind him of his limited water supply. There was still no sign of Nguyen. Caleb waited behind his scope, scanning the irregular rows of thatched huts that ran more or less north/south along two sides of a hard-packed dirt square. Small trees with dusty leaves stood scattered among them. The main gate was at the south end of the square and the RF barracks at the north end. A new well, complete with hand pump and water trough, all compliments of Uncle Sam, was on the northwest corner of the square, and the district chief's hut was right behind it.

About 0730, Nguyen appeared at his door with a little boy beside him. Caleb's 20 power scope brought them in so close he could even see the two of them squinting as they stepped into the outdoor light. He homed in on Nguyen who, even by Vietnamese standards, was a small man, with a thatch of white hair and a wispy Ho Chi Minh beard. He was smiling down at the little boy whose hand he held, and his nut brown face was creased with deep good humored lines that radiated from his eyes.

The two of them crossed the square, still hand in hand, and walked over to a plywood sided building tucked right up against the palisade fence. It was an outhouse, a six holer by the looks of it, built to US Army Field Sanitation and Hygiene specifications, and plainly also compliments of Uncle Sam. *Clean water and a place to shit*, thought Caleb, smiling to himself. That had to be a hard act for the VC to follow.

The boy came out first, then Nguyen. They washed up at the well and went on to another hut all the way down at the far end of what by then Caleb had labeled the West Side. A pack of urchins came tumbling out the door to climb all over the old man. A woman followed, trying to restore order, but without much success. Even from the top of the Rock Pile, Caleb could hear the excited little voices that arose from Ba Hom's orphanage.

And so the day unfolded. The farmers, whom the RF sentries had checked out through the main gate in the morning, returned in the afternoon, muddy from the rice harvest. No one seemed much upset by the delay at the gate as each man had his ID checked. There was a lot more skylarking than Caleb would have expected from men who always seemed so silent when he passed them on patrol.

The school children had come back earlier. He couldn't figure out how school worked. Some kids went. Others didn't. The little delegation that had marched with their books out the gate in the morning was made up of all shapes and sizes. He'd heard that nuns ran the district school and wondered if it was just the Catholics that got to go to school.

At one point he took a break from the scope to rest his eyes but was drawn back to it by a great racket from below. A pig roundup was in full swing. Yelling kids and squealing pigs were charging all over the village.

It looked like a game and the pigs knew the rules. After fifteen minutes or so of playing hard to get, they all settled down and allowed themselves to be herded out the gate to root in the already harvested paddies.

Nguyen, meanwhile, wasn't doing much of anything. He came and went from his hut, stopped to talk with anyone who came his way, and in general acted as if he didn't have a care in the world. Caleb lost track of him for a while towards evening when the sun was low in the west and he couldn't use the scope for fear of it becoming a signal mirror and giving him away. But when just after sunset he did find Nguyen again, the old man was carrying on as usual. Never once did he go outside the gate. He did talk briefly with the driver of the truck that hauled away a load of rice. As far as Caleb could tell, that was his only contact with the outside world.

Evening came. Caleb got up to stretch, not much the wiser for his day of spying, and by the time he had crawled back into his ravine the lanterns were lit again in Ba Hom. The RF platoon executed colors. Small groups of villagers gathered around the square. He could see the glow of cigarettes and hear bursts of high-pitched laughter.

It seemed just a night like any other night. But he did clear up one puzzle. He'd spotted an olive drab box next to Nguyen's hut and had wondered all day what was in it. Around 2100 he heard a muffled hum and looked over the edge just in time to see electric lights go on in the village chief's hut. He swung the scope back onto the always open door and saw Nguyen sitting inside reading a book. Evidently the old man allowed himself at least the luxury of a generator.

Caleb was spared from running out of water that night by the arrival of the monsoon. The rains were a month overdue, but when they came, they came hard. The wind swung around into the north. The sky turned ink black. He heard a couple of big drops land on his poncho tent and then all hell broke loose. His comfortable little ravine turned into a rushing stream bed and he had a couple of frantic minutes groping around in the dark to save his gear from washing right over the edge. But he was able to use the neck of the poncho as a funnel to fill all his canteens.

The next morning brought with it a majestic sunrise and he looked down to find Ba Hom washed clean. Leaves glistened and pigs wallowed in new puddles, but otherwise life went on as before. He spent the day either too cold or too hot as torrential rains alternated with steamy sunshine, but he learned nothing new.

The only excitement was at the orphanage. Nguyen stopped by there in the afternoon and was met with the usual enthusiastic reception. The same frantic woman rushed out, trying just as unsuccessfully as before to restore order. But this time Nguyen raised his hand. The kids formed a laughing circle around him. The village chief took off his hat and passed it around. Each child dropped something in it and then they had a drawing. Nguyen presented his hat ceremoniously to the now smiling woman. She screwed her eyes shut, reached inside the hat, and held something up for everyone to see. The kids crowded around. Caleb could hear shouts and arguments. One tiny little girl began jumping up and down. The rest looked disappointed, and Nguyen and the little girl went off hand in hand. It was her turn to spend the night at Granddaddy's house.

When he heard the hum of the generator that evening, he crawled behind his scope and focused in on an old man reading bedtime stories to the little orphan girl who sat on his lap.

Day four passed the same way as the one before. Nguyen held another drawing at the orphanage that afternoon and a timid little boy with a horribly twisted foot won the night with Granddaddy.

Caleb was running out of patience. Nguyen's life seemed to follow an unvarying ritual and there didn't seem much more to be learned from watching the man going endlessly through the same steps. He decided to head back that night, relieved in many ways that he was no closer to getting at his target.

He crawled back behind the scope, more to pass the time than in the hope of seeing anything he hadn't seen before. But there was something different going on. Nearly all the women and village elders were gathered down by the main gate at what appeared to be an open air market of sorts. He was traversing the scope over in that direction for a better look when he caught something out of the corner of his eye and swung back quickly onto Nguyen's hut. Four black clad men were filing out his door.

Where the hell had they come from? All the village men were still out in the fields. And he'd never seen anyone else but children in the district chief's hut no matter what the time of day.

He kept the four of them in the scope as they walked over to the Quonset hut barracks. One of them seemed to be in charge and his three men stayed a couple of paces behind him. The RF sergeant, who Caleb had concluded was the platoon leader, came bounding out of the barracks to meet them, and the five of them stood around talking like old friends. Ten minutes later Nguyen showed up.

Caleb could almost sense the others stiffen to attention. The leader of the mystery men broke off from the group. He and the district chief moved out of earshot of the others and began talking earnestly. Nguyen seemed upset. The two of them argued back and forth for a few minutes. At one point they both turned and looked long and hard up at the Rock Pile, making Caleb duck instinctively even though he knew they couldn't see him. Then Nguyen threw up his hands disgustedly and started back for his hut, followed by the four strangers. All five disappeared through the door but only Nguyen came back out again. Caleb stared at that door until it was too dark to see. The four men never reappeared.

He started back at 2200. Getting down from the Rock Pile was a lot easier than getting up and the hike back to Chu Lai was uneventful except for a repeat of the strange experience he'd had on his way out. As he'd hiked inland those four long days before, it had been as if he were also hiking towards the center of Hume's onion. The further he'd moved away from the security of his own lines, the more layers had peeled away until he found himself almost a different animal, duller certainly to the kind of feelings his friend had considered the mark of their humanity, but infinitely more receptive to all the signals that were coming to him out of the night.

As with every hunter, he'd experienced some sharpening of the senses when he'd gone after deer, but this was a whole order of magnitude more than that. He'd become a narrowband receiver, precisely tuned not only to his three sensory antennae but also to that fourth vestigial one he had first experienced by the river. Everything else was filtered out. There was only now, and it was a now of such intensity that it was as if he were tripping on some drug. It was an intoxicating brightness, a kind of tingling awareness that came from being focused so intensely on the moment.

But as he made his way back to the base, that brightness faded to be replaced by the image of an old man sitting in his simple hut reading to the little girl who sat in his lap. He passed back through the wire just before dawn and went straight to the Battalion Command Post to tell Colonel Riccio that he wasn't the right man for the job.

The Wop had been out running. Caleb walked along beside him while he cooled down. He told his CO about the VC on the river, about Nguyen's unvarying ritual, about the four suspicious men, and about the little orphan girl who had won the raffle. "I can't do it, Sir," he said finally. "Nguyen's just a kind old guy who wants to be left alone, just like every other poor jerk in this miserable country."

"Sure," said the Wop. "That's the way it looks to you. So maybe I'll tell you something that happened to me when I was a little kid. OK?"

"Where I grew up," he began, "our next door neighbor was a baker. Old guy. Loved kids just like Nguyen. We'd go by his shop and he always gave us *cannolis*. Then one night when I was eight maybe, I woke up and there's these red lights flashing on my ceiling, so I looked out the window and the cops are busting the baker. Next day, the bakery's got a lock on the door but there's still this big wedding cake sitting in the shop window and every day after that, when I'd walk home from school, I'd see the little plaster bride and groom on top of that cake and they're slowly tipping over. I watched them tip a little more each time I passed by, and that made me sad because I loved that old guy.

"But when I got a little older and started hanging out with some guys who maybe I shouldn't have been hanging out with, I found out that baker was still running all the call girls in Manhattan from inside the slammer. I found out his people were recruiting twelve year old runaways, and if a girl tried to quit on them, she got her face cut up. This by the same guy who'd been giving me *cannolis*!"

"I see what you're driving at, Sir," said Caleb, "but Nguyen's no criminal. He's…

"Yeah?" interrupted the Wop, "you're sayin' Nguyen's got a big heart because he looks out for those orphans. But you gotta ask yourself who made those kids into orphans? Who gave the Gooks the M-1s they're shooting at you with?"

Caleb just shook his head, suddenly too tired to argue. The Wop punched him on the shoulder. "Get some sleep, kid. I'll talk to Colonel Kant. OK?"

"Thank you, Sir. I know I'm letting you down, but I..."

"No worries! But what you gotta understand is just because a man's bad don't mean he can't do some good things along the way."

Caleb had just fallen into a troubled sleep when one of the battalion's admin clerks shook him awake again. "I don't know what you done, my man," the clerk warned, "but the Regimental XO is waiting for you up at the CP. He's all by himself an' he says he don't care if you report in your skivvies so long as you get your ass up there double time."

Caleb reported as ordered. "I understand you're having second thoughts," said the Ice Man.

"Yes, Sir, I am. I'm sorry, Sir. I guess I'm just not your man…"

The Colonel had shed his utility jacket and was wearing no rank. "I see," he said. "Well then, that's that. Good luck to you, Sergeant Caleb."

Caleb did an about face and was half way out of the tent when the Colonel called him back. "You lost a man not too long ago, didn't you?" he asked. "Hume I think his name was. A corporal?"

"Yes, Sir."

"Damn shame. We had orders to send him home."

"Home, Sir? Why?"

"All I know is HQMC wanted him back. Seems one of his former professors is now working for DOD and asked for him specifically. It was a mine that got him wasn't it?"

"Yes, Sir. One of our own mortar rounds wired up to a battery. I found the tail fin."

The Colonel seemed to be digesting this information in silence. "Capricious, isn't it?" he said finally. "The way the Grim Reaper swings his scythe? If somebody in the S-1 Shop had just processed his orders a little faster, Corporal Hume might that day have been on a plane home instead of on patrol with you."

"Yes, Sir," Caleb choked. "Is that all, Sir?"

"Yes. . . No, there is something else. Something I'm curious about. In Korea we called the Chinese Slopes, short for Slopeheads. What do today's grunts call the VC?"

"Gooks, Sir. We call them gooks."

"You ever thought why?"

Caleb shrugged. "No, Sir. We just do, that's all."

"What if I suggested that in our line of work it makes the job easier if we can turn our enemies into something less than human? If we think of them as Slopes or Gooks, killing them becomes not all that different from shooting rats." He looked up quizzically. "I'm guessing you could have shot Nguyen easily enough if he'd remained a Gook. But now that you've come to know him as an individual, it becomes a different story. Am I right?"

"Yes Sir, you are. I watched him with those kids. . ." Caleb's voice trailed off.

The Colonel nodded. "I can see that, never myself having been very good at turning the Chinese into Slopes. My problem was that my wife's a Chinese girl, so whenever I'd look out over those piles of dead Chinese heaped up in front of our lines, I'd wonder if maybe one of her family were lying out there." He smiled. "I knew the odds were against it—there's six hundred million of them at last count—but once I'd had that thought, I couldn't see Slopes any longer. I saw individual men in my sights, and the only thing that kept me pulling the trigger was knowing that if I didn't kill them, they sure as hell would kill me." He smiled thinly. "That's not exactly a noble sentiment, is it?"

The front legs of his chair came down on the tent's wooden floor with a thump. "I couldn't hate those Chinese any more than I can hate the VC. The real bastards are the ones who start wars and the bloodsuckers who profit from them, not the men who fight them. But the sad fact is that it doesn't matter a damn whether Nguyen's a good man or bad man. Fate has landed you and him on opposite sides of the fence and you can be sure if the situation were reversed, he'd understand the need to get rid of you just as clearly as I'd hoped you'd understand the need to get rid of him."

Caleb shook his head in confusion. "Oh Christ, Sir, I... I just think somehow it's wrong. . ."

"Wrong!" The word exploded like a pistol shot. "You tell me, how the hell do you define wrong? We're on the other side of Alice's looking glass now, and everything's turned around backwards. When it's our job to ratchet up the enemy's level of fear and suffering to the point that he throws in the towel, how can anything be called wrong if it contributes to that end?"

"I can't answer that, Sir. I don't know what to think anymore."

"Stick to your guns, goddamnit, Sergeant! Convince me that it's wrong. You argue your case. I'll argue mine."

Caleb's confusion gave way to anger. "It's not my place to argue with the Colonel, Sir."

"It damn sure is. While we're alone here, we're just two poor jerks trying to find our way down a road without sign posts. So forget rank. If you can come up with a better alternative than mine, sit down and tell me what it is."

Caleb found a seat on the same ammo box he'd occupied earlier. "Can't we talk to him, Sir?" he asked. "Tell him we know what he's up to and that there's no middle ground? That he's either for us or against us?"

"We could, but he's already too badly compromised and he knows it. Hanoi's got people watching him just as we do. So let's say he did come over to our side and gave us the whole network they've set up to funnel our stuff to the VC. He'd be dead in a minute unless we took him into protective custody."

"That'd beat killing him, wouldn't it?"

"Saigon wouldn't think so. That government's too shaky to risk word getting out that their number one national hero's in fact a VC collaborator." The Colonel leaned back again in his chair. "So we're the ones who'll have to take him out and make it look like it was the VC who did it. That way everyone's ass is covered."

"I don't see that, Sir. His own people could get to him one hell of a lot easier than we can. Why not let them do the dirty work?"

"Because Saigon's got more leaks than a rusty bucket. For one thing, Nguyen has enough friends in the government's inner circles that he'd hear about it as soon as the idea was floated. And for another, they're scared shitless of the guy." He grinned. "They realize, and you should too, that your kindly old man didn't land at the top of the French's most wanted list just by hugging orphans! They'd much rather let him go on playing his double game than risk having him defect openly to the other team."

The Colonel stood up and stuck out his hand. "So there it is. Good luck to you, Sergeant Caleb. I respect your stand on principle even if I don't agree with it."

They shook hands. Caleb came to attention, did an about face, and was half way out of the tent when the Colonel called him back a second time. "I got something here I forgot to show you." He handed Caleb a piece of paper. It was a requisition form of some kind. "Take a look at the third item. 81mm mortar rounds, isn't it?"

"Yes, Sir."

"They were supposed to be going to an ARVN unit but they never got there. Your friend Nguyen grabbed them."

A long moment passed. "I. . . I guess I'm back on board, Sir," Caleb found himself saying. "I don't know if I'll be able to pull the trigger when the time comes, but I'll try, Sir."

"Good! But you'd better pull that trigger, Sergeant, because if it ends up with Nguyen pointing his gun at you, you can be damn sure he won't have any second thoughts about pulling his."

CHAPTER NINE

Later that same day, Caleb found himself back up at the CP, but this time it was Colonel Riccio who was picking his brains. He wanted to know about those four VC who had appeared out of nowhere from Nguyen's hut. Caleb's only theory was that they must have come into the village after dark, holed up there until the following night, then left again. But he couldn't explain why they'd gone to all that trouble. They'd acted like old friends with the Regional Force troopers, so why hadn't they just come and gone like everyone else?

"Maybe Best's people will come up with some answers," said the Wop. "I've sent Recon back out there again to see what there is to see."

Caleb went back to his tent to collapse exhausted into his rack. But he got only a couple of hours of sleep before that same admin clerk was back to summon him once again to the CP. The sun was just beginning to show above the horizon when he got there. The Wop and the Bull were waiting for him, coffee cups in hand. Colonel Riccio handed him a cup of his own and the Lieutenant began his report.

"I used both my squads, Sir," the Bull began. "We went through the wire at 2030. Sergeant Turner took his squad to the river and Corporal Sachs took his to the village. I went with Sergeant Turner. We reached the river at 2330, a mile to the east of Ba Dom, at about the same place where Sergeant Caleb first saw the VC, and we dropped off one team at that point. Then we continued on to this point here." He pointed on the map to where the Song Lo turned abruptly towards the village, "and that's where we dropped off the second team. Sergeant Turner went with his last team on up the river, another half mile or so above the village. I stayed with his second team.

"Corporal Sachs' squad got as close as they dared to Ba Dom and spread their people out so there was no way anyone could approach the village from the direction of the river without being seen.

"Then we waited. Around 0240, Turner's first team called me on the radio to report that three boats had just passed by his position. At 0310 those same three boats passed us. So I called Sergeant Turner to alert him that they were headed his way. Half an hour went by without Sergeant Turner seeing them. I knew the current runs harder further up stream so I told him to keep waiting. But when he radioed back at 0400 to say they still hadn't passed his position, I figured they'd still have to be somewhere between us and him. So I started up the river by myself to see if I could find them.

"I hadn't gone far—maybe a couple of hundred yards—when I spotted the three boats pulled up into the weeds right here." He pointed with an enormous finger to where the river turned west again, just about at its closest point to Ba Dom. "But the VC were gone. I couldn't wait for them to come back, as it was already first light and we had to get out of there. So I radioed Corporal Sachs, figuring he must've seen those men heading towards the village. But he said he hadn't seen anything all night.

"That's my report, Sir. The only explanation I can come up with for how those men could have disappeared is that they've got a tunnel running from the river to the village."

"That's it!" Caleb blurted. "That tunnel must come out right under Nguyen's hut. That's how those guys got in and out."

"Could be," said Colonel Riccio noncommittally. "Anyhow, Lieutenant, that's a fine job you and your people did. Any chance you were spotted up there?"

"Always that chance, Sir. But I don't think we were."

That night Caleb went back to the river. He spent three soaking wet days hiding in another thicket near the spot where the Bull had found the boats hauled out. On the third night the VC came back. Caleb had with him a Starlight Scope mounted on an M-14, and through it he watched three low-sided skiffs, each manned by four paddlers, nose into the bank about thirty yards from where he lay. The men waded ashore, and then the rain started again.

The Starlight Scope works as a light-intensifier, so didn't work at all when there was no light to intensify, and there wasn't much light that night. The VC appeared to be loading equipment onto their boats. Caleb could make them out dimly through the scope when the clouds thinned but then lost them altogether whenever the rain began again. They moved silently back and forth between some point inland and the bank, carrying what looked to be ammunition boxes down to the river and going back empty for another load. One man was taller than the rest. Caleb timed him from when he saw him leave the bank to when he came back, trying to estimate from the time he took roughly how far inland he'd had to go. The tall Gook made the round trip consistently in less than two minutes, so the mouth of the tunnel, if it was a tunnel, had to be nearby.

Loading went on for about half an hour. Caleb could their hear footsteps squishing through the mud, but other than a few muttered grunts not a word was spoken. Another rain shower came through to blind him and when it had passed he found the VC all standing down by the boats.

Five minutes went by. They were still standing there. Then he spotted two more of them down on their knees, crawling jerkily backwards towards the bank. The sky lightened momentarily and he could make them out working methodically, raking branches back and forth to cover their tracks. They reached the boats, climbed aboard and disappeared back downstream into the night.

Caleb wasn't sure what to do next. If he waited until dawn to look around, he'd almost certainly be spotted from the village. On the other hand, if he went blundering around in the dark, he'd have to worry about leaving his own footprints. He crawled along the water's edge to where the boats had been and, for lack of any better ideas, sighted through the scope more or less in the direction he figured the VC had been walking. "Sonofabitch!" he said almost out loud. Their trail stood out clear as daylight.

They'd outsmarted themselves. The rain had stopped. Among the leaves they'd scattered over their footprints some had landed dry side up, and these reflected so much more of the night light than the wet ones around them that they almost glowed in the scope.

He followed the trail to where it seemed to end at the base of a gnarled old tree and then the rain started up again in earnest. He ducked in under low branches, looking for shelter even though he was already soaking wet, and sat down to wait out the downpour. Five minutes later the rain dropped off to a drizzle. He waited, listening to the drops filtering down through the branches above, and gradually he became aware of a different sound, almost like a waterfall right beneath where he was sitting. He started to roll over and, as his weight came onto his hand, the ground gave way beneath it and he collapsed, face in the wet leaves, with his arm stuck in to his shoulder through the wooden lattice that disguised the VC's private entrance to Ba Hom.

He lifted off the cover and dropped down as silently as he was able into the tunnel entrance, landing ankle deep in the water he'd heard cascading into the hole. It was pitch black. There was a faint smell of fish and kerosene lanterns. He looked up for a last time into the gray of the open hole above his head and sloshed off into the darkness. He had a flashlight, but didn't dare use it. The other problem was his rifle. An M-14, even without a bulky Starlight Scope attached to it, was not the weapon of choice in a tunnel. Carrying it in one hand didn't work. He needed both hands free to feel his way along. Carrying it slung, which he tried next, made it useless if he came around a corner and ran into a Gook. So, reluctantly, he left it leaning against the wall.

He went on a ways, had second thoughts, and went back for the rifle. He lugged it back out of the cave and hid it under the tree. If any VC followed him into the tunnel, he didn't want to leave a calling card at the door.

At first the tunnel floor pitched fairly steeply upward and he was soon out of the water. He moved in a half crouch because of the low ceiling, using one hand to sweep the darkness ahead and the other one to feel his way along between the wet narrow walls. About twenty paces in, he came to what appeared to be a fork. In the process of trying to figure out what was where, he got himself so completely disoriented that he had a moment of panic until he remembered to get out his compass. It wasn't much help. He could just make out its phosphorescent dial glowing too faintly in the palm of his hand to be able to read. He got out his flashlight, pressed the lens tight against the dial, covered the whole works up as best he could with his jungle hat and charged up the radium with the light. Five minutes later he had a working compass and a broken flashlight. He'd dropped the light trying to get it back into its pouch on his cartridge belt, and when he'd found it again after a frantic search around his feet, what was left of the bulb was rattling around loose behind the lens.

He went on, choosing the left, more southerly branch of the fork. A hundred and twenty paces further along he came to another fork and again kept to the left. He felt the walls turn from mud to rock and then, suddenly, he felt no walls at all. He groped around, first with his left hand, then with his right, aware that he must have blundered into some kind of a larger room, but no longer sure where the entrance was behind him. He could smell fresh air, either from a ventilation shaft or else an entrance, he didn't know which. He turned around, moving too fast in his anxiety to get back to the security of a wall, and stumbled heavily over something that caught him at shin height and sent him crashing down onto the dirt floor.

Somewhere in the darkness a child screamed. Caleb froze. He heard a man's voice. Then footsteps right above his head. There was some shuffling around, the clink of glass, and finally a faint square of light, outlining the edges of what appeared to be a trap door into the room above. The child's terrified wailing subsided into sobs and then again there was silence.

Nguyen's footsteps retraced their path above his head, followed a moment later by lighter ones. He heard Nguyen laugh, the child giggle, and the sound of the two of them settling into bed. "Well, I guess that's it," he muttered, kicking himself for not having factored in the possibility that one of the orphans might be spending the night with Grandpa. He started to grope his way back into the tunnel and then stopped again in an agony of indecision. He knew he'd never come back a second time. The old man lying just feet away from where he stood was becoming too close to him now, too much a fellow human being. It was now or never.

Suddenly and inexplicably, the long suppressed image of his dead mother all bloody in the bathtub flashed across his mind. Then followed a whole kaleidoscope of other images. Here was the Iceman challenging him to define wrong in war; now came his father trying to tell him something he couldn't hear; now Blandon on the beach saying he'd let others make his moral choices for him; now Hum struggling to cry out a warning with blood gurgling in his throat; now the Iceman again, holding up a requisition form for the mortar rounds Nguyen had syphoned off to the VC.

"Oh, that bastard!" he said, now hating the man who had by proxy killed his best friend. "That miserable, fucking bastard!" And from that moment he became a killing machine, nothing more. Everything else vanished as he focused, laser-like, on the job at hand. He turned around just in time to see the thin rim of light disappear as Nguyen blew out the lantern. Then he waited for what seemed like an eternity, motionless so he wouldn't lose his bearings on the trap door. Nguyen began to snore.

Caleb made his way across that black void on hands and knees, startling himself with the occasional sounds of his own progress and fighting off the impression that he was moving in aimless circles. At last he fetched up against a ladder. He took off his cartridge belt, held his knife in his mouth and pulled himself slowly upright, moving hand over hand from rung to rung until he was crouching, with his feet still on the floor and his shoulders against the bottom of the trap door. Ever so slowly, he began to straighten his legs. The door lifted an inch or two. There was something heavy on top of it.

He should have expected that. Nguyen would not have left his secret entrance uncovered. Caleb lowered the door back down and dropped onto his knees again to search for something he could use as a prop. There wasn't anything within reaching radius of the ladder so he cut off one of the laced on rungs. Then he started inching that door back up again, holding his breath against the possibility that whatever was on top might go sliding off with a crash. About six inches up, he felt the weight begin to shift, making what sounded like a terrible racket to his ear, pressed up as it was right under the door. He lowered his shoulders enough to stop the sliding, then levered up again slightly, trying to coax the load silently off the top.

Nguyen suddenly stopped snoring and Caleb froze again, awkwardly bent over under the weight of the half-open door. He heard the old man rustling around and waited until finally, when he thought his legs were about to give out, he heard snoring again. He got his prop into position under the door, then slowly wormed his way out onto the dirt floor of the hut. He recognized the child curled up in a ball next to the sleeping old man as the boy with the club foot. He picked him up gently from where he lay and, praying he wouldn't wake up, started across the room, to lay him down on the pile of rice matting he'd spotted stacked below a window. Then he turned back and did what he'd come to do.

Hands sticky with blood, he grabbed Nguyen's lantern, climbed back down into the tunnel, and fell to his knees retching. The spasm passed and he crawled clear of his vomit. *Maybe the bastards who caused all this will step in it*, he thought grimly.

The underground room, or at least what he could see of it after he'd lit the lantern, appeared to be a large cold closet filled with baskets of rice. In one corner was a pile of camouflaged canvas tarps which he recognized as US issue shelter-halves. He spotted the mouth of the tunnel he had come through and hightailed it back towards the river entrance, stopping only long enough to check out the two tunnel branches he had passed on the way in. Both of them led to rooms at least as large as the one beneath Nguyen's hut. One was an armory, its walls lined with rows of M-1 rifles, Browning light machine guns and even a couple of 3.5" rocket launchers. The other was a magazine, full from floor to ceiling with cases of ammunition. All of which should have left him feeling less sick to his stomach but didn't.

He had to hole up by the river until the following night, and by the time he got back to Chu Lai the news of the district chief's murder had preceded him. Colonel Kant's reaction was to send a criminal investigation team into Ba Hom, allegedly to assist in finding Nguyen's murderer. But it was no accident when in the course of their investigation they discovered the tunnel and retrieved the biggest single VC arms cache found so far in the war.

The Ice Man had not anticipated the VC's reaction. Three nights later, the VC overran Ba Hom. Their attack was so quick and savage that by the time a relief force arrived the village was in ruins and the VC gone.

The Marines got some of them with air and artillery as they pulled back into the hills, but that could not have been much consolation to the shell shocked villagers Caleb found when he accompanied Colonel Kant and a delegation of reporters on an inspection tour the morning following the attack.

Most of the RF platoon had just melted away. The few who had stood fast, men with families in the village, were all dead. The VC had run through Ba Hom throwing satchel charges into the huts. Smoke still rose from smoldering thatch. The well, the outhouse and the RF barracks were all in ruins. So was the orphanage. With no families to pick them up, shattered little bodies still lay like rag dolls all around the blasted hut. Caleb couldn't bring himself to look. But the TV crews had a field day.

Groups of survivors stopped poking through the wreckage to watch silently as Colonel Kant's party walked down the length of main square, past Nguyen's hut which was still standing, and on to the far end of the village where they found three nearly naked RF soldiers strung up on the palisade. Their balls had been cut off and stuffed in their mouths. The Ice Man would not oblige the press with a comment. He just shook his head, turned, and led his group back to the choppers.

"Why the hell did they do it?" asked the Wop when they'd gathered later at the CP. "It was their village, wasn't it? There's no way they could have operated there on the scale they did without everyone in Ba Hom at least knowing about it."

"I don't know," said the Ice Man. "They must have figured somebody in the village had informed on them so they made everyone else pay the price. Brutal, but still an effective lesson on the consequences of disloyalty. Ba Hom wasn't of any further value to them so they used it as an object lesson."

He smiled bleakly. "Charley cut his losses. He managed to turn a major setback into a psychological advantage. I have to admit I admire that."

*****

Caleb's days following his return from the tunnel passed in a haze of guilt. His orders were to talk to no one. Saigon was busy eulogizing the martyred Nguyen. MACV was being raked over the coals by reporters demanding to know how the VC could run right through an area that was supposedly pacified. The ARVN High Command was rewriting history to the effect that their Regional Force platoon had heroically defended Ba Hom against overwhelming odds. And at home, the antiwar people were milking those pictures of the dead kids for all they were worth. So the word had come down from the Ice Man that everyone involved was to lay low.

The only respite from his shame came when he pulled two men out of a burning bunker during a rocket attack. Colonel Riccio put him in for another Bronze Star. "K-Bar's hit the glass ceiling," laughed Blandon. "Been an officer who'd done that, they'd have given him a fuckin' Navy Cross!"

Caleb hung around the S-2 shop, hoping someone would give him something to do. Nobody did. Rumors were going around that he'd played some role in the events that had led to the massacre at Ba Dom, but since nobody knew whether they were supposed to consider that one a win or a loss, they weren't sure if he was a hero or a goat.

He knew what he was. Soldiers killed other soldiers who were trying to kill them. Murderers killed defenseless old men in their beds. He went to see the Wop. He pleaded with him to give him back his squad or to bust him down to private, he didn't give a shit what, but at least get him back in the field so that if he had to kill again, the man in his sights would be carrying a rifle.

The Wop understood. In his clumsy, good hearted way he offered what comfort he could. "You saved lives," he said. "You should think about all the Marines those weapons you found might have killed. So don't feel bad. I mean, what about the guys who fly the B-52 s? Christ, they do their killing from five miles up. Do they worry about it? Hell no! Fly back to Guam. Have a few beers at the club and forget all about it. Just part of the job. That's the way you got to think about it, Kid. Just part of the job."

*****

"I have a story of my own to tell you, Gunny," said the Vulture when Caleb finished his account of the days following his return from Ba Hom.

"After the Nazis picked us up, the officer whose job it was to decide which of us were fit enough to work and which would go straight to the gas chambers was a slightly overweight man with a rather ordinary face.

"That surprised me, as in general the SS looked the part—cruel chiseled features, cold blue eyes—you know the stereotype. But this man had the bovine expression of the petty bureaucrat putting in his hours at a repetitive, mildly distasteful task. I learned later to my sorrow that he was a doctor.

"He was very efficient. In that, at least, he fit the mold. He came briskly along our ranks, stopping briefly in front of each man. The stronger looking, he tapped with his baton on the right shoulder; the weaker on the left.

"Only a very few of the men whose fate he was deciding had the courage to show their contempt for this loathsome man. Most of us fell instinctively into the fawning role of the weak confronting the strong. We didn't beg or plead. He didn't allow us time for that. Instead, ours was a sort of psychic servility. Like cringing puppy dogs, we conveyed our subservience through our expressions and body language.

"When he came to me, the SS officer did a double take. 'Haven't I seen you somewhere?' he asked. 'In the circus, maybe?' The man beside me tittered obsequiously, thinking my interrogator was making a joke on my appearance. 'Yes, I've got it!' the officer went on. "You're the Mighty Midget, aren't you? From the *Cirque des Merveilles Macabres*?'

"'None other, Sir!' I simpered. "And still capable of the prodigious feats of strength and agility you saw me performing then.'

"With that I seized the man who had laughed at me by the belt and lifted him with one arm above my head, where for a long moment I let him hang screaming.

"The officer smiled a rubber-lipped smile and tapped me on the right shoulder. The terrified half-starved man I'd tossed into the air he tapped on the left one. Then he continued on down the line, deciding with monumental indifference who should live and who should die."

The Vulture paused. "Why do I tell you this?" he asked finally. "Mainly because I suspect that if you were to ask him, that SS officer who sent me to the labor camp would echo your Colonel Riccio. 'Just part of the job, kid,' he'd say. 'Just part of the job.'"

He smiled apologetically. "But I'm interrupting again! How did it turn out? Did you end up the hero or the goat after killing Nguyen?"

*****

A week following the Ba Hom massacre, Caleb was called back up to the Battalion CP and found there the same familiar cast—the Ice Man, the Wop, and the Chart and Pointer Man. They'd been talking about the effects of all the publicity Ba Hom was receiving, and he caught the tail end of that discussion when he came into the tent. "The anti-war movement's got no depth to it," Major Price was saying. "It's just a game for college kids looking for a cause. I mean, just look at their spokesmen—bunch of goddamn hippies! Crazies like that Joan Baez—does anyone really think the majority of Americans are dumb enough to listen to her?"

The Wop was nodding agreement. "You take those pictures of that massacre," he argued. "Those pictures are going to unite the country behind this war! The average guy isn't dumb—hell, I'm an average guy—and if I were home watching TV, I'd damn well know who'd killed those kids."

"I don't give our public that much credit," said the Ice Man. "The way I see it, Pete, the average guy is just sitting in front of his TV soaking up images, and the strongest images are the ones which'll stick in his silly head. He's going to remember the dead kids. If it weren't for this pissant war, he wouldn't have to look at dead kids. It doesn't matter to him who did the killing. He just doesn't like feeling uncomfortable looking at dead kids, so he's against the war.

"No," he went on, nodding to acknowledge Caleb's arrival, "Sergeant Caleb's just handed the VC one of their biggest setbacks since we got here, but the whole Ba Hom thing has become too controversial now for me to use in making the case for changing the way we're fighting this war."

"Maybe not, Sir," Major Price ventured. "Dead orphans and martyred heroes aside, we're still left with the fact that one well conceived operation using limited manpower hit Charley harder where it counts than we did in Operation Piranha last month. Between our guys and ARVN's, that was damn near a division sized operation, and what did we get? Maybe 200 VC?"

"You'll get no argument from me about that," said the Colonel. "But the only way we could take credit for discovering that arms cache would be to go public with our role in killing Nguyen. That would contradict Saigon, who've quite cleverly come up with the fiction that the VC chose to hide their armory right under the great man's nose because nobody'd think to look for it there. Saigon's saying Nguyen discovered what the VC were up to which is why they killed him.

"Damned smart, actually. Saigon's covered its ass, made Nguyen into a martyr for its cause, and muzzled us, all with that one story!"

"So what now, Boss?" asked the Wop.

"We ask Sergeant Caleb if he'll be our scalpel for a second time."

"Jesus Christ!"

"Hear me out. We know the VC and the NVA both have been using the Highlands as a safe haven. They can fade away into the mountains. Train, regroup, whatever it is they need to do. They're masters at camouflage and at dispersing their units, both of which skills limit the effectiveness of air power. Nor does that terrain lend itself to large scale operations. So what I propose is that we deploy the smallest unit of all—one skilled man with a rifle—and send him up into the Quang Tin mountains to take the war right into the enemy's backyard."

The Wop shook his head in disbelief. "One man! That's gotta be the *dumbest* goddamn idea I've ever heard. Send in a Recon Company, maybe. Run it as a deep penetration raid. That kind of thing we know how to do."

"Maybe. An operation of that size might inflict more damage but it would cause less panic. I want to do to the NVA what Jack the Ripper did to London. The Vietnamese are a superstitious lot. My one man materializing at random out of nowhere to kill and then disappearing again to come back another day at another place to kill again, that kind of thing would spook them a lot more effectively than would your raid."

"Yeah, for about two days, which is about how long that one man would last."

"I grant you the idea sounds far-fetched," countered the Ice Man. "But don't forget, it wasn't all that long ago that trappers, mountain men and prospectors spent big chunks of their lives alone living off the land in our own hostile wilderness. Sergeant Caleb's already shown us that he has the skills and temperament to do the same thing." He paused, sucking at his cheek. "But you may be right. A two or three man team might stand a better chance than one man alone."

"Two men! Three men! What the hell's the difference? "You send 'em up there, they won't come back!"

The Ice Man nodded at Caleb. "Nobody's ever accused your CO of not speaking his mind. What do you think, Sergeant?"

Caleb didn't answer right away. He wasn't worried about going alone. He felt a lot safer on his own than he had as a squad leader. But even at that point, even after murdering Nguyen, he had not, in the Ice Man's words, entirely shitcanned his sense of decency. He knew from having been there that there was a place within him where decency didn't exist. Honor, compassion, fair play, all those Noble Warrior sentiments he had brought with him to Viet Nam were meaningless in that place where there was only the intoxicating brightness of the here and now. He was scared of who he might become if he again let himself be tempted by that addiction.

But he knew also that he was already committed. The Ice Man's logic had been his justification for killing Nguyen. He knew he couldn't turn back now from where that logic led without denying the rightness of the original course. "Yes, Sir, I'll do it," he said finally, "but only if I go alone."

The Ice Man stood up to indicate the meeting was over. "I don't know when or how I can get you up into those mountains, Sergeant. About all you can do for now is get yourself ready to go. So whatever you need, just ask for it, OK?"

*****

"A place within where decency doesn't exist," mused the Vulture when Caleb paused in his story. "Can there be such a place?"

Caleb didn't answer.

"Well, by coincidence, I've been reading a paper by a man who's done some interesting work suggesting that we're born with a rudimentary moral sense. He's run experiments with infants which, if they're valid, indicate that we all come into this world programmed with some notion of loyalty, kindness and fairness.

"So maybe instead of there being a place within us where decency doesn't exist, it might be more accurate if we were to consider something analogous to the Holocaust survivors who suppress their memories of the camps. Maybe it is possible to suppress that innate moral sense, but if so, I have to ask the same question as I have before. What's the cost if one does?"

Caleb lay silent.

The Vulture shrugged resignedly. "It seems the watchers are back at their posts. So let's just get on with your story."

CHAPTER TEN

Caleb's tent mate, "Dinger" Charlton, the battalion armorer, was a ham-handed, unflappable good ol' boy who took naturally to shooting and drinking beer. His pride and joy was the old Springfield the battalion carried on its Table of Equipment as a sniper rifle. He'd replaced the standard issue Weaver two power scope with a Redfield variable power one, and reworked the action so that the bolt felt like it slid on bearings.

Dinger wasn't happy about giving up his Springfield, and Caleb wasn't sure he even wanted it when he found out that with the scope mounted it could only fire single shot. They took it down to the beach, paced off 500 yards, and set up a five gallon oil pail lid for a target. Dinger dropped three rounds into Caleb's hand. Then he unscrewed the turret caps from the scope and scrambled up the sight settings. "OK, Hotshot," he drawled, "if you can hit that lid with any one of these three rounds, then maybe we can do business."

"Fair enough. Only I'm going to use a rest."

"Use anything you damn well want."

"Also going to make myself a nine hundred inch range, OK?"

Caleb took off his skivvy shirt, tied the sleeves together, and filled it with sand. Then he paced off seventy-five feet and set up a tin can for a target. He removed the bolt from the rifle, handed it to Dinger to hold for him, and hunkered down prone behind the Springfield. It was an overcast day with five to eight knots of wind gusting in off the water just about broadside to his line of sight—what shooters call a "full value wind." He noted that it was likely to give him trouble.

He got the barrel solidly wedged into his improvised sandbag and sighted in on his can through the open bore. Then, being careful not to move anything, he shifted his eye to the scope. The tin can wasn't even in the field of view. "Jesus Christ!" he muttered, "you really did fuck up this sight!" Dinger laughed.

Caleb went back and forth between the bore and the scope until he'd moved the crosshairs onto the can. By the time he'd got things adjusted to his satisfaction the wind had picked up to a hard breeze.

The next step was the hardest. He knew that, because of the curving trajectory of the round, the sight setting was the same at seventy-five feet as it was at two hundred yards, and he was confident he had pretty good dope for that distance. But he wasn't sure how much additional elevation to add on for five hundred yards. So he guessed ten minutes of arc and set that on the sight. Windage was also pretty much of a guess. He cranked in five minutes of left windage. "OK," he said, "say goodbye to your lid!"

Dinger handed him the bolt. He slid it back into the receiver and chambered a round. He steadied up the crosshairs on the lid and took up the slack in the trigger. The rifle bucked unexpectedly against his shoulder. "Fuck all!" he said in disgust. "You didn't tell me about that hair trigger. I can't even call that shot."

Dinger slapped his knee. "Two left!" he chuckled.

Caleb wasn't going to make the same mistake twice. He dry-fired five or six times to get the feel of Dinger's hair trigger. Then he tried again. He waited for a lull in the wind, squeezed off the round, and saw it hit low and a hair right. He dialed in two and a half more minutes of elevation and took off a half minute of windage. Then he chambered round three. Dinger was decent enough to keep quiet.

A gust of wind rocked the barrel. He moved the crosshairs back onto the lid but he'd lost his concentration. So he slipped on the safety and took a break with his eyes closed and his head on his arms, forcing himself to relax. A long minute went by. He heard Dinger start to shuffle around. "You gone to sleep down there, Staff Sergeant?"

"Nope," said Caleb. "Just making you sweat a little, that's all. Watch now, that lid's good as dead."

"Shee-ut. Safest place on this beach'd be right behind the gawdamn thing."

"We'll see." Caleb fired off the third round. The lid arced through the air and landed back in the sand.

"Not bad!"

"Not good. I didn't hit it. Hit right below it."

"Looked like a hit to me. But it don't matter. Main thing is you know what you're doing. Here, let me try. We can't leave that target without no hole in it."

Dinger fired offhanded, nailing the lid with all three shots. But, Caleb reminded him, he hadn't scrambled up the dope. They spent the rest of that afternoon making up a range card for distances out to a thousand meters.

"Remember," said Dinger as they hiked back to the base, "you only got one shot at a time with this old girl. So don't get yourself in a spot where you need to shoot quicker than you can reload."

*****

Caleb's chance to get up into the VC's backyard came faster than anyone expected. On the night of 16 November, the First VC Main Force Regiment, thought to have been largely wiped out some months before in Operation Starlite, emerged phoenix-like from the mountains to overrun Hiep Duc in the valley where the Song Trinh River runs down from the mountains of western Quang Tri.

MAG-16, flying out of Chu Lai, heli-lifted two ARVN battalions in to counterattack and Caleb went with them. It was a rough flight. As the chopper pitched steeply down into the rain and mist that hung in the narrow walled valley, VC heavy machine guns opened up with sheets of antiaircraft fire. The door gunner returned fire. They banked jerkily into a hard turn and were hit by a giant sledge. Caleb watched a line of holes stitch themselves across the floor, and when he looked over at the US Army battalion advisor sitting beside him the man's right leg was hanging from a shred of meat. The ARVN corpsman couldn't stop the bleeding and the Army captain was dead by the time they landed.

It took two days of hard fighting for the ARVN battalions to drive the VC back up into the mountains. Then the I Corps commander decided he couldn't afford to leave enough men behind to re-garrison Hiep Duc. The recaptured town was abandoned and the ARVN troops began heli-lifting back to their base in Quang Ngai. Caleb stayed behind.

It took him two more days, traveling at night, to make his way into the mountains. He climbed out of the valley's heat and into the cool quiet of the upland jungle. And as he went up he also went back into that more primitive, more alive state of being he'd known before. On his fifth day alone in the mountains he had to force himself to check in with the outside world.

At 1730, a half hour ahead of the schedule he'd worked out with the Ice Man, he climbed out on a rocky outcrop and turned on his little aviator's emergency transmitter. He lay there, chewing on a bamboo heart and looking down over the clouds in the valley below, and he felt a great wave of happiness sweep over him. The war seemed as far away then as it had during that lazy afternoon with Hume in Da Nang's old city. But at precisely 1800 the Colonel's voice came rasping over the transmitter to remind him that it wasn't.

"Othello, Othello, this is Iago, over."

Caleb grinned. He'd read Shakespeare in high school and he'd picked those call signs in hopes that the Ice Man would know who Iago was.

"Iago, this is Othello. No contact yet. Over."

"Othello, this is Iago. Roger. Good hunting. Out."

They'd agreed to keep their transmissions few and short in case the VC tried to home in on him with a radio direction finder. Caleb heard a far off engine and looked out to see a little spotter plane bank around and head back towards the coast. He had another five days to himself before the next check-in. But the spell was broken. It was time to get on with what he was being paid for.

He was in no particular hurry. He'd snared his first bandicoot, a rat-like rodent which was to become a staple of his diet while he was in the mountains, but he had to wait until dusk to cook it so as not to show the smoke from his fire. So he stowed the radio and took a lazy look around in the late afternoon light. To the east, the coastal plain stretched away to the sea; and to the west, ridge after ridge of jungle-covered mountains disappeared like waves into the distance.

Across the valley, in the shadow of the setting sun, he thought he saw something move. He twisted the selector ring on Dinger's scope up to eight power, thought better of it, and backed off to six power for a wider field of view.

At first all he could see was unbroken jungle canopy. But then half way up, on a part of the ridge where the slope was almost vertical, he caught sight of a flash of khaki. A man appeared out of the leaves, gingerly edged himself sideways around a narrow rock ledge and disappeared back into the jungle on the other side. Another man followed. Then another.

Caleb estimated the range to be somewhere around eight hundred yards, remembering that targets generally look further away with the sun behind them and closer when seen across a valley. He calculated that those two factors would pretty well cancel each other out. The Redfield scope had two parallel reference lines above the horizontal crosshairs. For ranges greater than six hundred yards, Einar had taught him to adjust the power ring until he could bracket a 36-inch-high object between the reference lines and then double the range shown on the scale that appeared in the lower right quadrant of the sight picture. He did this to see how close he'd come to correctly estimating the range.

The next man he saw start around the ledge evidently had a fear of heights. He inched his way timidly along, presenting Caleb with a fine full face target as he went. Caleb framed him between the references lines. He figured that from knees to shoulders on his target should be about thirty-six inches. Eight hundred yards plus a little bit said the scale. He consulted the range card he and Einar had worked up, split the difference between the elevation setting for eight and nine hundred yards, and dialed the right dope into the scope. There was no wind.

He chambered a round and laid out three more beside him. The light was fast fading on that far slope as the sun sank behind it. His timid target made it across the rocks and disappeared while Caleb debated whether to risk so uncertain a shot. He watched the ridge's dark shadow march across the valley floor and waited for the next man. The setting sun was starting to shine right in his eyes.

A man appeared on the ledge, ducked back into the leaves, and then showed up again walking backwards at one end of a stretcher. Ever so slowly he began backing his way along the narrow path. The man carrying the other end came into view. Caleb shifted the cross hairs onto the second man, then briefly onto the heavily bandaged figure he was helping to carry, and then back onto the man in front. They were half way across.

Unexpectedly the image in the scope grew dark. Rain clouds were boiling over the valley, blotting out the sun. He backed off the power a notch for better light gathering and zeroed in again on that first man. A long low clap of thunder came rumbling out of the west as he squeezed the trigger.

The scope bucked as the round went off and then settled back onto the target. Caleb kept the crosshairs on the lead man, watching him stiffen and then slowly begin to crumble. He let go of the stretcher, seemed to watch horrified as the man in it bounced down the mountain, and then he too fell off into space. The other man just stood there, still holding onto his end of the stretcher.

The thunder had muffled the sound of the shot. An officer appeared out of the leaves. He too just stood there, staring down to where the two shattered bodies lay far below. Caleb chambered round two and sent the officer bouncing down the mountain. He left it at that. His job was to terrify. He'd done enough of that for one day. So he hiked back a couple of miles into the jungle and ate his bandicoot. That night it rained.

*****

It was raining also in Philadelphia. Darkness had fallen early, the afternoon light obscured by low scudding clouds. A gust of wind rattling the window next to his bed brought Caleb back to the present. He watched the lights above his head flicker and then go out.

"So that was the man on the stretcher," observed the Vulture, still writing in the light from the emergency lamp which now dimly lit the examination room. Caleb was spared from answering by Randall who poked his head in the door. "Power gone off in half the city, Sir," he said. "Hospital's emergency generators supposed to be kickin' in any time now." As if on cue, the overhead fluorescent lamps flickered back to life. Randall left, silently closing the door behind him.

"I think we'll call it a day, Gunny," declared the Vulture, closing his notebook. As he spoke he was fumbling with the latch on his briefcase. Without thinking, Caleb reached across with his good hand and unsnapped it for him.

"Much obliged, Gunny. But if you wouldn't mind closing it again, I'd rather do it myself. It's become a game of sorts, learning to live with these tremors of mine."

"Sorry, Sir. I thought..."

"You thought I was just being my usual awkward self?"

Caleb grinned.

"I wish that were the case, but I'm afraid it's now gone a step further than that. It seems I have Parkinson's Disease." He paused, still intent on the latch. "Only reason I mention it is that it may mean some changes for both of us. I've petitioned the authorities to let me continue my work here, but we'll have to wait and see what the Grand Poobahs decide."

"Bastards!" Caleb exploded. "Some desk warrior in Bu Med who doesn't know shit gets to sit in judgement on the best... best..." Embarrassed, his voice trailed off.

The Vulture nodded vaguely, fumbling again at the latch which at last sprung open. "See?" he said grinning, "What was before a routine act now becomes a great and satisfying triumph. So there you have it. When fate deals us a different hand, one can always find ways to play it out, sometimes even better than with the one we held before. Good night, Gunny. We'll pick up tomorrow where you left off."

Randall returned to wheel Caleb back to the bone ward.

Where you been? wrote O'Malley on his pad.

"Getting laid!"

"Don't you wish!"

*****

"Shall we pick up where you left off?" asked the Vulture when they met again the following day. "If memory serves, you were eating a rat."

*****

Caleb ate his bandicoot and turned in, listening to the rain pelt down on his improvised poncho shelter. He slept fitfully, and at first light thrashed his way across the valley looking for the trail the VC he'd shot had been following. Finding it at mid morning, he holed up until dusk and then set off to see where they'd been heading. There was still light enough when he got to the ledge across which the stretcher bearers had tried to pass that he could still see blood and gristle splattered against the rocks.

He traveled most of the night along the west wall of the valley and then the path turned south, up over the ridge and down into the valley beyond. Morning found him on a more heavily traveled trail. That vestigial instinct of his began sending off alarms and he moved south again into the jungle where he spent the day napping by a fast running stream which he hoped was making enough noise to drown out the sound of his snoring. When he woke up it was dusk and he knew right away that he was very close to other men.

Once night had fallen, he started wading upstream, not sure where he should be heading or even exactly what he was looking for, but expecting the underbrush to thin out as he moved higher out of the valley. Half an hour of hard going later he came to a log bridge. He crawled underneath it and waited, thinking the night was too silent.

Then he heard a voice, so close it made him jump. Somebody yawned. There was some rustling around, twigs snapping and then the flash of a match, no more than twenty yards upstream from where he lay. He crawled over to where he could get a better look. Some men were building a fire down by the water's edge, evidently counting on the thick jungle canopy to hide the light from any plane passing overhead.

Caleb watched heads appear and disappear in and out of the ring of light. Shadows danced across the stream. It was hard to tell how many there were. He guessed they were an outpost assigned to guard the bridge. Nobody seemed to be taking the job very seriously.

He heard a muffled squawk followed by laughter and a few minutes later a raft of waterborne feathers passed by him under the bridge. Charley One—he was beginning to recognize them as individuals—seemed to be the head chef. He filled a steel pot from the stream, and there followed a little ritual where each of the four men stepped up to the fire and poured from out of the long sock he carried slung around his neck his ration of rice into the common bowl. Charley Four appeared to be a little parsimonious. There were admonitions from out of the darkness. Four grinned and poured in a little more. Charley Two reappeared at the fire carrying a not very well plucked chicken. He squatted down by the stream, chopped up his bird into little pieces and threw the whole works—head, feet, guts and all—into the pot. Charley One rummaged around in his pack and produced a jar which he held up for all to see. There were happy smiles all around. The chef ceremoniously added some of the contents of his jar to the pot and the smell of nhouc mam, the Vietnamese answer to ketchup, filled the air.

What Caleb did next was an act of recklessness he was to blame on forgetting his mantra. But he was riding an adrenaline high and he was also hungry enough that the smell of cooking chicken tempted him to folly. The bridge had backed up enough water to form a pool on the upstream side. Leaving the Springfield where he lay, he slid down into the water and made his way on hands and knees against the current with only his head above water. He was counting on the VC to have lost their night vision from staring into the fire and on the sound of rushing water to drown out any noise he made himself. He pulled himself over to the stream bank just outside the ring of light and threw a stone into the bushes behind them. Conversation stopped. He threw another stone. Charley One muttered something and got up. Three picked up his rifle and started to follow the chef into the darkness. Four said something sarcastic and One and Three came back into the light, looking sheepish. Caleb threw a big handful of pebbles in another direction. That time they all got up to investigate. He eased their pot into the stream, hoping it would float.

His dinner went bobbing off into the night. But he hadn't counted on the hiss of a hot pot hitting cold water. Four heads snapped around. The head chef let out a shout and kicked his fire into the water. The VC floundered around in the sudden darkness. Caleb let the current carry him back downstream. The pot had fetched up against the bridge. He snagged it, retrieved his rifle, and then remembered a trick his father used to play on him.

He launched into an insane cackling. The sound, echoing hollowly out from under the bridge, sent the panicked VC pounding off down the trail, and he stayed where he was eating their stew in silence. There was more than he could finish. He dumped out the rest, rinsed the pot, and left it hanging by the trail, figuring that would spook them again. So was born the Mad Cackler.

VC security was surprisingly slack when he first came into their valley. The regiment's training areas, hospital, bivouacs and supply depots were widely separated. They'd taken elaborate precautions against being spotted from the air, but evidently felt secure enough from attacks on the ground not to see the need for many sentries or outposts.

Early on, he staked out one of the Regiments latrines, which were nothing more than foul smelling slit trenches dug some distance from the encampments they served. He tunneled into thick brush not ten yards from where VC soldiers squatted with their trousers around their ankles, and, during the hours that he waited patient and unmoving, he noticed a pattern. Soldiers would often come down the path leading to the latrine, see that someone else had gotten there ahead of them, and turn back to wait for the chance to be there alone. Caleb saw the possibility of denying even that one small comfort to the enemy.

The next soldier to use the latrine alone he left laying face up in the trench with a jagged bloody gash across his throat. He had a moment of remorse when he saw the worn packet of letters that his victim had been holding and which now lay half buried in the shit beside him. But by then he was so much the Iceman's creation that he just shrugged and melted silently back into the bush. His hunch proved correct. From that point on sentries were posted at all the Regiment's latrines and their users came in groups. His had been a very effective act of terror.

He tried to make his appearances as random as possible. He'd set up a base in the jungle, work out of it for a couple of days, and move on to somewhere else. He left a few careless VC dead and scared a lot more with his cackling. His life settled into a rhythm of sorts. He'd go for several days at a time without eating much of anything. Then he'd stuff himself on bandicoot or snake or rice taken off a dead VC, sleep an entire day and start the cycle all over again.

The only interruptions to his routine were his radio calls to Iago. The Achilles' heel to their communications plan was that in those early days of the war all the aviator's emergency radios such as the one he carried were set to the same narrow frequency band. Knowing that, the VC routinely scanned the band with their radio direction finders in hopes of homing in on downed pilots. Caleb never transmitted twice from the same place. Even so, he suspected he was being heard.

The greater problem with those contacts was that they forced him to shift gears. On December 7th, his fourth radio check with the colonel began as it always did. The Ice Man came up as usual right on schedule. Caleb started to answer, got as far as "This is Othello," and couldn't go on. He put the radio down and sat beside it, feeling a little sorry for the Ice Man who'd just lost control of his experiment. But he knew he couldn't do the things the colonel wanted him to do or be what the colonel wanted him to be until he freed himself from the radio.

The little set crackled back to life. The colonel sounded worried. "Othello, Othello, this is Iago. I hear you weak and garbled. Repeat your last transmission. I say again, repeat your last transmission. Over."

Caleb didn't answer.

"Othello, Othello, if you can read me, key your set three times." He repeated slowly and distinctly "KEY—YOUR—SET—THREE—TIMES, THREE TIMES. Over."

He picked up the radio, hesitated, and then keyed the mike three times. Even over the drone of the airplane engine he could hear the relief in the Ice Man's voice. "OK, Othello. I got that. Go to our alternate schedule. We're coming to pull you out. Acknowledge with three clicks. Over."

Caleb didn't acknowledge. Their emergency schedule called for him to monitor the set for the first ten minutes of every hour after they put it into effect. He didn't do that either. Instead he stowed the radio in his pack, and there it stayed for the next two months.

CHAPTER ELEVEN

Some days later, he was kneeling by a stream, stripped to his waist when the round hit. The log next to where his head had been in the instant before he'd leaned forward to slop water onto his face exploded into jagged splinters. He dove instinctively into the brush above the stream bank and only after he'd landed, torn and bleeding in the jagged foliage, did he become aware of the searing pain that burned across his mouth. *Shit*, he thought. *Seems two can play this game!*

The second round hit the tree against which he'd leaned his Springfield. The sniper was smart enough to be aiming at his rifle. But Caleb couldn't get to it himself without becoming an easy target. So he watched helplessly as a third round sent the Springfield flying to land hard on its scope in the mud five yards from where he lay.

He inched his way towards it. The sniper followed his progress, firing blindly into the brush whenever he saw a branch move. Bullets smacked into the ground around him. He rolled sideways into a shallow gully which gave him some protection. The Springfield still lay just out of reach.

Something was wrong with his mouth. He reached up gingerly and felt the splinter that had driven itself in under his lower lip and out below his upper one. Another round hit close enough to splatter him with mud and remind him that he had more immediate problems. He rolled again, landing on a broken branch that stuck painfully into his arm. Working it loose from under him, he was able to use it to hook the Springfield through the trigger guard and pull it to him. The sniper's round had creased the fore grip, doing no serious damage. But there was no telling whether after landing on its scope the rifle would still hit where he aimed it.

He worked his way downhill along the gully until he reached a place where he could again see the stream curving away eastward into the jungle. There he waited. "Let the deer come to you," his father used to tell him, and in this case he hadn't much choice. He lay with his chin on his blood slick rifle stock, forcing himself to systematically scan from right to left and then back again across his field of view. The afternoon sun broke through a hole in the high canopy sending shafts of light slicing through the jungle gloom. "Angel fingers," his aunt had called them. He realized he was getting lightheaded.

The sniper was waiting too. Caleb used his stick to hook a branch as far to the left of him as he could reach and shake it. Almost instantly a round smacked into the dirt just below the shaken branch. He couldn't be sure, but thought he'd spotted a brief flash of reflected sunlight near a large rock at about a hundred meter's distance on the far side of the stream. The light faded and then returned as the sun passed across another break in the canopy. He saw the flash again and fired. It was a snap shot and he hadn't much confidence in it.

He lay unmoving until it was fully dark. And then, gritting his teeth, he pulled the splinter from his mouth and used mud to staunch the bleeding. All the rest of that night clouds of mosquitoes added to his misery, and by dawn the next morning he found himself barely able to stagger to his feet. He climbed up to the ridge line that paralleled the stream and worked his way along it to a point that he estimated would be well beyond the sniper's rock before descending once again to intercept the stream.

Then, moving silently, he returned in the direction from which he had come until he spotted the boulder and the body that lay behind it. The sniper's rifle was a Russian-made Mosin Nagant with a 3.5 power scope. Caleb's round had hit the scope mount and driven it into the sniper's cheek, leaving a huge jagged hole below his right eye.

The rifle was useless so he left it there. But he did take the long cloth tube filled with rice that the man had carried slung over his shoulders, and with this he climbed out of the valley and down into the next one where he stayed, living on rice, until his mouth had healed into the crooked line which was to become part of his trademark.

Without radio calls to orient on, he started to lose track of the days. Christmas went by without his noticing it. On January 9th, 1966, he broke his self-winding watch and time stopped with it. The life he had led before coming up into the mountains faded so far into memory it all seemed part of a different incarnation.

Whenever he'd see his reflection staring back at him from some puddle or pool, the Mad Cackler scared even himself. He wore bits and pieces of clothing taken from his victims. One of the two pairs of utility uniforms he'd carried with him fell into rags, and the other he had the foresight to stow in his waterproof bag and bury where he could find it so that he wouldn't look like the enemy when the time came to walk out. He did at least retain that much sense of future.

Back in the long ago days when he'd been a squad leader, he'd more than once smelled the VC before he'd seen them. He didn't want them smelling him, so he took cold, soapless baths in clear mountain pools. Keeping himself clean proved a lot easier than keeping the Springfield clean. He'd run out of oil early on, taken a can from a man he'd killed, run out of that, and finally had to resort to using bandicoot tallow.

His childhood spent knitting bait bags for his father had introduced him to the art of sewing, a skill not often found among Marines. Hume, who marveled at this talent, had declared that GL actually stood for Granny Let-me Fix-That-For-You, and the rest of his squad would grin at the sight of their *Uber*-Marine leader hunched over in some corner meticulously stitching together someone's torn uniform or piece of gear.

Now in the mountains, he was almost as careful of the needles in his sewing kit as he was of the Springfield. He'd known from his earliest days "in country" that the pressure points created by belts, bandoleer straps and other tight fitting pieces of clothing led inevitably to chafe, rash and almost certain jungle rot. By himself and no longer bound by regulations, he was free to improvise. Early on, he'd managed to steal an entire tent from a VC unit that had been called away to listen to a harangue from its political officer, and from this he fashioned a loose fitting jerkin that made him look like the Robin Hood he'd seen in the movies of his youth. Despite his best efforts, the VC did spot him from time to time, and this utilitarian but ghostly garment along with his roughly trimmed black beard is what led the ever more terrified Regiment to name him *Ke Hut Mau* or Vampire.

The mosquitoes were thick during the monsoon season, but even after he ran out of Atropine tablets he never caught malaria. His feet gave him trouble until the day he lost the sole on one of his boots and began going barefoot. Leaches were an ongoing problem. He discovered an astringent sticky brown sap which made them release their grip, but more often than not he just let them drop off. He lost weight and had on-again off-again problems with split calluses on the soles of his feet, but otherwise he stayed healthy.

He had no way to know about the Tet cease-fire that was supposed to have been in force between the twentieth and twenty third of January, 1966. He did have a vague idea that the Vietnamese celebrated their Lunar New Year sometime in January and, not long after his watch broke, he began to notice a kind of holiday feeling in the air around the VC encampments. Working his way closer for a better look, he found a bunch of soldiers swimming in a mountain pool.

They looked like children whooping and hollering and diving naked into the water. But he could see their rifles neatly stacked and their uniforms neatly folded by the stream. He watched them frolicking, trying to decide which one to target. His rule was to look for rank, but naked as they were there was no telling who wore the stripes. He picked the noisiest one and shot him. The rest took off into the jungle.

It was a poor shot. The man he'd hit floundered around, half in and half out of the pool, while the water turned red around him. Caleb's rule was never to shoot twice from the same location, but in this case there didn't seem much risk in putting the man out of his misery. He was chambering another round when one of the other swimmers came back out of the bush.

That man must have known he'd be an easy target. He got his hands under his wounded friend's shoulders and started pulling him up the high steep bank. Twice he slipped and the two of them fell back into the water.

On his third try, Caleb shot him. He'd learned by then that a terrorist could not be selectively heartless.

*****

"Cut!" commanded the Vulture who had been writing furiously as Caleb talked. "I've got a cramp in my hand." He looked back over what he had written. "I must say, Gunny, if I were reading all this as a work of fiction, I'd have to say it stretches the bounds of credibility."

"Yes Sir," Caleb agreed. "Thinking back on it now, some of it seems more like a dream even to me."

"I can understand how you could have mastered fear. In the camps we learned to live with the constant possibility of death. But your physical discomfort during all that time must have been appalling. How did you handle that?"

Caleb shrugged. "As Hum used to say, you learn to tune it out."

"I suppose. That's the genius of our species, isn't it? We can adapt to nearly anything." As he spoke, the Vulture was massaging his right hand with his left. "There, that's better," he said. "I'm ready to write again. So onward, Gunny."

*****

He woke up to an unaccustomed silence and realized that what he wasn't hearing was the distant nonstop rumble of planes and artillery. All that day there were sounds of revelry from the VC. He waited until evening. There were already signs that the regiment was feeling less secure in its jungle safe haven. They'd posted a lot more sentries, always in pairs, and they were sending patrols out to comb the ridges. So, with all this noise to suggest that they were letting down their guard, Caleb set out at dusk to make what hay he still could.

Looking back on that night later, he called it his night among the sheep. He called it that because once when he'd been a boy, a dog had gotten in among the neighbor's ewes which were pastured right outside his bedroom window. The morning afterward he'd walked among the bloody carcasses that littered the little field behind his house, and he'd wondered then why those sheep had waited so silently for their end. They'd been ripped to pieces not twenty yards from where he slept and he hadn't heard a thing. That had been a puzzle to him.

His own night among the sheep had been an orgy of killing drunken men. He'd staked out a group of revelers—he could never figure out if the VC socialized by unit or by rank—and as he watched that high spirited band laughing and joking around their camp fire, one of their number got up to take a piss. Caleb intercepted the man as he stepped into the underbrush tugging at his fly. The soldier froze, as paralyzed as a rabbit facing a snake. Caleb took the three steps that separated them and drove his knife up under the man's ribs. His victim made only a faint rabbit squeal, drowned out by the laughter of his squad mates. His eyes never left Caleb's as he sank slowly to his knees and fell face down into the leaves, vomiting up blood.

So Caleb understood the sheep. He also understood the dog. That night he reached the very center of the onion. He was that dog.

*****

In the week that followed, it seemed as if the whole VC regiment had turned out to chase him down. He climbed over the ridge into the next valley, where he marked the days he spent in a stupor of eating and sleeping by cutting notches in a tree. Nine notches later he returned to the Regimental area to find the VC troops making up their packs and the whole encampment buzzing with activity.

He watched these goings on through his scope. A group of officers came into his field of view. He was centering his sight on the senior man when he saw one of them stoop down to lift up a camouflaged curtain. The others ducked in under and the junior man followed.

It took him the better part of an hour to work his way down from his lookout on top of the ridge to another vantage point close to where those officers had disappeared. What from higher up had appeared to be jungle canopy turned out to be a large net strung between trees and covered with a lattice work of leaves and branches. He could hear voices from underneath. He moved in closer. The VC least expected the Mad Cackler right in among them during daylight, and he'd become almost brazen about crawling right up to their doorstep.

The same brush they'd piled up to hide their command post also served to hide him. He made himself a little nest and peered in under the net. Twenty or so officers were standing around a large mud and stick model of the kind of concrete blockhouse complex the French had left behind. What Caleb could see of it was remarkably detailed. Barbed wire, bunkers and guard houses were all modeled to scale.

The regimental commander was tall and lean with the weathered face of a man who'd spent his life outdoors. His officers all jumped deferentially out of his way as he bounded around the table, pointing out features on the model. Other officers contorted themselves around the table trying to visualize field of fire and avenues of approach. From the number of times he heard the name repeated, he gathered that the fort they were preparing to attack was at An Hoa.

The meeting broke up at dusk. The Gook officers filed out in one direction and Caleb left in the other. He circled back, trying for a shot at their CO, but by then it was too dark.

The next day the regiment began moving out of the valley. Caleb climbed back up onto the ridge and dug out his radio from where he'd buried it a lifetime earlier. He had no idea what day it was and little hope that Iago was still monitoring his frequency, but he hoped he could raise someone to warn of the impending attack on An Hoa. He switched on the set and jumped at the sound of static. The battery condition gauge registered on the low end of the scale. He tried calling out once or twice, startled at the sound of his own voice, and then sat all that night and on into the next morning listening to the faint crackle of static, watching the little needle on the gauge slide further into the red, and waiting for the sound of another voice. None came.

The spell was broken. It seemed suddenly important that he shave. He rummaged around through his pack and came up with a tiny chunk of soap. Then he found a still mountain pool, scooped water onto his face, and waited for his reflection to come into focus as the ripples settled out of his watery mirror. He set to work with the K-Bar, scraping off as much skin as beard, but gradually there reappeared a face he recognized from somewhere long ago. He put on his one remaining uniform and looked at himself again in the pool. "Where've you been all this time, Staff Sergeant?" he asked the stranger who looked back at him.

His map had fallen apart. He pieced it back together again as best he could and looked for An Hoa. There were two An Hoas, one to the north, not far from Hiep Duc, and the other to the south, thirty kilometers or so west of Quang Ngai City. He guessed the regiment's objective was the second one, as its men were headed south. He calculated the distance they would have to travel as being sixty kilometers if they marched as the crow flies across the mountains and twice that if they dropped down onto the coastal plain and skirted along the edge of the highlands. He knew they were packing the same heavy AA machine-guns they'd used at Hiep Duc and also some big 4.2 inch mortars, so he figured they'd probably take the low road for easier traveling.

If he made a beeline across the mountains there was a chance he might beat them to their objective. An Hoa lay in a valley that cut back deep into the mountains, and since there was no other unforested valley in between, all he'd have to do was head southeast until he hit cleared land.

That hike was to be his last voyage back into the light. Past and future, both briefly reawakened, slipped away and that primitive state returned again in all its pristine brightness. He walked through two sunsets, stopping only once to eat rice and a rat. Even so he was too late.

He first heard the sound of distant gunfire sometime during the second night and, by the time he broke out of the jungle on the ridge overlooking the An Hoa valley, the battle for the strong point was already underway. Far off to his right, he could hear the flat cough of heavy mortars and see the night sky light up with the flash of exploding shells.

He'd intercepted the valley well west of the village. He dropped down the side of the ridge into the gentle hills of the upper valley and turned left towards the sounds of battle. He slogged along, aware for the first time of the heaviness in his eyes and legs.

Wet muck dragged at his feet. He went on automatic pilot and the next thing he became aware of was the *chuff* of a mortar firing not very far away on his left. He looked up in time to see the trail of the round arching off into the night. Seconds later came the *whump* of the exploding shell, then another *chuff*, that one to his right. He stopped and listened. *Chuff-whump, chuff-whump, chuff-whump*, all in perfect cadence. Four tubes firing.

He crawled up to the crest of the hill he'd been climbing, and from there spotted muzzle flashes. The nearest one was almost directly in front of him, about two hundred yards down the forward slope. There was another to the left of it and two more to the right, all precisely spaced ten yards apart. In the distance lay An Hoa, silhouetted against the flash of exploding shells.

He watched the mortar men walking their rounds methodically back and forth through the fort. There was a deadly cadence to it. The left hand gunner led off. Two, three and four followed suit, each one dropping his round just to the right of the last one. Then number one dropped his elevation a notch and the four tubes began stitching another dead straight line across their target. An Hoa's defenders were still shooting back. Pinpricks of light flashed from the blockhouse and the south wind carried with it the crackle of small arms fire.

Caleb watched impassively. He was outgunned. The eight rounds he had left for the Springfield wouldn't go far against four mortar crews. So he lay low. The mortars kept up their hypnotic rhythm and the firing from An Hoa grew lighter. The mortars fell momentarily silent. He heard a radio crackle. The lead gunner barked a series of commands, paused long enough for the others to adjust their aim, and hollered "BAN!" The four tubes fired as one. More commands, another "BAN!", and another four rounds went crashing into the old French fort. The VC mortar men were walking their salvos across the bunkers towards the blockhouse with their infantry following close behind the exploding shells. Fire from the defenders had all but stopped. In his mind's eye he could see them in their bunkers, flat on the ground, pinned down by the hail of shrapnel that tore the air around them.

"Get up!" he heard himself whispering. "Get up or they've got you!" And then, hardly knowing what he was doing, he was on his feet running catlike down the hill. He stopped twenty yards or so behind the number four tube and let out a low cackle. Then he moved a ways to the left and cackled again, louder this time. He heard panicky chatter and above it the shout of the lead gunner trying to restore calm. Then another "BAN!" but this time the salvo was a ragged one.

The moon broke briefly through the clouds, and he snapped off a shot at the number three loader as the man stood crouched, silhouetted against the night sky, waiting for the command to drop his round into the tube. His shot missed, hitting the tube itself. The loader jumped back. For a split second it looked like he was juggling with the heavy round. Then he dropped it. There was a blinding flash, a tremendous *WHUMP*, a second of stunned silence, and then an awful concert of cries and moans. Caleb himself had hit the deck only a split second before the shock wave washed over him and shrapnel scythed through the brush above his head.

He cackled again, barely able to hear himself over the ringing in his ears. The few mortar men still standing bolted. He waited until he could no longer hear them crashing through the underbrush and then crawled down to the abandoned firing position to check if any of the mortars were still serviceable.

Dead and dying men lay all around him. A staticky Gook voice started shouting right by his feet. He jumped, then saw the radio. He guessed that voice was the infantry CO, wondering what had happened to his covering fire, and he drove the butt of the Springfield into the set. Far down the hill, the number one gunner was yelling again, trying to rally his remaining troops. Caleb yanked the safety wires off as many rounds as he could make out in the darkness, figuring the mortar men would stumble over at least one of them if they returned, Then he ran back up the hill.

The mortar crews never came back. Firing around An Hoa continued for the rest of the night. Caleb holed up to wait for dawn. He woke up to the sound of A-4s and Phantoms screaming across the valley, pouring out napalm. Then came the choppers, wave after wave of ungainly green insects dumping out their cargo of Marines. He was almost home.

He started down the hill past the bodies of the mortar men. One of them was still alive. He found a canteen and tried to give him a drink, but the wounded man stared at him with such terror in his eyes that he gave it up. He left the canteen where the man could reach it, bashed in the four mortar tubes with a rock, and went on down into the valley.

The outfit he'd watched landing was Third Battalion, Seventh Marines. He walked up on two very green clerks who were supposed to be providing CP security and scared them almost as badly as he had the dying VC mortar man. He told them he was an escaped POW. They sent him over to the H&S Company Commander, who escorted him up to the CP and left him there.

Caleb waited, feeling self conscious in his bare feet as radios crackled and staff officers came and went, all too busy to pay any attention to him. Finally a tall, wiry Lieutenant Colonel broke away from the group clustered around the situation map.

"Come on, Two," Caleb heard him say, "the war'll wait. Let's go see that guy who escaped from the VC." He and a gangling First Lieutenant with S-2 stenciled on his steel pot walked over to where Caleb waited.

Caleb came to attention. "Staff Sergeant Caleb, Sir. H&S Company, 2/4. I'm..."

The Colonel glanced at the Springfield. "Caleb? I've heard about you." He stood there a minute, sucking at his cheek. "You're in luck, Sergeant Caleb," he said, "2/4's the other half of this cluster-fuck. I'll get the next available chopper to fly you over to their CP."

He turned to his S-2. "You take care of that, will you, Jim? Meantime, Sergeant Caleb, don't say shit to anyone until you're debriefed. OK?" He started back to his map, turned back and grinned. "That is, unless you got something you want to tell me now."

Caleb remembered the armed mortar rounds he'd left up on the hill in case the VC came back and pointed out their position on the map. The colonel whistled. "Jesus! They had 4.2's there? We owe you one, my friend. Those mortars would have raised hell with our landing."

The S-2 was looking at him wide eyed. "So you're the famous K-Bar Caleb? I thought that stuff we were hearing about you was just scuttlebutt!"

They flew him over to 2/4. Colonel Riccio's hilltop CP could have been the twin of the one he'd just left, but the reception he got there was a lot more friendly. 3/7 had radioed ahead that he was on the way. The

Wop grabbed him in a great bear hug. "Sonofabitch!" he roared. "Sonofabitch! I thought you'd gone native up there! I didn't think you'd ever come back!"

2/4 and 3/7 swung the tide in the battle of An Hoa, but Caleb wasn't there to see it. Colonel Riccio flew him back to Chu Lai with a load of walking wounded and he spent the days that followed in a strange kind of limbo. The doctors kept him in sickbay a week for observation, but they couldn't find anything wrong with him other than that he had shed twenty pounds off his already lean frame. Which, along with his yellowed complexion from the Atropine, had left him looking very much like the men he had been hunting.

He pissed in a bottle, produced a worm free stool, dazzled the dentist with the brightness of his teeth, and had long interviews with a Navy psychiatrist from Massachusetts who used that connection as grounds for presuming immediate intimacy. This too eager doctor asked his prize catch if he hadn't been afraid, up there alone among the enemy. Caleb thought he was talking about the kind of sudden, gut wrenching, shit-your-drawers kind of fear that triggered a great rush of adrenaline and left him sweating. Sure, he said. He'd been scared up there. Who wouldn't have been?

He did not tell the doctor about the back burner kind of fear that had rarely left him and which, as nature's way to keep flowing whatever chemicals it took to maintain all his senses on full alert, had been the narcotic that had hooked him. Nor did he tell his new friend from Massachusetts about his night among the sheep. So eventually the doctor had to give him a clean bill of health and let him go. He was debriefed by staff officers from Division and MACV, and by hard looking civilians who flew in on an Air America C-47. He was cooperative. They were polite. But there was a lot left unsaid.

He drank a few beers with Dinger, ate at the mess hall, and hung around the S-2 Shop. Everywhere he went he sensed that he made people uneasy. The story had got around about some renegade Marine wingnut running loose in the highlands. There'd been a rash of defectors from the First Regiment who asked for amnesty under the *Chu Hoi* Program and told stories about the cackling madman of the mountains. The rumors had grown from there.

And every day that passed since he'd come down from the mountains, he could feel himself buried deeper under the fast thickening blanket of Hum's civilizing veneers. As that blanket grew, so grew his uneasiness about the things he'd done. But so also grew his sense of loss, because he knew as the brightness faded that he would never again be as fully alive as he had been on the night of Tet, 1966.

CHAPTER TWELVE

Wee Willie and the Vulture were sitting on opposite sides of an empty fireplace in the large house where Wee Willie lived alone. His was one of the Philadelphia Navy Yard's Senior Officers Quarters, a large Victorian house dating back to the period when officers were assigned household staffs and expected to play their parts in a never ending round of stiffly formal entertainments. But those days were long past, and the Vulture had driven down empty streets through the largely decommissioned Navy Yard to find the block of decaying mansions that spoke of a more gilded age.

He was enjoying the visit. They'd spent a long hour in the cellar surrounded by the tools of the watchmaker's trade. More interesting to him by far was Wee Willie himself, bounding boyishly from lathe to milling machine, explaining the function of each, and showing off with ill-concealed pride the tiny parts he fabricated with these tools. Watching him so cheerfully uninhibited had left the Vulture wondering what had happened along the way to so submerge this seldom seen side of the dour, much feared Chief of Orthopedics.

The two men were now back in the sparsely furnished living room and their talk had turned again to Caleb. "He ever say anything more about that guy on the stretcher?" Wee Willie asked.

"He did. But I have to confess, Will, I'm facing a bit of an ethical dilemma myself. Technically, our conversations are confidential, but I justify revealing them to you on the grounds that we share responsibility for his treatment." He smiled. "Even so, my colleagues would tell me I'm walking a fine line. But it does turn out the man he shot was actually carrying the stretcher. The result was the same. The man on it rolled off and fell down a cliff."

Wee Willie grunted. "Japs used to do the same thing. They figured if they could take out the Doc, the Marines in his unit would keep their heads down, knowing nobody'd be there to patch 'em up if they got hit." He picked up the bourbon bottle. "More?"

The Vulture shook his head. "Even with what I've seen in my own life, I still find it hard to believe the things wars make sane men do."

"I don't. I mean, shit, I'm not naive enough to think you can have wars without atrocities. Only difference between what I'm hearing about now and what happened in my day is we knew when the line had been crossed. It didn't always stop us from crossing it, but we knew when we'd done it. Not like that pissant Army lieutenant who's strutting around like a goddamn hero after letting his men gun down all those women and children.

"Funny," Wee Willie went on, pouring himself another giant slug of whiskey, "as a kid I used to daydream about knights in shining armor and chivalry and war as the ultimate test of manhood. All that good shit. Of course, when I went to war myself, I saw a lot of stuff that didn't fit that picture by a long shot. But I also saw a lot that did.

"I remember once in Korea. It could've been a scene right out of World War One. We were in our holes and the Chinks were in theirs. Not a hundred yards between us. The Chinks had a machine gunner who'd let fly at anything that moved. Anyhow, our lieutenant had more balls than brains. I guess he figured if he kept his head down he could crawl close enough to take out that machine gun with a grenade. So off he goes and gets himself zapped halfway between their lines and ours. He's out there thrashing around like a squirrel that's been hit by a car. That Chink gunner's holding his fire and we all figure he's just waiting to pot anybody fool enough to go after the lieutenant."

"But that's my job—I was a corpsman then and dumber than I am now—so off I go. I'm damn near shitting my drawers but I get the Lieutenant under the armpits and I'm starting to drag him back, and all the while that Chink's just has to have me in his sights. He never pulled the trigger."

Wee Willie paused a long moment. "I dunno," he said finally. "Maybe his gun jammed. But I don't think so. I like to think he had a sense of honor. I like to think he was the warrior I thought all warriors were when I was a kid. If we were all like him—if there really was a warrior's code of honor—then we'd fight wars as they should be fought! We'd not be shooting men on stretchers."

"Better yet, Will, let's not fight wars at all."

"Yeah, maybe you're right. Because we called in air. A Corsair came screaming over and laid his napalm right on top of that Chink gun. About the only thing left of that gun crew was the smell of cooked meat!" He shrugged. "I guess that's closer to the real thing than my dreams were. You hungry?"

"You don't leave me much in the mood for meat," smiled the Vulture. "But yes, I could eat something."

"Haven't got much in the house. Mushroom soup OK?" Wee Willie disappeared into the kitchen without waiting for an answer.

"Anything I can do to help?" the Vulture called after him.

"All I've got to do is open the can." Wee Willie returned with two lukewarm mugs of soup and they sat down at the card table that was the only piece of furniture remaining in an ornately cavernous dining room.

"Despite the majesty of your surroundings, Will, you live a pretty Spartan life," laughed the Vulture.

"The wife took the furniture when she left. Fine by me. Glad to be rid of the stuff. Her too. But there's some son of a bitch Supply Corps captain way junior to me who's trying to get me evicted. Says that seeing as I got no family I don't rate these quarters. Bastard! If he'd just asked me, I'd have let him have the place, but the cock-sucker tried to go over my head, so fuck him!"

"How long were you married, Will?"

"Twenty-three years. Still would be, I guess, if it weren't for this fucking war."

"The war? But how. . . ?"

"Boy wouldn't go, and my wife backed him. First he burned his draft card, and then the two of them began joining the protests. Got so bad I turned on the TV one night and saw them waving banners saying

'Military Families Against the War.'" Wee Willie's face was taking on its usual ferocious scowl.

The Vulture looked fondly over at his enormous friend. "Would I be risking a thunderbolt from heaven," he asked, "if I were to suggest that perhaps events are proving them right?"

"Right? What the hell's right got to do with it? Hell, I agreed with them that we shouldn't be in this fool war! But once the shooting starts, that die's already been cast. Other men's sons are going off to fight. Mine's place was there with them. Simple as that!"

"I'd say it was anything but simple. With you as his father, it must have taken enormous courage not to fight! You might think of it that way."

Wee Willie shrugged. "Too late now," he said, looking away. "But he could at least have cut his goddamn hair!" He stood up abruptly. "Come over here and look at this picture."

He led the way over to the fireplace above which hung a large print of an aircraft carrier. "That's the *Randolph.* A CVA she was then, although now she's a CVS."

"I'm sure that's an improvement!"

"Wise-ass. CVA's an attack carrier. CVS means she's anti-sub. I was on her for my first tour after I finished my residency." Wee Willie was standing by the mantelpiece, pointing. "See this gun turret here ahead of the island? Marine Detachment manned that one. They'd always outshoot the squids. Used to piss off the CO when they did, but I had divided loyalties. In those days, I'd spent a lot more years with the grunts than I had with the blue jacket Navy."

He pointed to one of the open gun turrets. "World War Two vintage five inch thirty-eights, those guns were. Fire control system was just as obsolete as the guns, and they expected us to shoot down goddamn jets with those things. *Jets* for chrissake! Now, if you look over here..." He was off and running. The Vulture listened with good humor to his friend's animated dissertation on the Randolph's strong and weak points. And yet, as he tried manfully to understand the shortcomings of hydraulic catapults when compared to the more modern steam driven ones, he felt an enormous sorrow for his friend whose life appeared to be as lonely as was his own.

His own life had always been a solitary one. He figured that was as much an aspect of his deformity as were his stubby arms. People would sometimes be drawn to him out of pity, but he would not accept their charity. To the person too effusive or too solicitous he would politely but firmly close the door. He had his patients, of course, but that kind of relationship was no substitute for the real one. Which raised one of the puzzles about Gunny Caleb. What was it about this enigma of a man that made him harder to keep at arm's length?

Wee Willie was waxing poetic about flight operations—the almost ballet like choreography of the flight deck crew, the indescribable noise of the planes catapulting off the deck, the heart stopping moment when those fuel and armament heavy monsters would seem to sag towards the water, then finally their fiery contrails disappearing triumphantly into the night—and as the Vulture half listened to all this the other half of him was wondering why anyone with a choice in the matter would, as his friend had apparently done, elect the company of machines over the company of his fellow man.

"So there you are," concluded Wee Willie. "Next time someone mistakes you for a real naval officer and asks you something about ships, you'll be able to tell him!"

The Vulture winced. "And here I was thinking I could pass for the real thing." He pointed to a citation hanging next to the print. "How about this one, Will? I didn't know you had a Silver Star."

"Not many people do. I don't wear it because I didn't earn it. They gave it to me for rescuing that fool lieutenant. But I was just doing my job, same as everyone else. I'm prouder of the one next to it."

The Vulture bent over to have a look. "It says here that you qualified as an Officer of the Deck Underway," he read. "I thought we medical types couldn't stand bridge watches."

"We can't. But I did. Got pretty damn good at it too. *Randolph*'s CO was a helluva good man. He ok'd it for me to stand watches and gave me that letter when I left. 'Course he couldn't make it official, so it doesn't mean shit to anybody but me."

"The Navy's your whole life, isn't it, Will?"

"Only one I got left."

"Do you think it still holds a future for you?"

"I hope so. I'd like to get command of a major hospital. Not Bethesda. That one's too political. But maybe Chelsea or even here at Philadelphia. I'd give my ass to show those jerks at BuMed how to run a hospital." He nodded towards the soup pan. "You want more of this shit?"

"No thank you. Very good though."

"Who you kidding? Only reason I buy it is it's cheap!" Wee Willie carried their plates into the kitchen and came back, wiping his hands on a dishtowel. "You know another one of Caleb's stunts that sticks in my craw? That's when he killed that old man. He ever say anything more about that?"

"Only that he'd done it. But I sense that there is more to the story than he's letting on." The Vulture held out his glass. "Perhaps I will have a bit more of your whiskey?"

"Good for you! I was beginning to think I should've got you some pussy wine instead of this stuff!" They drank in silence, each watching the reflection of the light in the amber liquid.

"I sometimes think I should disqualify myself from Caleb's case," said the Vulture finally.

"Why's that?

"It's odd. He seems a decent man, a sensitive one too—he worries about hurting my feelings—and yet he's done things I can't accept as inevitable in combat. I'm drawn to the man and appalled by his evident brutality, all of which makes it very hard to maintain the requisite level of clinical detachment!"

"Well, for chrissake stick with him at least until my bone bridge has a chance to take, OK?"

"I will. To tell the truth, I think I might need Gunny Caleb every bit as much as he needs me."

*****

"You talk of a brightness," began the Vulture when he and Caleb next met. "That's not a word I can relate to at all in this context. It fails to illuminate." He grinned. "That was a pun, Gunny. I hope I don't have to explain it."

But Caleb was in no mood for puns. His jock rot was gone, replaced by bedsores made doubly unpleasant by the indignity of having to bare his ass to Short, who Wee Willie had with malicious pleasure assigned as the attending physician for this problem.

"I don't know how else to describe it, Sir," was all he said as he squirmed around trying to find a more comfortable position.

"I see. One wonders if this primitive, almost animal like state you describe yourself as having fallen into is the only way to achieve that . . . that brightness? Can the artist or the composer or perhaps the scientist—all men who are working at the outer limits of their potential—can they achieve the same exalted state of being?"

"Not likely, Sir," said Caleb, still attempting not to get drawn into this conversation. "They're not putting their lives on the line."

"Aha!" said the Vulture. "There's a clue! But the athlete, maybe? The long distance runner? Someone who must break through pain to achieve a higher level of performance?

Caleb shrugged. "I dunno, Sir. Maybe you should find one of those guys and ask."

"No, I'll stick with you, Gunny. But we'll come back to this on another day. It seems right now you have more pressing problems to worry about. He considered a pun built around the word 'pressing' but thought better of it. He started packing up his notes.

"You're leaving already, Sir?" Caleb asked, realizing too late that he hoped not, that talking might be an antidote to his bedsores.

"Only if you want me to leave, Gunny."

"I don't, Sir."

"Good! Then let's go on."

*****

The day after the troops got in from the An Hoa operation, Caleb ran into the remainder of the Tribe in the mess tent. There were a lot of new faces. Turk was gone, killed by a mine. Blandon was the new squad leader. Caleb carried over his mess tray. "You guys up for company?"

"Free country," Blandon said, sliding over to make room.

"Nice to feel wanted!" Caleb laughed. "How you all been?"

A few of the old gang grinned. Blandon answered. "Been? We been hanging in there. Countin' the days. That's how we been. The difference between us and you, K-Bar, is that we don't like it here. I mean, it's different strokes for different folks. Right?"

"If you say so, George. I've never known you to be wrong yet."

"Yeah? I've been wrong about a lot of stuff. This fuckin' war, for example. I volunteered for this hell hole. Can you believe that? And you know what else I was wrong about, K-Bar? I was wrong about you. You were my hero. A fuckin' for real John Wayne!"

Caleb stood up to go but Blandon kept on pushing. "Hey," he said, "don't run off so quick. I mean, I haven't even had the chance to introduce you to the new guys." He rapped on his canteen cup for silence. "Gentlemen," he said, "let me introduce third squad's former leader, Staff Sergeant John Caleb, known better to his many admirers as the famous K-Bar Caleb!"

"Jesus!" said someone. "So that's the guy!"

Blandon took the cue. "That's right, folks! Before your very eyes! The one, the only *K-Bar Caleb*! A one man killing machine, folks! A grunt who got his start using his best friend's body to bait an ambush. So let's hear it for him, folks! Let's have a big hand for K-Bar!"

There was an embarrassed silence. A couple of grunts laughed. A couple more clapped half heartedly. Caleb tried to leave but Blandon wouldn't let up. "Speech, K-Bar! Speech! Tell all the young Jarheads here how it is to cut a man's throat when he's got his hands tied! Tell them, tell us all, what you were doing up there in the mountains."

Caleb grabbed George Blandon by the collar and lifted him one handed off his feet. He let him hang there pop-eyed for a long moment, dropped him and walked away. That scene only confirmed his reputation. Then a magazine reporter got wind of the story. The Marine Corps had no comment, but there was enough unofficial gossip floating around that the writer had no trouble tracking him down. Caleb wouldn't talk to him. "I'm going to file this story no matter how much you stonewall me," threatened the thwarted interviewer. "Do you want me to base it on fact or rumor?"

Caleb told him he didn't give a damn what he did. So the reporter came up with a piece of fantasy and ended it with the observation that *"In wartime it is often the sociopaths who become the heroes. How society will help these men to readjust to a nonviolent world when they come home remains an unanswered question."*

Colonel Kant was TAD in Saigon when Caleb first arrived back at Chu Lai. They didn't meet until a week later. The Ice Man hadn't changed. "The Prodigal Son returns," he said with the trace of a smile. "What happened up there, Sergeant? I sent you in for three weeks, not three months."

"I guess I just got into it, Sir. I had that regiment pretty well tied in knots. Didn't seem any reason to quit."

"You got into it? What's that mean? According to a lot of panicky Chu Hois, there was some kind of foaming at the mouth madman up there."

"You sent me up there as a terrorist, Sir. I did my best to be one."

"Better even than I might have wanted."

"Sir?"

"I almost didn't dare claim you. But it worked out. You've made us some converts in high places. We're even starting up a sniper school in Okinawa. I'm thinking to get you assigned there for the rest of your tour."

"No, Sir," said Caleb. "I want to go back to the mountains."

The Ice Man raised his eyebrows. Caleb bulled ahead. "You had three battalions at An Hoa, Sir. Two Marine and one ARVN, probably four thousand men in all, and you got 400 or so VC. Sixteen of those were mine. I made your point for you, Sir. I was pretty damned cost effective."

"No question about it. But no, Staff Sergeant. No more solos. It's time you went home."

"The closest thing I've got left to home is where I just came from, Sir. Down here, everyone's looking at me like I'm some kind of a freak."

"That's why I won't send you back."

"Sir?"

"I'd hoped not to have to tell you this," said the Ice Man, looking as close to uncomfortable as Caleb had ever seen him. He sat a long time silent, tapping his pencil absentmindedly on his desk. Then he took a deep breath and began. "You see," he said, "we killers have to be the ones who most hate the killing. That's the great irony of our profession. It's our revulsion to bloodshed that drives us to the hard choices weaker men sidestep by hiding behind their peacetime principals."

He paused again. "Something happened to you up there, Sergeant. Somewhere along the line, it seems you started to enjoy your work."

Caleb was too stunned to speak.

"I'd like to think you're still the man who beat up that Vietnamese lieutenant. I hope you still are that man, and if you aren't, I have myself to blame."

"Yes, Sir," said Caleb. "Is that all, Sir?"

"That's all."

Caleb snapped to attention and did an about face. The Ice Man called him back. "Forgot to tell you," he said, "Colonel Fowler over at 3/7 is putting you up for another Bronze Star for taking out those mortars. What'll that give you? Three?"

"Yes, Sir. Thank you, Sir."

"Don't thank me. If you ask me, we shouldn't have medals. Anyhow, as long as we play these silly games, I had to go Fowler one better. So I've written you up for a silver one. Had to improvise a bit on the citation but I think it'll fly." He smiled thinly. "We don't really have the right award for what you did up there, but maybe we should. We could call it "The medal for bravery when nobody's watching," or, better yet, "The Medal for Solitary Heroism!" Either way, you can be damn sure not many of us would qualify for it." He stood up and extended his hand. "You certainly would have. Goodbye, Sergeant Caleb."

"Goodbye, Sir." Caleb pushed aside the tent flap and walked numbly out into the night.

GEORGE CADWALADER

CHAPTER THIRTEEN

"I come bearing gifts!" announced the Vulture, lurching into the exam room where Caleb lay waiting for him the next day. "Or more properly, it is Randall who bears the gift." Randall followed him in, holding aloft a whole sheepskin with the fleece still attached.

"Direct from the farm to you, Gunny! I hope you like it!"

"The answer to all my prayers, Sir!" laughed Caleb. "What am I supposed do with it?"

"You supposed to sit on it," said Randall. "So hike up your scrawny ass so I can shove this thing in under you."

"It's the lanolin in the wool that's the operative ingredient," explained the Vulture. "A folk remedy for bed sores which I learned from a Gypsy woman during my circus days."

Caleb found himself doing a circus act of his own, trying his best to levitate off his mattress while Randall worked the sheepskin in under him. "You be gettin' mighty skinny," the irreverent corpsman grinned. "You ask me, Gunny, you be better off eatin' sheep than sittin' on one."

"The two aren't mutually exclusive," noted the Vulture, settling himself into his purloined armchair. He went through the usual routine of adjusting his glasses and rummaging through his briefcase, but instead of extracting a notebook as he usually did, he pulled out a much the worse for wear Old Testament. "*Jeremiah 11:19*," he began, "which I will share with you, preparatory to admitting to a mistake—two mistakes actually." Clearing his throat, he read '*I was led like a lamb or an ox that is brought to the slaughter; and I did not know that they had devised plots against me.*'"

He carefully closed the old book, replaced the rubber band that held it together, and returned it to his briefcase. "The 'they' in that passage I saw as Colonel Kant and his minions, all men who I believe to be guilty of the same kind of soulless calculations we too often see being made by the men in Washington who are orchestrating this war.

"You were my Jeremiah, Gunny. I saw you as a fundamentally decent man led unsuspecting by your Colonel's Machiavellian reasoning to override your conscience and do his bidding." He smiled. "The ox simile seems more appropriate to you than does the lamb."

Caleb remembered a similar remark from George Blandon. He didn't smile and the Vulture continued. "This latest chapter in your saga, however, leads me to rethink all that. Instead of being amoral, the Ice Man you've just described apparently sees himself as part of an elite priesthood of sorts; a priesthood of like-minded men who, as he would have it, sacrifice their humanity on the alter of war and kill to end the killing." He paused. "I have to admit, I have trouble with that concept. I can't fault the logic behind it. Nor do I any longer doubt your Colonel's good intentions. But I can't help thinking of the Spanish Inquisitors coercing confession to save the souls of the men they were stretching on the rack. Or of those Germans who saw themselves as doing God's work by killing my parents. They too perhaps had all the best intentions, but there does seem to be something a bit wrong with their methods, wouldn't you say?"

Caleb said nothing.

"So now let's talk about you, Gunny," the Vulture continued. "Where was I wrong there? We've talked of idealists morphing into zealots. Is that what happened to you? Did Colonel Kant harness your idealism for his purposes and then watch helplessly while you ran off with the bit in your teeth? It does seem he was concerned that the man he'd sent up into the mountains was not the same one who came back down."

Caleb found himself caught between tears and anger. "He set me up, Sir," he choked. "Goddammit, he set me up and then he blamed me for going too far. So I'll ask you what I asked him. How could I go too far? He sent me up there to demoralize the enemy. The more horrible the things I did, the better I did that job. So you tell me, Sir. How could I go too far?"

The Vulture sat a long time contemplating his trembling hands. "I'll answer that with a question of my own," he said finally. "Was this orgy of killing you went on really driven by a reasoned belief that you were carrying out the mission you'd been assigned? Or had something else taken over? This brightness, perhaps, which you speak of so often? Had that brightness taken you to that place where messages from the Heart are no longer being heard?"

"So what if it had?" Caleb almost sobbed. "I had a whole goddamn VC Regiment scared shitless. Do you think I could've done that if I'd had heart palpitations over every man I had to kill to do it?"

"No Gunny, I don't. But it's not your effectiveness in the mountains that concerns me. My concern is about what you did has done to you. About the steam. Remember?"

Randall poked his head in the door. "Be someone else comin' for you tonight, Gunny," he said. "Boss Man's got a taxi waitin' to take him home an' the meter's runnin'." He helped the Vulture to his feet and the two of them left together, with the little doctor leaning heavily on the corpsman's shoulder.

That someone else from the ward was Nurse Reardon. "How's the leg?" she asked.

"Pretty near healed, thanks. . ." Caleb let the sentence hang, not sure what to call her.

She inspected his leg. "Good! That'll give me more room to maneuver."

A half hour later she was behind his bed pushing it towards the door.

"You going to be able to move this thing, Nan?

"Not easily," she panted. "But it'll help explain why I look so mussed up!"

"If they ever caught you at this, you know they'd throw the book at you, don't you? Conduct Unbecoming of an Officer. Fraternizing with an Enlisted Man. Lewd and Lascivious Behavior. Christ, Nan, you could even end up in front of a court martial!"

"Not to worry, Gunny. It's my ass." She grinned. "I didn't mean that literally!"

CHAPTER FOURTEEN

Caleb left Viet Nam in April of 1966. His orders were to Parris Island, where he spent the next three years as a drill instructor. The entire time he felt himself in a kind of limbo, stuck somewhere midway between the Quang Tin Mountains and the peacetime garrison life that had once been his sanctuary but was no longer. He couldn't leave Viet Nam behind. Nor could he escape his reputation. K-Bar Caleb got a lot of ribbing at the NCO Club. It was good natured on the face of it, but with uneasy currents beneath. He made people uncomfortable.

There was a lot of theater at Parris Island, a lot of rip out their eyeballs kind of stuff, all for the announced purpose of turning eighteen year old kids into killers. It worked on one level. Drill Instructors could whip up some pretty authentic savagery on the bayonet range. But with the exception of the very dumb or the very sick, nobody ever entirely bought into the act. For most of the men who went through that training, there was always something inside saying, *this isn't really me out here shouting* "Kill! Kill! Kill!"

K-Bar Caleb served as a reminder that it was all for real. He saw himself somehow as a corrupter of innocence. His was a vague, unfocused unease, a kind of faint discordant background music, annoying but tolerable. His nightmares worked as a kind of catharsis. When the background music grew too loud, he'd wake up soaked in sweat, heart pounding, and usually unable to remember anything of the dream itself. Then the music would fade again for another couple of months until the whole cycle repeated itself.

On Christmas Eve, 1967, at a party at the NCO Club, he spotted an old acquaintance from 2/4 at the bar. "Hey, K-Bar," the man called across the room, "You hear about the Ice Man? He got out. Came home from his second tour and turned in his badge. Don't know what the hell he was thinking of. Guy was a cinch to make flag and he just up and quit."

The party was getting rowdy. Everyone who had a family was home with the wife and kids. At Parris Island, as at every other NCO Club the world over on Christmas Eve, the bar was lined with cynical, foul mouthed, hard drinking, misfit, career NCOs all drowning loneliness in alcohol. Normally, that was Caleb's world. That night, he wanted none of it.

He went outside and spent the rest of that strange evening wandering aimlessly around the base. Midnight found him over by his training battalion's obstacle course. He sat shivering under the climbing ropes, reminded by the bells of the chapel pealing out the arrival of Christmas Day of a long ago time when he and his father had nailed a little spruce tree to the mast of their *Sarah B.* while listening to the same carols ringing out across the water.

He woke up with someone shining a light in his face. "Reveille, Sarge!" an MP was saying. "Looks like you been into too much of the sauce. I know what it's like. You ask me, Christmas is the fuckin' pits!"

The MP drove him back to the NCO Quarters. He staggered into his bunk and dreamed that he was talking to the Ice Man. "I'm scared, Sir," he was saying. "My Dad gave me some pretty solid moorings to hang onto, and now you've cut me adrift from all of them."

The Ice Man was trying to tell him something. Caleb strained to hear him. "We're the ones who have to keep our bearings when civilization's signposts have all fallen down," his old CO was saying. "We pick the lesser of evils. That's the best we can hope to do."

"*How do we know?*" Caleb shouted after him. "*How do we decide?*" But the Ice Man was gone.

He woke up hung over and shamefaced at the memory of his drunken performance for the MP. He took it out on his recruits. If they'd expected a break on Christmas Day, they didn't get it. Caleb was all over them, as the DIs liked to say, "like flies on shit."

*****

"How *do* we decide?" asked the Vulture. "That is the key question, isn't it?" He'd come this day in a wheel chair, pushed by Randall, and Caleb, who'd been occupying himself conjuring faces out of the latticework of plaster cracks in the exam room ceiling, felt pity enough for his indomitable little doctor that he risked a candid answer, even knowing that he was heading for uncertain ground. "I don't know, Sir," he admitted. "I didn't know then, and I still don't now. I guess it's like I said before. You just trust your gut. What else can you do?"

The Vulture smiled. "I see we've moved once again from the heart to the gut. Is the one a better guide than the other, or are they both synonyms for what we more literal types call conscience?"

"It's all one and the same, Sir."

"Agreed. But wouldn't your Colonel deny you even that signpost? Wouldn't he say that conscience is just another peacetime luxury that weak men hide behind to avoid the hard choices wartime demands? Wasn't that his argument in persuading you to kill that old man?"

"It was, Sir, and I bought it. I still do."

"Which means your gut was silent on the matter? Or that you killed him despite the objections from your gut?"

"The last, Sir. Chrissake, do you think I *wanted* to kill him?"

"And yet you did. How does that square with trusting your gut?"

Caleb shrugged. "As the Colonel said, Sir. You don't have to shitcan your sense of decency. You just can't let it get in the way of doing your job."

"It's that simple? Those messages from the gut, or as I prefer, the heart, are to be listened to or ignored depending on circumstance? Is that what you're proposing?"

Caleb hadn't thought about it that way. "Yes, Sir," he said finally. "I guess it is."

"Would your friend, Corporal Hume, have agreed with that?"

"Hum? Not in a million years! He'd go on about the scientific method—how you have to follow facts to where they logically lead. He'd tell me you can't let superstitions or prejudices or religion or anything else get in the way. But when you get right down to it, he couldn't do that. The Ice Man could but Hum couldn't."

"Why do you say that?"

"You remember when he was telling me about that spy who was ratted out by his own people to fool the Germans? He understood why the Brits had done it. He even admitted they'd saved a lot of lives by sacrificing one man. But even so, he told me he wouldn't have done it. He *couldn't* have done it. As he liked to say, when your Heart is telling you one thing and your Head another, Heart takes rank."

"Yes, I recall his words. 'God gave us Heart as a check on runaway Head.' Which I think was admirably put, even if I don't accept God's role in the matter. I'd agree more with my secular friend, the one I was telling you about who did the work suggesting that we're born with a rudimentary moral sense. He'd have it that our higher sentiments—kindness, loyalty, fair play and such like—all endow their possessors with an evolutionary advantage. But it doesn't really matter, does it? Whether we attribute conscience to God or Darwin, if it does come built in, then—as I've said so many times before—we ignore it at our psychic peril."

"Meaning Hum was right and the Ice Man wrong?"

"I'm not passing judgment. But I will say that of the two, Corporal Hume probably slept better."

"OK, Sir, let's play that out. Let's say Hum or someone like him is the guy running that spy in France. Odds are he knows the man he's setting up to betray. Maybe they trained together. Maybe they're even friends. So when push comes to shove he can't do it. His heart won't let him. He doesn't rat his guy out. The Germans don't shift all those divisions to Calais and thousands more men are killed on the Normandy beaches. How's he going to sleep then, Sir?"

"Not well, but in his nightmares he is haunted only by faceless masses. Which is easier to bear than if the accusing face he sees in his dreams is that of the one man he sent to his death. Stalin understood that distinction. As he put it, 'one death is a tragedy; a million is a statistic.'"

Randall arrived and they left it there.

*****

The Vulture had fitted out his wheelchair with an American flag and a large blue and gold sign reading *Commander Ernest Throttlemeyer USNR (Retired)*. "My hope is that passers by will be sufficiently impressed by my martial presence to see me as some doughy old warrior now fallen on bad days."

"I'd buy your act," Caleb laughed.

"The Bureau of Personnel evidently didn't. The powers that be have decreed that I am no longer fit to wear a uniform."

"Can't you fight it, Sir? You said yourself they need you here."

"They still do. In their wisdom, they are allowing me to revert to my former role of consultant. So for us nothing will change. But a new commander, a *real* commander is being brought in to take over the department."

"Far as I'm concerned, Sir, you're still the real commander. You can tell the other guy that for this wingnut it's you or nobody."

The Vulture's face lit up. "Randall says much the same thing. So perhaps with the people that count I still belong to the fraternity." He paused, looking pensively at his prostrate patient before continuing, "But I'm deluding myself to think that, aren't I?"

"How so, Sir?"

"My mistake was to think that simply by putting on the uniform I might become a part of your world. You see, I envied the camaraderie I saw there. I admired the code of honor and the self discipline. I saw the ranks of young, fit men, in contrast to whom many of my own students seemed all the more selfish and self absorbed."

His right hand began jerking spasmodically, causing him to drop his pen. He leaned forward to pick it up, managing only to push it under his chair, before abandoning the effort and hauling himself painfully erect again. "You weaned me from my romantic infatuation," he said, still short of breath from his exertions. "Your story brings home to me what it's really all about." He smiled ruefully. "I couldn't have done the things you did over there, and the odd thing is that Colonel Kant's argument is convincing enough that I'm not sure any longer whether or not that's to my credit."

Caleb didn't know how to answer that. "I remember when we were in the Dominican Republic," he said finally, "This guy was sniping at us from a rooftop. He couldn't shoot worth a damn so he was more of a nuisance than anything else. But anyhow, I rounded him up and we had him restrained between two of those wire litter baskets the Navy uses on the ships. We'd tied them together face to face so it was like he was in a cage. And I can still see the way he was looking out at me through the wire. Christ, it was as if the hate was radiating off him almost like heat. I could damn near feel it!"

Caleb shook his head in wonderment. "I'd never experienced anything like that before. That guy didn't know me from Adam but that hate of his was personal, aimed right at me. Given the chance, he'd have ripped out my throat with his bare hands.

"There's a lot of others out there just like him, Sir. There's whole *countries* filled with guys just like him, and if you ever run into one, you're either going to have to kill him before he kills you or else hope like hell someone like me comes along to do it for you."

The Vulture nodded. "So tell me then, Gunny—and understand that I ask this question as one for whom swatting a mosquito is a big game hunt—tell me what is the physiological impact of killing on the killer? I mean, does one's heart rate increase, one's palms sweat or one's nose itch? What exactly happens at the moment one pulls the trigger or wields the knife?"

"Everyone's pretty well wound up in combat, Sir."

"I'm not talking of combat. I mean when one kills with premeditation. As you did with Nguyen."

Caleb was too angry to answer. He lay silently, jaws clenched, trying unsuccessfully not to conjure from the latticework of cracks in the ceiling the outline of Nguyen's face staring back at him.

The Vulture too was silent for a time. "My colleagues would take me to task for asking you that question," he admitted. "But I asked it with malice aforethought. You see, there's a side of you that you've yet to show me. Your colonel's arguments give me the intellectual rationale for the things you did; but, as any honest academic will tell you, it's far simpler to arrive at solutions in the abstract than it is to actually carry them out. You, however, did put theory into practice. In your capacity as the Ice Man's scalpel, you committed acts which, if I were simply to list them at any psychiatric seminar, would earn you the unanimous diagnosis as being seriously unbalanced.

"Yet here you are, on the face of it a thoroughly sane and decent man. That's the enigma I've yet to solve." He paused, rearranging his notes and then glanced up, looking almost embarrassed. "Which brings me to a confession of my own, Gunny. Since childhood, I've always led an active fantasy life. In my daydreams I'd imagine myself in one heroic role or another, but whatever my fantasy, I'd always be tall and handsome with beguiling maidens falling at my feet.

"These fantasies faded as I grew older and became more reconciled to who I am. But lately they've returned, perhaps because of the drugs I'm on. Now however, they're always the same. I'm once again the tall imposing figure of my childhood fantasies—looking much like you do, as a matter of fact—and I'm about to kill that sadistic doctor I told you about. As I think I intimated to you earlier, I had good reason to hate him.

"In my fantasy I have a knife I've fashioned from a flat bed spring. The craven doctor is cringing in front of me. His flaccid face is twisted in terror. But I am beyond pity. I draw my arm back to strike, intending to drive my knife up under his ribs just as you've taught me to do.

"Until this point my fantasy is extraordinarily vivid. I can feel the knife in my hand and the coarse weave of my inmate's uniform chafing against my skin. Even over the stink that pervades the camp, I can smell the cowering SS Officer's sour breath. But there my daydream ends.

"The problem is that never having killed a man, I can't even imagine what it feels like. Does the knife slice smoothly or does it take force to drive it home? Is there an eruption of blood? Escaping gas from a ruptured gut? Sucking noises when the knife's withdrawn? I don't know. And what do I feel at that moment? I don't know that either. So you see, Gunny, there is an ulterior motive for my question. I suppose it does me no credit, but I want to finish killing that monster."

Caleb just shook his head. "It's best that you don't, Sir. Even if it's just in your mind, don't go there if you don't have to. It'll only drag you down closer to the same kind of world that Nazi doctor lived in."

*****

Caleb was promoted to Gunnery Sergeant in August of 1969, and got orders back to Viet Nam a month later. He wasn't sorry. His last act at the end of each training cycle was to hand out assignments to his graduating recruits. With so many of them going, he felt he should go himself. Even knowing that the only reason they were still fighting that hopeless war was to give Washington time to negotiate some face saving way out of a mess of its own making, he still felt he ought to go back. Even knowing doing so would be playing with fire, he felt he had no choice.

Nixon had announced the phase-out of US troops. "Vietnamization" was the buzz word. The plan seemed to be to try to prop the ARVN up with enough firepower to allow them to hang on for a polite period of time after the US bugged out. Like everyone who'd been there, he knew the ARVN hadn't a snowball's chance in hell of actually beating the NVA. But it was easier to go back himself than to keep on pushing kids through Parris Island who he knew would end up cannon fodder in a cause America had lost the will to win.

He flew out to San Francisco at the end of October, and after a day of shots administered three at a time by virtuoso medics at Travis AFB, he climbed onto an Air Force Starlifter to start his journey via Wake and the Philippines to whatever was left of Viet Nam. The big plane's backwards-facing seats held mostly dogfaces with a few Marines and sailors sprinkled in among them. Caleb spotted some Viet Nam Services Medals, but for most of his fellow passengers this was going to be their first trip. He wondered how many of them would come home in body bags.

The seat belt sign blinked out and people began milling around the aisles. Caleb was just about asleep when someone hit him a whack on the shoulder. He looked up, foul tempered, and there stood Bull Best, now a captain, grinning hugely.

They both had orders to the Seventh Marines. Bull was going to 3/7. Nobody had told him so outright, but he thought he was being sent there because that battalion was having race problems. "The natives are restless," he laughed, "so they're sending in the Bull to quiet 'em down."

They spent the rest of that long flight talking about how a war they'd thought they could not lose had turned into such a disaster. Caleb blamed the peace movement for convincing Hanoi to hang on until Washington caved in. Bull's indictment was broader and more bitter. He blamed Johnson for lacking the political courage to mobilize the reserves, MacNamara for a draft that picked too many apples from the bottom of the barrel, and the Chiefs of Staff for not opposing the thirteen month tour of duty which made men more concerned with watching the clock than winning the war. By the time he'd come to the end of his list, they were landing on Wake.

*****

A television set had materialized in the exam room. Nobody could say who it belonged to or where it had come from, but the suspicion was that the mysterious appearance of the Vulture's armchair and now this TV were somehow connected. As before, Caleb's advice to his doctor was to launch no inquiries.

Another mystery was how to turn it off. Caleb was powerless even to change the channel, and the Vulture, now almost equally immobile in his wheelchair, refused to have anything to do with it. The sound had providentially been turned off, so the set sat in the corner, its screen flickering with nonstop images while Caleb and his doctor talked.

But Caleb found it impossible not to watch it. Try as he might to ignore *As the World Turns* and other such distractions, his eyes were invariably drawn to the screen and to the procession of mute characters who marched across it. The Vulture too was not immune to that temptation, and on this day the show was a violent one that they were both trying with an equal lack of success to ignore.

"We never were exposed to anything even remotely like that when I was a child," remarked the Vulture, conceding defeat. "Children in my day retained their innocence to a much later age than they do today."

"You got that wrong, Sir," Caleb shot back with a vehemence that surprised his doctor. "Sure kids today see all that acted-out killing. But they don't get sticky with the blood. They don't get to smell the stink of guts spilled open or to know what it's like to wipe someone else's brains off their shirt. So, no, Sir. They don't lose their innocence any quicker. It just gets poisoned by the bastards who put that kind of crap on TV."

"A sentiment somewhat at odds with your reputation," murmured the Vulture, writing furiously. "But let's move on. When we last left off in your narrative, you were headed back to Viet Nam. That's become a place where whatever innocence a man might bring with him won't last long, hasn't it?"

"It sure has, Sir. But this time I didn't last very long myself."

CHAPTER FIFTEEN

Bull Best and Caleb returned to Da Nang on the last day of October, 1969. Three years before, there'd been optimism in the air. No more. Sullen, long haired clerks wearing peace symbols processed them through Personnel. The Bull pulled strings and got Caleb assigned to 3/7. They took off for Landing Zone Ross to join the battalion, both of them glad to get clear of Da Nang. Morale was supposed to be better in the field. The once familiar country they flew over on their way to LZ Ross was an unrecognizable patchwork of abandoned rice paddies, uprooted trees and empty villages. Looking over that devastated landscape, Caleb saw that Hum had been right. We had wrecked it for them.

Morale was no better in the field. Bull's new command, Lima Company 3/7, was in worse shape than Caleb would have thought possible in the Marine Corps. More than half the company were new arrivals from the Third Marine Division, openly bitter at being left behind while the rest of their old Division was being pulled back to Okinawa. A couple of days before Caleb got there, twenty or so black Marines had refused to turn out when the company formed up to go back into the field. Lima Company had stood down and watched shamefaced as the rest of the battalion lifted out. Their company commander had been relieved.

In any other war, those twenty would have been run up for mutiny. But Viet Nam in 1969 was not like any other war. Nixon's announced troop withdrawal had taken care of that. "Who wants to be the last man killed in Nam?" was the new refrain. Caleb relieved a burnt out Platoon Sergeant in the Third Platoon. The old veteran was shaking his head when he left. "Good luck, Gunny," he said. "You're gonna need it. Thirty years I've been in this lash-up—World War II, Korea, an' one tour over here before this one. I never thought the Corps could sink to this."

The first thing Bull did was to fall out the company. Caleb's platoon straggled out to the impromptu parade deck on the helo pad. "Jesus fuckin' Christ," he heard one of them mutter. "New CO's callin' for a goddamn rifle inspection out here in the bush. That's gotta be a fuckin' first!" He formed them up and took his post in front to wait for the Platoon Commander. "Asshole!" said somebody behind him. "Silly shit must think he's still at PI!"

He spun around fast enough to see who it was. It was a black kid, a tall, still smirking Lance Corporal, the third man in the second rank. *Well*, he thought, *if not now, I'll just have to do it later.* He stuck his face close up to the Lance Corporal's. "Was that you calling me an asshole, boy?"

The man's eyes went hard and Caleb realized he'd made a mistake. Every recruit could be 'boy' in boot camp. Out here it was a fighting word. "Don't you ever call me boy, motherfucker!" snarled the Lance Corporal.

Caleb decked him. Nobody said a word. "Anybody else here want to call me an asshole?" he asked the platoon. The Lance Corporal climbed shakily back on his feet. There was hatred in his eyes. Caleb went back to his post just in time to report to the Lieutenant.

"Trouble, Gunny?"

"No, Sir, none at all. Third Platoon all present, Sir." The Lieutenant gulped. He'd forgotten his lines. There was an awkward silence. "Shall I take my post, Sir?" Caleb prompted.

"Post, Gunny!" Caleb heard snickering in the ranks. He took his post behind the platoon. *God help us*, he thought, *this is going from bad to worse*. Bull took over the formation. "Sweet Jesus!" whispered somebody in the platoon. "Look at the size of that guy!"

"Knock it off," Caleb growled.

"Platoon Commanders!" roared the Bull, "Fall out your people an' have 'em gather around Ol' Bull up here so we can all get acquainted. Do it now an' do it quick!"

The company fell out and milled around the captain. "Moooo!" said somebody. "MOOOOOOO!" took up the rest. The Bull's face split into a grin. "Now all you moo cows had best pay attention!" he said. "Because what I'm going to tell you, I'm only going to tell you once and what happens after that depends on how well you listen. Do I make myself clear?"

Whatever smiles there had been were gone now. Tension almost crackled in the air. Caleb looked out over a sea of sullen faces, some pretending not to give a shit, others outright hostile, and he wondered if Bull could pull it off. Lima Company seemed very close to beyond salvage.

"Today is the third of November," continued the Captain. "'In another week it'll be the tenth, and on that day the Marine Corps is going to be one hundred and ninety-four years old. And you know something, people? In all that time, Lima Company 3/7 is the first company of Marines ever to refuse to fight. That's right. The first one! And that makes me ashamed.

"You say you don't want to be the last man killed in this fucked up war? I can understand that. I don't want to be that man either. But let me tell you something, people. Your chance of getting killed is a whole lot better when you're in the worst company than if you're in the best. And right now you *are* in the worst company. If this outfit's going to go out in the field still feeling sorry for itself like it does now, we're going to get our asses kicked. That's the truth! If you want to go home standing up, you'd best stop lying down right now!"

Bull wiped the sweat off his face. "I'm black," he said. "In case you hadn't noticed!" There was an explosion of laughter. Caleb felt the tension go out of the back of his neck. But the Bull wasn't smiling. "You know somethin', people?" he went on. "Right now, sitting here today, we're all black!"

He chuckled. "Now I know there's some crackers out there, some good ol' boys, who don't like hearing that! But I'll tell you why we're all the same color. We're all brothers because every man in Lima Company today, *every man,* black, white, 'Rican, I don't care what you are, you're gonna have to fight to get back your pride and your dignity just as we black folk got to do every day.

"So that's the story, people. Mr. Richard Nixon may disgrace himself! Mr. Henry Kissinger may disgrace himself! Mr. Robert MacNamara may disgrace himself!" At each name the Bull's rumbling voice rose a notch. He was winding them up. "BUT WE AREN'T GOING TO DISGRACE OURSELVES!" he thundered. "WE'RE MARINES! WE'RE LIMA COMPANY AND LIMA COMPANY'S SAT OUT A FIGHT FOR THE LAST TIME!"

They were on their feet cheering. The Bull had worked his magic.

When Caleb fell the platoon back out again an hour later for CO's rifle inspection, he sensed he was in front of an outfit with some snap in it. There were still some surly faces, that Lance Corporal's in the second rank among them. His troubles weren't over. But they were fewer than he would have thought possible earlier that day. They stood at ease while the Captain inspected the First and Second Platoons. He didn't skip a rifle, and each one he grabbed, you could hear the slap a mile a way. The Bull had iron hands.

"*Ten-Hut*" barked the lieutenant. The Captain and the First Sergeant were headed their way.

"Third Platoon, ready for inspection, *Sir*!"

"Very well," rumbled the Bull. "Put your second and third ranks at ease, Lieutenant." He moved down the first rank, the lieutenant ahead of him and the first sergeant behind, taking notes. All went well. The captain handed the last man in the first rank back his rifle and headed towards the second squad leader. Caleb waited for the lieutenant to call the second rank to attention. He didn't do it. The second squad leader began to squirm, not sure whether or not to come to attention without the command.

"Second rank, *ten-Hut*!" Caleb muttered. "First rank, at ease!" Bull grinned but didn't say anything. The lieutenant turned red. The inspection proceeded. Squad leader OK. First fire team leader, OK. He started to relax. He would have liked to run his own inspection before the company commander's. There hadn't been time for that. But they were doing well.

He watched the Captain face left in front of the man he had decked. The Lance Corporal came lazily up to inspection arms and he knew there was going to be trouble. "What happened to you, Lance Corporal?" asked the captain. "Whatever hit you in the head must've scrambled up your brain, because that's the most fucked up inspection arms I've ever seen."

"The Platoon Sergeant sucker punched me, Sir," said the Lance Corporal.

"He *did*? Now why'd he do a thing like that?"

"Ask him."

"Ask him, *Sir*," rasped the First Sergeant. The Captain snatched the Lance Corporal's rifle. He checked the breach, spun it around to look down the bore and handed it back. "If I was your Platoon Sergeant," he said, "and you showed up with a rifle as cruddy as this one, I'd have smacked you too. Except I'd have done it harder! Now you'd best square yourself away. Hear?" He moved on to the next man.

That evening the lieutenant came by Caleb's tent. "Round up the squad leaders, Gunny," he told him. "The Captain wants to see us." Caleb gathered up his three Sergeants and the five of them all headed up to the CP. It was raining.

The Bull was waiting for them. He bowed. "Welcome to my humble abode," he grinned. "Don't worry! You haven't done anything wrong! This is just a social call."

They filed into his tent.

"You all find yourself a place to sit," he said, "an Ol' Bull here'll run the bar." He fished a six pack from behind his cot. "This isn't exactly cold . . ." he was starting to say. Out of the corner of his eye Caleb saw the tent flap start to lift behind him. Then he saw the grenade.

Later, when he came to in the hospital, he remembered seeing the spoon pop off and hearing the hiss of the fuse. He remembered how the Bull's face had exploded into pulp. After that there was nothing to remember but pain and darkness.

CHAPTER SIXTEEN

Wee Willie arrived at Caleb's bedside carrying a plastic pill bottle. He came alone, unaccompanied by his usual retinue of staff. "This is the biggest chunk we pulled out of you," he said, dumping a shard of metal out of the bottle.

Caleb examined the jagged piece curiously. It was about the size of a quarter with some of its olive drab paint still visible.

"One of ours, wouldn't you think?"

"Hard to say, Sir."

"Horse shit! I know pretty much the whole story, Gunny. You and your CO both went for the grenade. Captain Best absorbed the brunt of the explosion with his body. Your arm took the rest. Thanks to you two, the other four men in the tent weren't even scratched."

Wee Willie was examining Caleb's arm as he talked. "Coming along nicely," he muttered. Then, more loudly, "We'll have to get you down to X-ray to see for sure, but I'd say you're about ready to come out of traction."

That normally would have been good news, but Caleb had other things on his mind. "How do you know this, Sir?"

"About your arm? Well, there's good granulation. Bone seems to be filling in nicely across the bridge. It all looks..."

"I mean, Sir, how did you hear how I was hit?"

"Someone from the Naval Intelligence Service came by just after you got here. You were in no shape to talk to him at the time."

"Just as well."

"I think it was. Particularly since the suspect in the fragging turned up dead. So the thinking seems to be that the whole thing's best kept under the table. That OK by you?"

"What about Captain Best, Sir?"

"His parents were told he died in combat. They gave him a Purple Heart."

"Then it's not OK by me, Sir. He'd be up for the Medal of Honor if it hadn't been our guy who threw the grenade."

"I know, Gunny. But there isn't much that's fair in life. Least of all how they hand out medals. You know that."

"It's not right, Sir. I can't. . ."

"You're going to have to. It's that or let Best's parents learn he was killed by one of his own men. How do you think they'd feel about that?"

"Same as I do. Did you say the man who fragged us is dead?"

"He is. Somebody in your company took care of that for you."

"I wonder if he got a Purple Heart?"

"Probably he did, Gunny. Like I said, there isn't much in life that's fair."

*****

The following day they wheeled him back down to the OR and when he woke up again the pin was gone from his wrist and, for the first time in many months, his right arm lay beside him. It was almost like a foreign object. He tried to lift it but it wouldn't move.

They got him out of bed but he was too weak to stand. He had to be wheeled down to Physical Therapy and, when he got there, it was as if he'd arrived at some cruel *Mad Magazine* parody of a gym. To the right of the door were the parallel bars where sweat-drenched Marines stumped back and forth on artificial legs. To the left of it, grimacing burn casualties lay on tables where therapists stretched out their atrophied tendons. At other tables, rows of fiercely concentrating men struggled to lift coffee cups with iron hands.

Caleb began by supporting himself on the parallel bar with his left hand and, when he'd regained enough strength in his legs to walk again, he took his place among the cup lifters to learn to use his own claw. He tried not to let the look of his right arm and hand bother him. But sometimes the sight of it would catch him unawares. He'd see that mass of purple, cratered flesh reflected back at him from a mirror or window and try not to stare, just as he would if that monstrosity belonged to somebody else. Most of the time he didn't think about it. With so many other deformed men around him, the horrible had become the norm. He grew used to the raw circles of meat that were the stumps of severed limbs and to the steel hook hands that men manipulated with wires that led to pins implanted in their biceps. For a time he even grew used to his own new self. But when he started taking walks in the park outside the hospital and saw people staring, that's when it hit him that he'd become an object of curiosity, which was bad, and pity, which was worse. The experience left him with an even greater admiration for the Vulture.

He was ashamed at feeling so self-conscious, and in his shame he remembered his father's amusement when as a boy he'd answered the advertisement at the back of a comic book for the Charles Atlas body building program. "Seems to me your friend Mr. Atlas has got things turned around," his dad had said. "I thought the Good Lord gave us muscles so we could do a day's work. I didn't think His idea was that we were supposed to work all day just to get muscles!"

He'd handed him his bull rake. "Here," he'd said. "If you want to make yourself big and strong, go out and rake up quahogs. That way you'll have something to show for it!"

His father's scorn for Charles Atlas had turned him off body building as an end in itself. But all that changed after he became conscious of those stares in the park. Whether his father and the Good Lord approved or not, he worked out furiously for no other purpose than just to build himself back up. He would kid himself during the hours he spent on the weights that he was just trying to get his strength back. The truth, as he had to admit, was that he wanted to turn himself into another Charles Atlas. Or at least into three quarters of a Charles Atlas. He thought if he could get the rest of himself looking like he belonged on the back of a comic book, then people might be less likely to notice the monstrous thing that hung from his right shoulder.

And when he got discouraged, he thought of the Iron Man who had been left paralyzed from the neck down by a piece of shrapnel in his spine. Every afternoon the therapists would strap Iron Man onto a tilt board. Then they'd raise him slowly up towards the vertical to exercise his heart while he struggled fiercely not to pass out, and everybody else abandoned their own particular hells to cheer him on.

The Iron Man's daily battle against the tilt board became their Main Event at PT. "We're going for two minutes at fifty degrees today, Sports Fans!" he'd announce in his reed thin voice. They'd all gather around him. Iron Man would begin by making a sad parody of a weight lifter's explosive breathing. The therapist would stop him at every ten degrees of tilt, letting him get used to it. The rest of them would fall tensely silent, trying somehow to will the poor kid from passing out. They'd watch the color start to drain from his face and they'd holler, "Come on, Iron Man! You can do it! You got thirty! You're almost there, kid! You're almost there!"

Tears of frustration would erupt from his eyes. His head would start to sag and they'd lower him back down again. On the day he managed to hang on without blacking out for a minute at forty-five degrees, they cobbled him up a trophy out of a barbell and a bedpan. The Iron Man cured them of any pity they felt for themselves. He died on the same day Caleb first managed to touch his new thumb to the finger next to it.

*****

Summer came. Staff Sergeant O'Malley was medically retired and transferred to a Veterans Administration Hospital. The nurses had a party for him on the ward. Everyone tried to put a good face on it, but it was common knowledge that only the chronically ill were sent to the VA.

Caleb began going on runs in the park. Sometimes Nan ran with him, her justification to a suspicious Short being that patients shouldn't be left to run alone. Caleb always kept her on his right side, thinking correctly that passers-by were more likely to look at her than at his arm. At the start, she was the more fit and he'd stop often, wobbly-legged and winded, while she annoyed him by continuing to run in place. But as the summer wore on, the shoe moved gradually to the other foot until the day came when she was the one who called the halt.

They'd run along the Schuylkill River, jumping back and forth across railroad tracks until they'd reached the Art Museum, and there she flopped down laughing on a grassy bank, saying she'd gone far enough. "You got any money, Gunny?" she panted.

"Nope."

"Damn! Neither do I. I could use a Coke right about now." She rolled onto her back. "Moneygunny!" she laughed. "I like the sound of that." She said it again. "Moneygunny!"

A man was coming their way walking his dog. Caleb stood up. "Excuse me, Sir," he said, grinning his half-smile, half-leer. "Could you spare a buck for a disabled veteran?" He held out his claw. The dog-walker looked up at the unsettling stranger who blocked his way, glanced furtively down at his claw, and nervously pulled out his wallet "Here, take five," he said and scuttled off, towing his dog behind him. "God bless you, Sir!" Caleb called after him.

"I don't believe you did that," Nan said. "You scared that man."

"I'm practicing for my new career."

She punched him lightly. He looked down at the radiant girl beside him and his face clouded. "You still on your crusade to bring comfort to the wounded?" he asked. It was a cruel question, but he couldn't help himself.

"No," she said, "That crusade began and ended with you. The logistics defeated me."

"I'll run get you that Coke."

She watched him jog off towards the museum. *He moves like a big cat*, she thought, and she realized suddenly that he scared her too. Caleb was back in a moment with the Coke.

"Hope it stays down on the run home," she laughed too brightly, handing him the empty bottle.

"I should have hit that guy up for ten. That way we could've taken a taxi!"

*****

Caleb had one last operation during which Wee Willie cut away the web of skin that limited his new thumb's range of motion. It was a simple procedure and he was back running two days later. He'd always liked to run, but now it was becoming an obsession with him. His breathing would fall into synch with his pace, the throbbing in his arm would fade to nothing, and when he'd again become aware of his surroundings, he'd find himself many miles from where he'd started.

On a bright fall day, he and Nan set out to run the length of Philadelphia's Fairmount Park. They started off at the Art Museum, ran down past the Water Works, and then out along the East River Drive. The air was crisp, the buttonwood leaves gone yellow and the maples a flaming red. For Caleb it was a perfect day.

Nan floated along beside him. She was an effortless runner and a pleasantly distracting one as she'd chatter away as she ran, unbothered by his monosyllabic replies. But this day she was silent. They passed the pioneer settlement at Schuykill Village and turned away from the river to run along the branch-covered banks of Wissahickon Creek. "Let's stop a minute," she said, drawing up. But Caleb was lost in his own private world and her words didn't register. He ran on a ways and, realizing that she was no longer beside him, turned back.

He found her sitting on a bench. "Sorry," he said. "I didn't see you stop." She was busy pushing a stone around with her foot. "You OK, Nan?"

She nodded. "Bob's asked me to marry him."

"Short?" Caleb sounded incredulous.

"He's fun," she said defensively. "He makes me laugh."

"I don't?" he said.

"Don't what?"

"Make you laugh. I thought I was a barrel of laughs!"

"I'm a little afraid of you," she admitted, her eyes avoiding his. "Like that man you hit up for money. You scare people, you know that?"

She maneuvered the stone over against his foot. "Would you marry a girl like me?" she asked finally. "I mean, I'm not asking you to. I just wonder if it's something you'd ever consider."

"I don't know, Nan. I..."

"You're not going to hurt my feelings if you say no," she said, trying hard to sound as if she meant it. "I know what you're probably thinking, Gunny. I know what Wee Willie calls me. His sex goddess." She snorted. "*His* sex goddess! Christ! I'd sooner crawl into the sack with Godzilla." She laughed again too brightly. "So it's OK if you don't think I'm the kind of girl you'd want to take home to meet your, mom. I can understand that."

Caleb started to protest but she cut him off. "It's for the kids on the ward, Gunny. They see me poured into a uniform two sizes too small and maybe just for a minute it's like they've got their arms and their legs again and they're back driving by the Dairy Queen cruising for chicks. I mean that's what I hope. I hope if I wag my ass a bit when I'm dumping their piss pots they'll think a girl can still come on to them, even all crippled up as they are." She paused, then punched him lightly. "Bob knows it's all just an act. That's why I like him."

"Like him? No more than that?"

"Like him. Love him. I don't know. All I know is that if this damn war ever ends I want to be the most conventional housewife there ever was." She grinned. "A husband, two kids, a station wagon and a dog! That's all I ask for." She punched him again, harder this time. "So how about it, Gunny? Would you take a girl like me home to meet your mom?"

Caleb sat stone-faced, remembering a time when as a child a monarch butterfly had landed on his hand. He'd laughed with delight at so beautiful a thing perched there on his finger and he'd cried when it had flown away. But then he'd been angry, and the next Monarch he'd seen he squashed. "I couldn't," he said finally. "Even if I had a mom, I couldn't do it, Nan. I'd want to... God, how I'd want to! But I couldn't."

She looked up at him questioningly. "Why couldn't you, Gunny?"

He shrugged. "I'd want to make you happy."

"So?"

"So I don't think I could. That's all."

"Wouldn't that be for me to decide?"

"You don't know who I am. Hell, *I* don't even know who I am. Not anymore I don't. That's what it boils down to." He pushed the rock back over to her and smiled his half-smile, half-leer. "If I ever get that sorted out, you'll be the first girl on my list."

"Give me your hand, Gunny," she said. "The bad one."

He reluctantly pulled his claw out of his pocket. She ran her five fingers through his three and put his hand on her leg. "Now squeeze!" she demanded. "Hard! As hard as you can."

As hard as he could wasn't very hard. "I'll remember how that feels," she said. "That's the way I'll remember you." They sat, not talking, with his claw in her hands. "Will you write me when you leave here?" she asked.

"What name should I put on the envelope? Reardon or Blankenship?"

"I don't know. But until I decide, I guess I owe it to Bob that this be our last run together." She held her face up to him. "So kiss me goodbye, OK?"

He did, and they stayed locked in each others arms until the street lights came on to remind them that their day was done.

*****

He went up before the medical board wearing his Winter Service Greens with ribbons and badges. He was assigned a Lieutenant to represent him. Three Officers sat on the board. Everyone was friendly. They asked to look at his hand which he showed them, and to raise his arm which he did as far as it would go. Then they declared him "physically unfit to perform the duties of his grade" and released him from active duty. His disability was rated at ninety percent "in accordance with the standard schedule for rating disabilities in current use by the Veteran's Administration."

"Congratulations, Gunny," said his counsel. "You hit the jackpot. Anything over eighty percent and you get your full base pay for a pension. Tax free, too. You made out like a bandit."

The board had met in an annex building a block from the main hospital. Erect in his uniform, Caleb walked in the winter's early darkness back along Broad Street to begin the process of checking out of the only world he still knew. Wet snow had fallen earlier that day and was now being churned noisily into slush by the rush hour traffic. He heard the hiss of air breaks. A Transit Authority bus pulled up to the curb ahead of him, and among the mix of civilians and sailors who spilled out onto the street he spotted Randall wearing sweatpants and a hooded jacket.

"Hey, Doc!" he called. Randall turned around. His face split into a grin and he came dancing over, shadow boxing as he came, "Oooo RAH!" he laughed. "They be gettin' ready to put you on a recruitin' poster, Gunny?"

"No way, Doc. They just canned my ass!"

"You be 'spectin' that, weren't you? Didn't come as no surprise?"

"Yeah, I was. But it still takes some getting used to." Caleb looked at Randall more closely. "What's that shit on your face?"

Randall wiped his sleeve across his cheek and inspected it. "Vaseline," he said. "I been sparrin'." He demonstrated, firing hooks and jabs which stopped just shy of Caleb's jaw.

"You never told me you were a boxer, Doc."

"Yassuh, I am. Good one too."

"Where do you train?"

"Gym down in South Philly. The Vulture took me down there when I first come to PNH." Randall grinned. "I been in all kinds o' trouble back then. They be runnin' me up for Office Hours about every other day!"

"The Vulture?" said Caleb, surprised. "I didn't think he'd be much on fighting."

"He don't mind it none. Long as I keep it in the ring. Won't be too long before you gonna be asking' ol' Randall here for his autograph."

Caleb handed him the manila envelope he'd been carrying. "Give it to me now, Doc. That way I'll already have it when you get famous." Randall wrote on it *Junior Randall*, started to hand it back and then added *middleweight contender*.

"Good luck, Doc. I'll be looking for you on the sports pages."

"Good luck to you, Gunny."

The two men stood facing each other under the light of the street lamps, both thinking of the many long nights they'd weathered together. Randall's face was lost in the shadow of his pointed hood. He kicked hesitantly at the snow and then launched a light jab in Caleb's direction. "I be watchin' you for a long time," he said, "an' I know you be a good man, Gunny. So don't you keep thinkin' you ain't. Hear?"

They shook hands, neither one of them awkward about the claw. "Thanks for that, Doc," Caleb said. "Here all along I'd been thinking it was the Vulture who was the wizard!"

CHAPTER SEVENTEEN

Caleb and the Vulture met one last time in the now familiar exam room.

"I envy Wee Willie," said the Vulture. "He can send his patients home fixed."

"Not entirely!" grinned Caleb, holding up his misshapen right hand.

"No, but there is a point where he can say, 'I've done all I can.' In my line of work, there's seldom so clear a finish." He thumbed through his notes. "Still, I do have to make some kind of final entry in your medical record, Gunny. What do you think I should write? I could say that you are in fact Everyman, more talented than most in the skills of your trade, but in all other respects exactly what you appear to be—a decent, thoughtful, intelligent, well balanced human being just doing your job.

"Or is there more to it than that? I've been doing some reading, trying to find some reference to that brightness you speak of. The closest I can come to it is a condition known in the vernacular as a 'danger junky.' It describes people—sky divers, mountain climbers and the like—who talk of the highs they get from these activities in very much the same terms as you describe your brightness. So would that fit? Are you compelled for reasons dark and secret to put yourself at risk?"

"I guess you could make it fit if you wanted to, Sir. You wizards play with a loaded deck. You can conjure up all kinds of subconscious shit, and how am I to argue when anything I deny you'll say I'm just suppressing?"

"That's a hard indictment for my profession to rebut," laughed the Vulture. "But what about that guilt hypothesis? Remember my Bishop? The one so driven by self loathing that he sinned as confirmation of who he thought himself to be? Anything there we can use?"

"There again, Sir, you can make it fit if you want to." Caleb was getting angry. "It's all there if you want to use it, Sir. 'Patient is obsessed with what he alleges to be his responsibility for the death of his parents. Confirms this warped self image by killing an old man in his bed. Goes on to commit further atrocities, using each one to justify the one before it.' How's that sound, Sir? Why don't you write that?"

"My Goodness!" laughed the Vulture. "It seems my story about that contemptible Prelate didn't fall on deaf ears after all. You did think that one through, didn't you?"

"I did, Sir, and it doesn't fit. All the pieces are there, but they don't go together."

"I agree. They don't. The Bishop fails the decent man test and hence the comparison collapses. Although perhaps not quite. Given the great stew of influences that combine to make us what we are, you might want to ponder the relevance of that story a bit further. But for the moment, I'm left with the problem of deciding what to write. So you tell me, Gunny, what *should* I put down?"

"Why not just write what you once said about yourself, Sir? 'Here's a guy who tried to do the best he could with the hand he'd been dealt?'"

"Good as far as it goes. Should I add that if this guy had had the wisdom of hindsight, he would have done some things differently?"

"Depends how far back that hindsight went," said Caleb bitterly. "If I could have foreseen how this war was headed, maybe I'd have tried to sit the damn thing out."

"Maybe we all should have sat it out, Gunny. It wasn't our war."

"Sure it was. Remember Hungary in 'Fifty Six? All those kids getting run over by Russian tanks? Wouldn't it be worth the fight, Sir, if we could stop that same thing from being repeated in Saigon? Because it will."

"I do remember Hungary, Gunny. I watched what was happening there with a sense of *deja vu*. But I also remember that Ho Chi Minh's people fought with us against the Japanese. I remember Ho himself in 1946 pleading with Truman to let him have his own country back, and I remember how we sold him down the river to the same French who had collaborated with the Japanese. So if you ask me, we forced Hanoi into the Russian orbit. If we had just let that benighted country settle its own affairs, I suspect we would have found that Ho's a nationalist first and a communist second."

"What's done is done, Sir."

"No regrets then? Not even killing Nguyen?"

Caleb winced.

"What about all that steam that's still bottled up? Should I mention any of that?"

"If you did, Sir, what would you write?"

"I'd write that you've still not come to grips with it. I'd express the hope that someday you'll be able to look inward with those clear eyes I was talking about. I'd hope that then, if you find yourself wishing you'd done things differently, you'd be able to face that fact with the same bravery you've shown so many times already. And once you'd done that, I'd hope it would open you up to a fuller emotional life than is possible for those tightly reined in Group Ones."

"Say I do all that, Sir. Say I keep on raking up all that muck. What the hell will it change?"

"It will change you, Gunny. Because guilt can be transforming just as it can be corrosive. You could even argue that within our capacity for guilt lies our best hope for becoming better human beings."

"You're sounding more like a priest than a wizard, Sir. 'Forgive me, Father, for I have sinned.' That kind of crap."

"No, you're wrong. I've always looked on the confessional as an easy out. I don't believe in absolutions from third parties. We've each got to face up to the lives we've lived entirely on our own. I'll have to leave you to do that yourself, Gunny." The Vulture held up his notebook. "This is number five," he said. "I've filled up four more like it." He reached shakily for his briefcase and pulled the others out one by one to stack them on the table beside him.

"That's quite a pile, Sir," laughed Caleb, his anger gone. "Looks like you've written a book!"

"So it seems. I lack only a title. Any suggestions?"

"None, Sir."

"None?" He nodded towards the pile of notebooks. "This is all just a record of idle ramblings? There's no unifying theme? No thread tying the whole thing together?"

"None that I can see. All you've really got is a guy blundering around trying to find his way without a compass. He's got himself lost on the colonel's road without signposts and he's still out there. So if that's a story, Sir, it's one without an ending."

Then perhaps I should call it *The Unmarked Road*. That would fit, wouldn't it?"

"Yes Sir, it would."

The Vulture looked slightly uncomfortable. "Another confession, Gunny. I've been being a trifle devious today. The truth is that I've already submitted my report. Had to get it in before you went up before the Medical Board. So rather than admit that you remain an enigma to me, I simply declared you sane as a judge and left it at that." He grinned. "I've been waiting ever since for the Great Psychiatrist in the Sky to strike me dead, but so far He has stayed his hand."

As he talked, he was leafing idly through the record of their time together. His tremors seemed to grow less when he applied himself to some specific task and now his hands were almost steady as he turned the pages he'd written. He smiled faintly at some entries and frowned at others. "Here's one loose end," he said, looking up. "That chicken."

"Yes, Sir," said Caleb, and now the watchers fled the gates.

"Would you tell me about it now? Just to complete my own record?"

*****

The rain had stopped while he was in the tunnel. A shaft of moonlight ran from an open window across the floor to where Nguyen lay on the opposite side of the room. His thin white beard was spread out across his chest and beside him on his rice straw pallet lay a child, curled up into a ball. Caleb looked around quickly to get the lay of the land. The rest of the hut was simply furnished. A wooden table, a makeshift alter, a tin lantern, a few woven baskets used to hide the trap door, a reading chair with an exposed light bulb hanging above it, another stack of rice mats under the window, that was all.

He moved noiselessly across the dirt floor, staying in the shadows. The child whimpered and ground his teeth in his sleep. Nguyen snored loudly. Caleb reached the bed and stood there, undecided what to do about the boy.

He laid his knife down in the moonlight where he could find it again and gently picked the child up in his arms. The boy's head rested on his shoulder and his twisted foot hung like a rag doll's as Caleb started with him back across the room.

He felt the child stir and froze, silhouetted in the moonlight. The boy stirred again. He felt the little head lift off his shoulder, saw the child's fright widened eyes staring into his own, and his mouth open in a scream which turned into a gurgle as Caleb snapped his neck.

Nguyen sat up. Caleb dropped the lifeless boy and crossed the room in a bound, scooping up his knife as he passed it. He pulled the old man's head back by his hair and drew the K-Bar savagely across his thin neck. Then he stepped clear of the fountain of blood that ran black in the moonlight and climbed back down the bamboo ladder, descending into darkness.

*****

Tears were streaming down Caleb's face.

"You'd do it again? Even that, Gunny?"

"Yes, Sir," Caleb sobbed. "Even that. I'd have to."

"Why?"

"For all the reasons Colonel Kant gave me, Sir. We didn't start this miserable war, but it was our job to end it as quickly as we could. The way I see it, nobody's come up with a better way to do that than he did. He's right. Even if it means killing a crippled little boy, he's still right." Caleb wiped futilely at his eyes. "I've got to believe that, Sir."

"I see," said the Vulture. "Although one might argue that your tears are evidence that you don't."

"No, Sir, they're not. I would do it again, which is why I was a casualty even before I was hit. We're all casualties. All of us who saw the things we saw and did the things we had to do. One way or another, we all come back damaged goods."

The only sound now was of Caleb choking back his sobs. The Vulture set clumsily about repacking the five notebooks. Caleb watched helplessly, knowing better than to try to help. Then at last the job was done and the old leather briefcase snapped shut with its familiar clunk. The little man looked up, smiling. "Well, Gunny," he said, "it seems this long odyssey you've led me on is at its end."

"Yes Sir. I'm sorry about my blubbering, Sir. I..."

"Don't be," interrupted the Vulture. "If it weren't for your tears, I'd have to think you a kindred spirit to the men who killed my parents."

CHAPTER EIGHTEEN

Wee Willie was pushing the Vulture's wheelchair and they'd come down to the lobby to see Caleb off. It was a busy morning. All around them patients and staff came and went. Some men hobbled across the granite floor on artificial legs, some passed by with missing arms, and still others maneuvered through the crowd in wheelchairs, but these sights were the norm here and went unnoticed, except by the shaken few who had come, perhaps for the first time, to visit what remained of the man they'd known as a son, boyfriend or husband.

Wee Willie spotted him first, coming with long strides up the ramp from the bone ward with his seabag over his left shoulder. They saw a nurse running towards him and smiled to see the tall Marine and the raven-haired girl standing motionless in a long embrace, both plainly oblivious to the sea of people that swirled around them. "Reardon," grunted Wee Willie. "Might have guessed it!"

Then she was gone and Caleb was effortlessly swinging his big seabag up again onto his shoulder. "He has you to thank that he can still do that, Will," said the Vulture.

"And you to thank that his head's screwed back on straight," grinned Wee Willie.

"Maybe, although I'm not sure it was ever screwed on crooked."

Caleb saw them and threaded his way through the crowd to where they waited. He stopped, instinctively started to salute, and caught himself.

"We're here to say goodbye, Gunny," said the Vulture.

"I'm here to make sure this pain in the ass is really leaving," thundered Wee Willie. He grabbed Caleb's claw and inspected it. "Not a bad job if I do say so myself! Looks like shit, but what the hell. You can't have everything."

"Thank you, Sir," Caleb grinned. "Doctor Blankenship tells me I'm lucky to have any hand at all. He didn't think you'd be able to save it."

"Blankenship said that? I'm surprised the two of you are still talking."

"He's not a bad guy, Sir. But he's no officer. Says so himself."

"Where will you go from here, Gunny?" interjected the Vulture.

"Home, Sir. To Woods Hole. I think I'll go back to lobstering."

"You'll be able to manage all right with that hand?"

"Guess I'll find out quick enough, Sir."

"Damn right he'll manage!" bellowed Wee Willie. "I built that goddamn hand! I know what it'll do!"

Outside, a bus pulled up to the curb. The lobby's automatic entrance doors hissed open, letting in a blast of cold air as the waiting passengers started towards it. "That's my ride," Caleb said. He stood awkwardly for moment, trying to find the right words. "I can't thank you both enough..." he began.

"Just doing our jobs," interrupted Wee Willie. "Now good luck and get going, Gunny. Otherwise you'll miss the goddamn bus and we'll be stuck with you here for another day!"

The Vulture held out his palsied hand. Caleb held it between his own, felt his throat tighten, and found himself unable to speak. "Next time Heart runs up against Head," smiled the misshapen little man, "remember what Corporal Hume told you. Heart takes rank!"

Caleb nodded, swallowing hard.

"Godspeed, Gunny."

The doors were closing. Caleb ran for the bus.

The two doctors watched him leave. "This country'd be in one helluva lot better shape if we turned out more men like that one," said Wee Willie.

"Perhaps," said the Vulture. "But then again, perhaps not."

"Horse shit!" said Wee Willie.

POSTSCRIPT

Captain William Williamson, MD, USN never did get the command he'd hoped for. At the end of his tour at PNH, he became Chief of Orthopedics, US Naval Hospital, Da Nang; a lateral move which he realized meant that he could expect to go no further in his career. He made no more friends in Da Nang than he had in Philadelphia, but even his most vocal critics could not fault his extraordinary skill as a surgeon. On his retirement in 1975, he gave up the practice of medicine and returned to his family's apple orchard in Medford, Oregon where he remained, a solitary man dividing his time between his trees and his machine shop, until his death in 1997.

Commander Ernest Throttlemeyer, MD, Ph.D., USNR took his own life in 1977, two years after his deteriorating health forced him into retirement. A note which was found in his typewriter and which, as evidenced by the number of keys hit in error, he had written at enormous effort, presented an *apologia* for what he was about to do, the substance of which was that a social order based on the related concepts of individual freedom and accountability could not without contradiction morally oppose a sane adult's right to decide when to end his own life. He left a substantial bequest to the Navy Relief Society, his personal papers to the University of Pennsylvania Medical School Library, and the remainder of his estate, including his house on Philadelphia's Delancey Place, to Junior Randall. In the summer of 1999 a doctoral student writing his dissertation on the role of dreams in Post Traumatic Stress Disorders discovered the notebooks that provided the background material for this narrative.

Lieutenant Junior Grade Nancy Reardon NC, USNR married Lieutenant Robert Blankenship, MD, USNR and is now a full time wife and mother living in Cambridge, Massachusetts. Dr. Blankenship is a rising star at the Massachusetts General Hospital.

Hospitalman Third Class Junior Randall USN submitted a request for early release from the Navy that was approved by the Bureau of Personnel, thanks largely to Captain Williamson's intercession on his behalf. He attended to Commander Throttlemeyer during the last years of his illness and, after the latter's death, returned to school to earn a degree in nursing. He now works as a Physician's Assistant at a South Philadelphia Free Clinic and coaches boxing at a neighborhood youth center. He and his wife, the former yeoman at the PNH legal office, still live at Delancey Place where, as the only black residents on that street, they have been welcomed somewhat too effusively by the young professionals who are their neighbors.

Gunnery Sergeant John Caleb USMC returned to his home in Woods Hole, Massachusetts and went back to lobstering.

THE END

ABOUT THE AUTHOR

George Cadwalader served for ten years in the Marine Corps. Wounded in Viet Nam and medically retired as a Major, he went on to found the Penikese Island School, a wilderness based program for delinquent teenagers, which he directed for twenty-three years and wrote about in *Castaways: The Penikese Island Experiment*. He lives in Woods Hole, Massachusetts with his wife, Yara, and worked until 2012 as a commercial lobsterman. He now divides his time between writing and rebuilding old wooden boats.

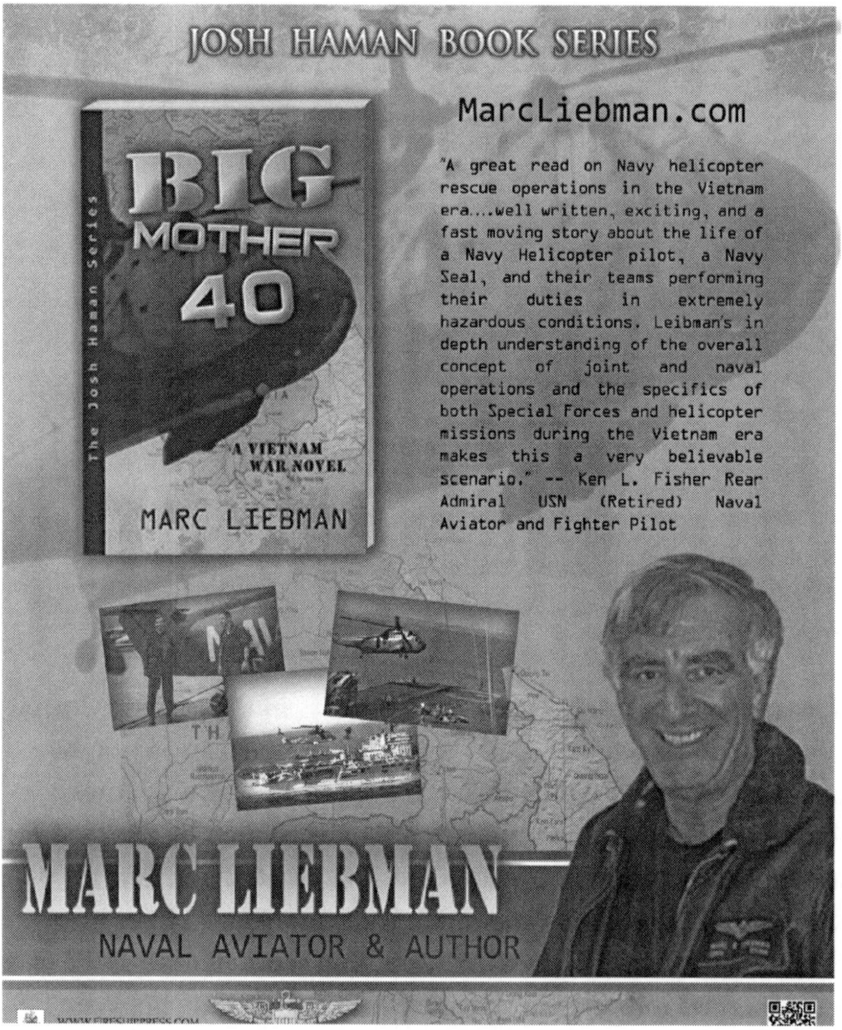
JOSH HAMAN BOOK SERIES
MarcLiebman.com
BIG MOTHER 40
The Josh Haman Series
A VIETNAM WAR NOVEL
MARC LIEBMAN
"A great read on Navy helicopter rescue operations in the Vietnam era....well written, exciting, and a fast moving story about the life of a Navy Helicopter pilot, a Navy Seal, and their teams performing their duties in extremely hazardous conditions. Leibman's in depth understanding of the overall concept of joint and naval operations and the specifics of both Special Forces and helicopter missions during the Vietnam era makes this a very believable scenario." -- Ken L. Fisher Rear Admiral USN (Retired) Naval Aviator and Fighter Pilot
MARC LIEBMAN
NAVAL AVIATOR & AUTHOR

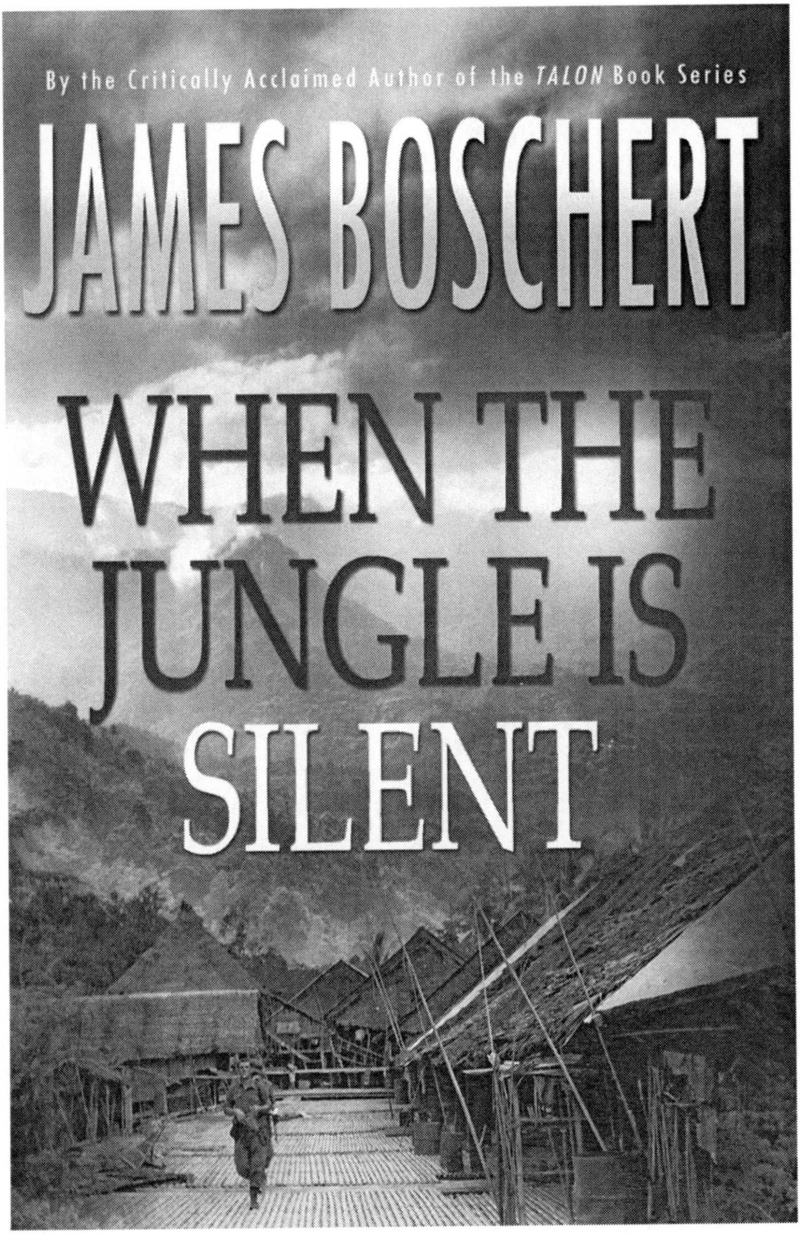
By the Critically Acclaimed Author of the TALON Book Series
JAMES BOSCHERT
WHEN THE
JUNGLE IS
SILENT

For the Finest in
Nautical and Historical
Fiction and Nonfiction

WWW.FIRESHIPPRESS.COM

Interesting • Informative • Authoritative

CPSIA information can be obtained at www.ICGtesting.com
Printed in the USA
LVOW070832080213

319196LV00004B/298/P

9 781611 792478